THE CRY OF THE DRAGON

The Dragons of the Mist Book 1

Brenna Bustamante

DEDICATION

To every woman afraid of stepping out of your comfort zone. You can do this. Amaze the world with who you are because without you, the world is a little less.

To my parents, who are the real dragons in my life.

To my sister and our constant sibling rivalry when we were younger. It inspired me to step out of your shadows.

To my husband, who accepts me despite all my shadows.

To my two dogs—Mojo and Nacho— and my cat, Mr. President for enduring the constant Taylor Swift music I played while writing this.

To my editor, who fluffed my wings too much and now I can't stop writing.

CONTENT TRIGGERS

Your mental health matters.

Violence, death and dying, sexism, racism, classism

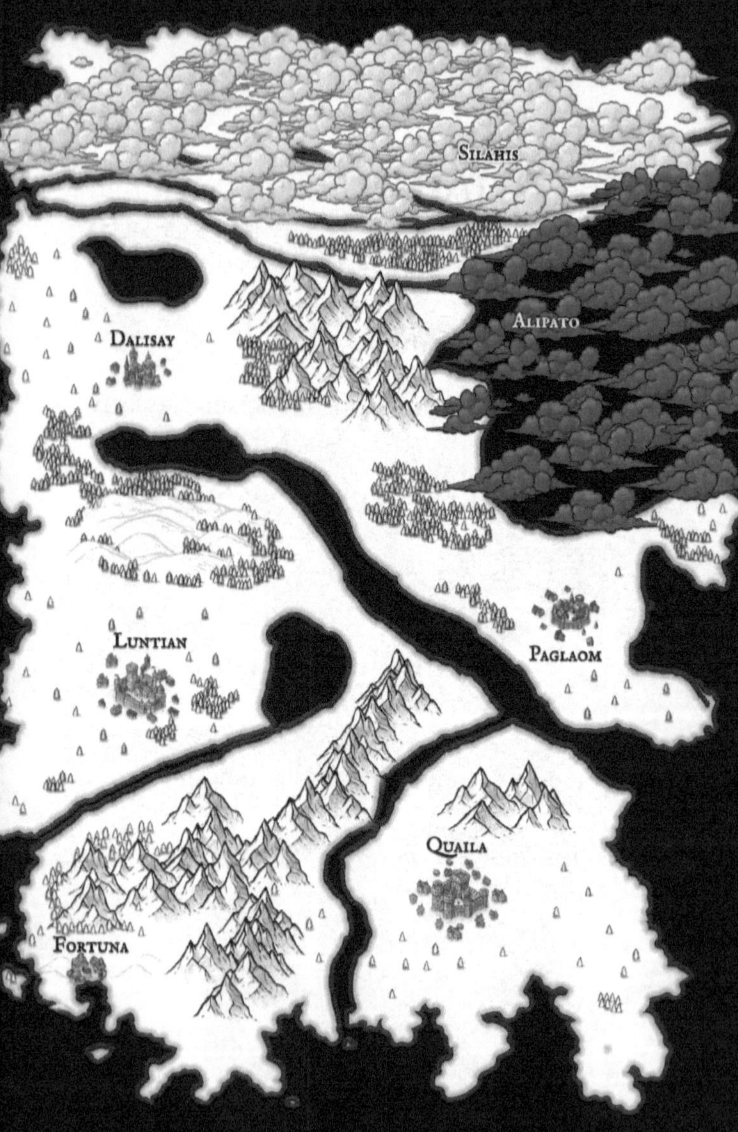

Silahis
Alipato
Dalisay
Luntian
Paglaom
Quaila
Fortuna

CHAPTER 1

Alex

"She's dying!"

I hear my brother's strained voice and instantly I'm up, the idea of deep sleep impossible now.

My mother sits at the edge of her bed, her entire body wracked with wicked coughs. Her dress is disheveled under all the sheets, and her long, dark hair is tied at the back of her head, with little frayed strands hanging beside her tired face. Lines on her forehead and cheeks seem more pronounced as she hovers over the edge of the bed. I'm next to her in a flash.

"What is it, Mother?" My brows knit as I put a hand on her back, supporting her as more coughs wreck her body. Her body's warm, like it's fighting off whatever infection has been in her body for years.

"P-p-pe," she manages before her entire body shakes violently.

She didn't have to say anything else; I knew exactly what she needed already––she'd been training me for years. I move towards the cabinet where we keep multiple small bottles containing various concoctions my mother and I have made through the years. I organized it recently alphabetically, so I scan to find the Ps. I frown. We're all out of what I'm looking for. Frustration pulls at me, and I run outside the house barefoot, Angus following behind me like a lost puppy. His eyes are wide, more from fear than sleep. But I ignore him, passing through all the plants we have growing at the side of our house. It's the middle of the night, and this disruption isn't unusual for my mother's condition. The moon's out, giving light to the otherwise dark surroundings. I see the fence of our property just beyond the horizon, where our cow grazes during the day.

As soon as I spot the leaves I need, I bend down, gently cutting them off and grabbing them with my other hand. I run back into the house, Angus on my heels yet again as I enter the kitchen, using a mortar and pestle to grind the leaves into a paste before I mix it into hot water.

"Go help Mother up while I mix her tea," I order the seventeen-year-old standing over my shoulder as I wipe the bottom of my feet against my other calf. He nods gravely, disappearing into my mother's room.

I finish mixing the paste into hot water and use a spatula to slowly dissolve the paste. My mother's coughs are so loud I can hear her from where I stand in the kitchen.

"I'm almost done!" I yell, tapping my foot as I wait for the water to boil.

Only heavy coughs respond, so I turn the heat up.

"Alex, hurry!" Angus yells from the bedroom. "She's coughing blood."

I don't respond, but I keep my eyes on the pot, bubbles slowly forming in and around the water. Once the bubbles are bigger, I turn the stove off, pour the tea into a cup, and race to my mother's bedroom.

Sticky red liquid pools on the floor. Her head is hovering over the ground, her body lying weakly as she heaves, breathless. Angus sits on the edge of the bed, rubbing her back. He looks at me, his eyes bulging with fear. My stomach knots as I settle on the other side of my mother, helping her sit up. She sits up, but her body is so weak that she doubles over.

"Mother," I say softly, "I have the tea. Come on, it'll only take a second, I promise."

She nods, coughing up more blood that sticks to her body and the bedsheets.

"Alex," Angus says, horrified.

I ignore him, letting my mother smell the tea before helping her to sit back up so she can take a sip. She slurps slowly, coughing even more than blood-red liquid coats her mouth.

"Come on, Mother, you've got this," I say softly as I offer her the tea one more time.

She takes the cup, taking a longer sip this time. When she sets the cup down, her tear-filled eyes are bloodshot, and a trickle of blood runs down her chin. She breathes deeply, her tea sputtering as she bursts into another fit of coughs. I rub my hands down her back, slowly patting as she gets the rest of it out. Her eyes are still wet, and tears stream down her face. I pull her into my arms, rubbing her back at the same time.

"It's okay, Mother, it's okay," I say softly, wiping the tears from my face. My eyes turn back to my younger brother, who's also staring back at me, fear lingering in his eyes.

My mother's been sick ever since I can remember. It started out slowly, morphing from random coughing every now and again to this. She can hardly stand these days. Most of the time she's in bed. We could never figure out what was wrong, and we've never had the money to send her to a healer. These days, only this tea makes her feel better. Nothing else.

"Alexandra," she manages, and I let her lay down on her pillow.

"What is it, Mother?" I ask, fluffing out the pillow next to her and pulling her blanket up to her chest. I reach for her hand. It's ice cold, so I rub my hands over hers.

"The deliveries for today," she breathes.

"It's okay, Mother. Angus can help me," I say, looking at him.

"I'm sorry," she says, her eyes drooping wearily.

"It's okay, Mother. We got it," I promise her, then add as I pat the nightstand next to her. "Your tea is here. It will make you feel better."

She nods tiredly, shifting to her side. I reach next to her, shutting the curtains and turning off the light. I slip out of the room, pulling Angus with me.

"Do you think she's okay?" Angus whispers.

For a moment, in the dark of the night, I remember Angus when he was just seven years old. I was fourteen, and he used to get so scared before falling asleep. He'd trembled with fear, and I'd crawled into bed with him so he could nod off. That was ten years ago, and here he is--not much different from then, maybe a bit braver, but always scared that Mother will die and leave us. I'm scared, too, but I don't tell him that. I have to be strong for him.

For her.

I pull him into a hug, forgetting for a moment that he actually towers over me now. He smells of crisp night air and river water, a smell he's always had ever since he was young. I miss the days when I could just tell him something and he'd do it. At seventeen, he's not like that anymore.

"She'll be fine," I whisper, but even I'm unsure. "Go to bed, Angus. We have work tomorrow."

He turns, disappearing behind his door, and it's dark in the house again.

I sigh. Angus, my mother, and I live in Fortuna, a few hours away from the main city where the palace and the royal family lives. They have property in the area, but honestly, we've never seen the royal family, and we've never seen their soldiers.

They've never cared, so neither did we.

My mother, when she was younger, decided she preferred the slow life of the mountains, so we moved here before I was born. We live on our little farm, supporting ourselves and a few other families nearby. It's a little lonely, but nice. I don't have to deal with the soldiers or palace people, and our house may be small, but we own it, so at least we don't have to pay rent—which is just as well now that Mother is too sick to work.

So, at least we didn't have to care about people who clearly didn't care about us.

A few minutes later, I lay on my bed, pulling my blankets up as I struggle to gather as much warmth as I can. Light has already started peeking through the clouds. It'll be morning soon. Tomorrow will be a rough day.

Just like every other day.

CHAPTER 2

Alex

My eyes open at the sound of a rooster. Oh boy. Chris is awake. I rub my eyes, breathing deeply as I wrangle myself out of the sheets. I only got a few hours of sleep last night, thanks to Mother's horrific coughing fit.

I get dressed, and quickly check on my mother, who's still sleeping, then put on a warmer coat, since it's been cooler in the mornings lately. Rubbing my eyes to wake myself up a little more, I drag myself into the chicken coop.

"Good morning," I greet Chris.

"I'm hungry." The lavender rooster looks up at me as I enter the chicken run.

"I know; that's why I'm here, grumpy," I grumble.

Chris crows again, noting his disappointment.

Yeah, yeah. I know. I break into the bin and start scooping out chicken feed, and Chris and a few other chickens instantly flock to the feeder.

"Thanks, Alex," Alyssa and the other Buff Orpington ladies say.

I nod, mentally counting the number of chickens. "Where's Virginia?" I demand.

The chickens all continue to peck at their food, ignoring me.

"Chris, where's Virginia?" I say again, this time planting a hand on his back. He turns, pecking me on the finger before turning back to his food. I roll my eyes, striding past the feeder to the run. Virginia's in the nest, laying. When she spots me, she cuckoos disappointingly, so I turn to check their water instead.

"See, I take my job seriously," Chris says when he finally turns to watch me refill the water.

"I was just checking. There's a lot of big birds around," I defend myself.

"Stop hovering over us, Alex, You're slow when you do," Alyssa says as she turns from her food. I roll my eyes.

"You're not getting bugs today," I mutter under my breath.

"Bitch," Virginia says in between clucking.

I grab some bugs and throw them in before scowling and heading out of the chicken run, locking it behind me.

"Bye," the chickens cluck behind me.

I heave a sigh as I walk over to the pen, where Sweet's already waiting for me, grazing on the grass.

"Good morning," I greet her, smiling as I open the fence.

"Good morning," she moos loudly, turning to me. I pet her face, rubbing the space behind her ears. She really enjoys that.

Of course, I've wondered how I can talk to my animals many, many times, only to be laughed at by Sweet, my cow, Chris, and Virginia. I don't know how; I don't know why. My brother can't talk to animals, nor can my mother. And yet, in this lonely house, so far away from civilization, my only friends are the cow, the chickens, who apparently sometimes hate me, and my cat.

"How are you today?" the cow asks me.

To others, she must just be mooing. But I understand every word she says.

I brush her body, and she wriggles with happiness.

"I'm okay," I respond, shrugging.

"Oh, Alex." Her voice is older, like a grandmother trying to sate my concerns.

"What?" I demand, scowling at her as I brush her faster.

"You haven't had a good sleep, yet again. At some point, your lack of proper rest will get to you, you know. You're not going to be young forever," the cow says.

"I know, Sweet. It's not like I can help it. Mother got really sick last night. No one else will be doing this. Angus isn't even awake yet," I respond. Once I'm done cleaning her, I bend down on my knees, putting a bucket below her.

"You ready?" I ask. I always like to ask because it makes them feel good, feel ready.

Sweet moos in response. I pull on her teat to release milk into the bucket.

"Are you going to be doing anything today?" Sweet moos again.

I laugh as I move on to another teat. Milk pours into the bucket. "Deliveries," I sing, trying to sound cheerful.

"Can't Angus do that?" she asks, lifting a leg as I move on to a different teat.

"True," I say absentmindedly. "But he's not even awake. He's not going to be up before ten am."

"Oh. Maybe be the big sister and tell him to wake up?" Sweet moos, but all I hear is a snicker. I scowl again, directing it at her, even though she can't see me.

I finish collecting all the milk from her, then carry the bucket back to the barn where I can bottle it carefully. I glance up at the clock in the barn, calculating the time I have before I need to start delivering. It's 7:22 am. I have only about two hours. I sit at the desk, reaching for the bottles to get them ready. Usually, my mother and I bottle the milk together as it's time-consuming. More often lately, I've had to do chores myself. At least my mother taught me how to do everything well before she got too sick.

Now, I can run the house, even when she dies. I pause for a moment, my heart sinking at the thought. I love my mother, I do. Shame and embarrassment fill me, and I shake away the thoughts. I owe my mother everything. I should be grateful she's still alive. I should be grateful I can return the favor.

I turn back to the task at hand, washing the bottles carefully before putting the milk in them. When I finish the last bottle, I wash my hands, drying them with a towel before putting a sticker with our phone number on it. That's how we get our income. We sell eggs and milk to some of our neighbors, giving us just enough to live on. It couldn't put Angus through school, but at least we're alive, right?

I bag all the bottles up, sticking a name tag onto each paper bag so I know which one goes to whom. Then, I slip each bag into a saddlebag before hanging it over Wayne as he nuzzles me affectionately.

"Hello," he says, excitedly stomping his foot.

"Hello, Wayne. Don't worry, we'll leave soon," I say while placing a saddle on his back. "I'll wash you after, don't worry."

"Sun. Movement, so exciting, Alex," he neighs.

I laugh, mounting. "Let's go." At least the roads are clear when we leave our farm, unlike most areas around here. The roads are lined with massive trees, most so high up that they create a cover for the road. Fortuna is very, very remote. The few neighborhoods there are mostly consist of farms. There's a single store, a few tiny restaurants, and maybe a post office. Other than that, it's just dirt roads and lots of trees. I like it like that, though. It's so remote, away from people who could hurt us. Away from the fake, the rich, and the people who take advantage. At least, that's what my mother always says.

My first delivery is at the local pub, at least about twenty minutes away on horseback from my home.

Serena meets me as I turn the corner to the pub. Serena owns the pub. She's about twice my age at forty-eight, but she's always been extra nice to me. She's beautiful, too, the kind of woman you wouldn't usually see in the middle of nowhere.

"Hello." She smiles, pushing her long blonde hair behind her back. She's wearing an apron today, over a red sundress. Her skin is light, and her eyes are blue. That's how most people around us look. We're the foreigners, the people who've traveled from who knows where and don't look anything like our neighbours. When we first arrived, I was three. Angus wasn't even born yet. I was always the odd girl, the girl that didn't completely fit.

When I first met Serena, I was a shy girl of sixteen; she took me in. She introduced me to people, accepted me, made me feel like I am human, despite the constant stares and whispers.

"How are you?" she asks as I hand her the bag of milk.

I shrug. "I'm okay."

Wayne neighs. "Are you though?"

I struggle to keep a straight face.

"Alex, you really should come out every now and again. You owe it to yourself. Even Angus manages to get out on occasion," Serena says, turning to me with her beautiful blue eyes.

I give her a face. "Of course he does. I'm sure we only need one Mauricio out and about," I say with a bite of sarcasm.

"I'd really rather it be you," Serena offers kindly, a soft look in her eyes.

I chuckle. "Maybe next time." I start to turn, but Serena catches my arm.

"You realize your brother's been spending time at the fields owned by the royal family, right? The moment he gets caught, they'll kill him," she whispers.

My eyes grow wide. "What?"

"You need to tell him to stop. He cannot keep doing this. They'll kill him," Serena repeats.

My mouth drops, but I turn to face her. "I...when did you see him?"

Serena's eyebrows rise. "Every day for the last few weeks."

"Shit," I say under my breath. "Thanks for telling me, Serena."

She nods, and my body tenses. They won't kill him just because he's trespassing. We're not considered *their* people. He'll be arrested for treason simply because his skin color is different.

CHAPTER 3

Alex

Wayne neighs happily when I return home and start grooming his coat. When I turn, I see Angus sitting on the desk. The heat of my anger threatens to burst out all at once. Not a great idea. So, I bury all of it for now and put on a smile.

"Did you sleep okay?" I ask.

"I slept." He shrugs. "Anything I can help with?"

I roll my eyes. "Angus, it's 2:00 pm."

"I'm sorry; I was up all night with Mother," he says.

It takes all of me not to tell him I was up, too. "Chores start at five. I could've used your help." I brush Wayne's sides as he neighs his approval.

"You need to be stricter with him, Alex. You're too nice." Wayne frowns.

I just look at the horse, pretending I haven't heard what he just said. He whinnies, but I'm sure it's him rolling his eyes.

"I'm sorry. I'll help tomorrow, I promise," Angus mumbles as he watches me clean Wayne.

I fight to keep my voice gentle. He doesn't respond well when he feels got at. "Where did you go yesterday?"

"What do you mean?" Angus asks, tilting his head in confusion.

Once again, I remember him as a little boy. But he's not young anymore. He's taller now, taller than I am, and his jaw is more pronounced. His eyebrows are thicker and darker, although they've always been like that, even when he was younger. He talks back so much more now.

"Where did you spend your time yesterday?" I ask again, frowning at him.

"Is this just you testing me? Or are you actually asking?" Angus asks, frowning back.

"Angus, just tell me," I say, heaving a sigh.

"I was with my friends," Angus grunts, but I can already tell he's lying by the way his eyes shift.

"Yeah? Which friends?" I ask.

"Alex, if you already know, then stop trying to torture me," Angus snaps, standing up from his seat, his eyes gleaming with anger. Maybe even hurt.

"I'm not trying to torture you. I'm trying to give you the opportunity to tell the truth," I say, standing my ground. It's rare that Angus and I fight, but to be honest, it's always been because I'm too tired. I just…I'm not a fighter. I'm fairly gifted at sarcasm; other than that, raising my voice always exhausts me.

He looks at me, eyes wide, his breathing hitching as he prepares to say something.

"Were you at the fields yesterday? And the day before?" I ask.

His palm goes up, and he turns away, his hands fidgeting.

"Angus," I try.

"So what, Alex? So what? I was just trying to have fun," Angus roars, turning around.

My heart breaks. "I know that, but you know who we are, and what we are to this kingdom. You know how they'll react if this continues to happen."

"You know fun? The thing that seems to be such a foreign concept to you?" Angus sneered. Sarcasm sits inside both of us, I guess. Family trait.

I click my tongue, forcing every bad emotion, every bad word, deep within me. "I'm too busy taking care of you and Mother."

"I don't need to be taken care of," Angus growls.

Yes, you do! I want to say so badly. But instead, I keep quiet, looking at my younger brother, at the tears streaming down his face. I fight the urge to comfort him, but I lose, stepping forward to wrap my arms around him.

"I'm sorry," Angus whispers against my ear. "I won't do it again."

"I'm just trying to protect you. I don't want anything to happen to you," I say.

"I won't do it again," he says. "It's just such a nice field, and it's so pretty during the day."

I frown, once again seeing the little boy who always liked to roll around in grass. He always did this—even as a little boy. Why did he have to grow up and become aware of the evil all around us? "I'm sorry. I'm sorry this is our situation."

"It's not your fault," he mumbles. "It's not your fault we're like this."

I know he means the color of our skin––the biggest thing that makes us different. The biggest thing that makes it more difficult to live.

It's not a fault, Angus, I want to say, but nothing comes out of my mouth. I don't want to lie to him. The people around me *do* see it as a fault. So instead, I sigh deeply, patting him on the back.

"No more going to those lands, okay?" I say.

He nods, his face crestfallen. "No more," he agrees.

"I'm sorry," I tell him. "I know how much you like good grass."

He shrugs. "It's okay, I can find someplace else."

"Can you go clean the coop?" I ask, changing the subject.

He nods, walking off.

"Are you sure it's the coop that needs cleaning?" a voice says, and I turn around to see Mouse sitting by the desk. Mouse is our highland lynx cat who loves to terrorize the mice in the area.

"What did you do?" I ask, giving her a look.

"Oh, nothing. I just had lunch," she says, licking her paws.

"Disgusting." I roll my eyes at her, turning my back to face Wayne again.

"You're too nice, Alex," Wayne says as I brush his coat once more.

"Yeah, Alex. Wayne is right. You're too nice. If I were you, I'd just, pah, pah, pah," Mouse agrees, raising her paws like she's punching something.

I laugh. "You look like you're pawing at the air, Mouse, what do you think you look like?"

"I'll rip your throat when you're sleeping, Alex, make fun of me again," she warns, her eyes narrowing, her ears laid back.

I can't help bursting into laughter. She looks at me warily, showing her six toes proudly. "Ooh, I'm so scared," I tease.

She jumps at me, scratching my pants.

"Ow, you little shit," I say, getting up to brush her off me.

"That's just the start, Alex. Maybe if you actually got a life, you wouldn't be so pathetic," Mouse says.

"Says the freaking cat!" I laugh.

"Exactly. That cat that you talk to," Mouse retorts.

"I do feel bad, you know," I say, sitting down.

"About what?" Mouse asks.

"That he never got to go to school. I think it still haunts him, just as much as it haunts me."

Mouse jumps up next to me. "Yes, it does." She turns to me, giving me a slow blink. "You may pet me," she adds, tossing her head. I chuckle, obliging and petting the space behind her neck.

"You've heard him?" I say, going back to the original topic.

"Yes. He cries about it at night every now and again. He doesn't think he'll amount to anything. I guess it's normal for someone who's never had a normal childhood," Mouse says.

My throat tightens. "Do you think he'll get over it?"

The cat chortles. "Of course not. Not with how society acts. Worth will always be assigned according to the money you have or the lineage you come from."

I fold my arms over my sinking heart. "Then how do I put him through school, Mouse? We barely survive."

"I mean, if you can sell the mice I catch, you'd be a millionaire," the cat says, turning to my palm affectionately.

If only.

CHAPTER 4

Alex

I finish washing Wayne and tell Angus to wash Sweet before I head back into the house to work on my mother's herbs. If there's anything that my mother brought from her family, it's this. My mother can make all sorts of concoctions. That was how she escaped her old, dangerous life to arrive here in one piece. She traded many concoctions, poisons, sleeping draughts, anything and everything that people can use to hurt, heal, or help someone. She'd just started teaching me a few years ago, before her condition got really bad. Nowadays, I mostly just make her a concoction of peppermint, slippery elm, and ginger, and it helps with the coughing.

"Hello, Mother," I greet her. She's still in bed , but her eyes are open, weariness written all over her face. Her blankets are crumpled at the foot of her bed, and she's on her side, her knees pulled up to her chest.

"Alex," she manages with a small smile.

"How are you feeling?" I stand at her door, leaning against it as I cross my arms.

My mother doesn't like to be hovered over; it makes her feel weak, so I've learned to avoid it as much as I can. To be fair, though, I haven't seen her since last night.

She coughs, propping herself up on her elbows. "Tired," she responds.

"Want me to make you anything? Food? Drinks?" I offer, holding back the urge to come and comfort her.

She shakes her head. "I'm not hungry, but if you have time, I'd love some of the cough syrup you gave me last night."

I nod my head. "I can do that. Have you drunk any water today at all?"

She gives me a wary look. "No," she admits.

I roll my eyes, turning from her to grab her some. "Mother, please drink water. It'll help you tonight, I promise."

I reach back to her, handing her the water bottle. She accepts it, and I watch her struggle to drink. I push the urge to help her away, turning to go back to the kitchen, grimacing when I hear her struggle.

The mortar and pestle I used last night still sit in the kitchen, pieces of peppermint leaves still stuck around it. I exit the house barefoot to harvest a few more leaves and grab some slippery elm, since I used the last of it last night. Angus is still outside , working on cleaning the coop. I can see him struggling to rake the chicken run while all the chickens cluck at him.

"Chris, Virginia, stop it!" I yell.

"I enjoy making it harder for him," Chris crows back as it flaps its wings, flying around Angus, who's clearly struggling.

I roll my eyes, walking around the side of our house to forage for supplies. Once I've gathered what I need, I place it in the mortar, before adding a piece of ginger onto the cutting board so I can also cut the leaves into pieces. Once I have little pieces, I drop them into the mortar before breaking them down into a paste. Then, I turn on the stove, adding a pot of water onto it so it can boil.

"Alex, can you make a sleeping draught for me too? I can't seem to sleep anymore," my mother calls from her bedroom.

"Okay!" I yell back.

My mother had only just started teaching me before her health worsened, but it's taking a lot longer because we can no longer go out into the forests to look at different plants. I can make a sleeping draught, and I can temporarily paralyze someone with a concoction, but that's it right now. I haven't been in the fields with her since I was twenty-one, the day she was pointing out the different types of mushrooms and what I can do with them.

I mix the paste with the hot water, then hand it to my mother. "Here you go," I say.

My mother accepts the mug, drinking it slowly. "Thanks, sweetheart."

I nod, turning around to start the work on a sleeping draught, scouring through our cabinets and closets for ingredients. Chamomile, lemon balm, lavender—I count off, pulling a bit of each to use for my concoction. I just need valerian root, so I head to our garden again to pick out a few leaves. But Angus is on his way back inside, holding an arm gingerly.

"Are you okay?" I ask, seeing him grimace and watching the blood drip from his arm.

"I accidentally scratched myself on the chicken run," he says.

All thoughts of what I was doing slip from my mind, and I rush to get medical supplies and usher him in.

Within seconds, Angus is sitting on a chair in the kitchen, his head and arm hanging over the table.

"I'm coming, Angus, I'll be right there," I say, noting the nausea roaming across Angus's face. He's never been great with blood. I grab a bandage and a needle in case I need to patch it up and drop them next to him as I inspect his wounds.

"It'll need stitches, Angus," I tell him as he nods, his gaze still fixed on the floor. I pat a towel over the wound to stop the bleeding and grab water for him. "Here," I say, trying to lift him up to drink. He does what I ask.

I make sure to sterilize the wound before stitching it up.

"What's going on?" my mother croaks from her bedroom.

"Angus got cut. Don't worry, I'm patching him up," I say, before handing Angus spilanthes, a flower to help with the pain. He chews on it, keeping his head down.

"Ready?" I whisper.

"Can I have alcohol?" he murmurs weakly.

I roll my eyes. "No," I say immediately. He groans. "It'll be painful. Hold on," I say before starting to stitch his wound up.

His face changes while I stitch his wound, from a grimace, to an almost-yell, back to a grimace.

"I'm sorry, I'm sorry, I'm almost done," I say, quickly finishing up the stitches. When I make the last stitch, I sigh a deep breath. "I'm almost done. I just have to bandage it, okay?" I pull a bandage from its cover and wrap it around his wound, tight but not too tight.

"Thanks," he manages, but his face is pale, and his lips have lost all their color.

"Okay, drink." I give him another glass of water, and he gulps it down, his eyes rolling to the back of his head.

"I gotta go lay down," he murmurs as he tries to walk.

I hold on to him, pulling his arm over my shoulder and helping him to his bed. "I didn't get to Sweet, Alex," he adds, burying himself into his sheets. I nod, a flare in my chest rising at the additional chore.

"It's okay, I've got it," I say, patting him on his back.

"Alex, my sleeping draught, please," Mother says weakly from the other room.

"Yes, Mother." I close the door to Angus's room before heading back into the kitchen. For a moment, I have to reorient myself. What was I doing? Oh, valerian root. I make my way back out to the gardens, picking up a few leaves of valerian root before heading back inside to make my mother's sleeping draught. Once I'm done, I give the glass to my mother and then head back out into the kitchen to clean up. Another day in the life of Alex. Rinse and repeat. Just more of me doing nothing else but everyone else's tasks.

I wash the dishes, putting them back into the cabinet, before I wipe my hands on my apron while looking around the kitchen for any more things to clean before I need to go wash Sweet.

A white envelope sits on the fridge door, one I hadn't noticed before. I grab it, opening the envelope and grabbing the white paper inside.

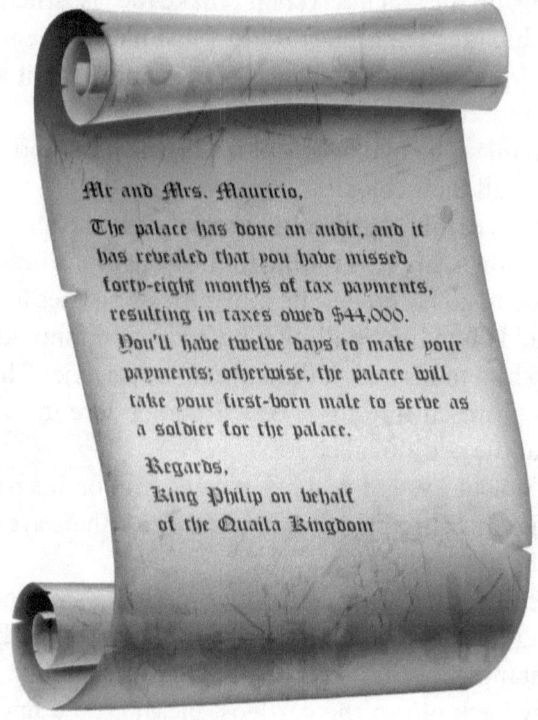

My mouth drops when I see the date on the stamp. We received this letter eleven days ago.

"Mother!" I yell, my blood burning hot at the fear and anger in my head.

"What?" she murmurs, turning over in bed.

"Why didn't you tell me about this?" I ask.

But her eyes have drooped, her breathing is steady, her body calm, and I know she's fallen asleep.

CHAPTER 5

Alex

The next day, I wake up extra early just to finish all of my chores, so I can count the money we have. There's no chance we have the kind of money being demanded by the royals. None at all. We live day to day, barely having any savings for things like emergencies. We can barely afford to pay even small installments of the amount they're asking. There is no way I can get them off our backs. How did we lose this? How did we stop paying taxes? I didn't even know we were expected to pay them. They haven't done anything for us, not in the last four years, not ever.

I sigh, walking to my mother's bedroom. She didn't have a great time last night, either.

My heart clenches, and a sob escapes around my words as I force them out. "They're coming to take Angus today, Mother. Why didn't you tell me about this?" I demand.

She peers at me from her pillow, a sad look stretching across her face. "I'm sorry, Alex. I forgot," she murmurs.

Forgot? Forgot? I'm going to lose my brother. You can't just forget this! I want to yell at her, but the way she closes her eyes makes me realize how weak she is already. There's no way I can shout at her for this. Angus comes out of his bedroom, whistling. I see the moment he realizes what I've4 just said, and I watch helplessly as the blood drains from his face, and his eyes darken. "Who's coming to take me?" he rasps.

I let out a shaky breath, turning to him as I hand him the envelope, forgetting for a moment that he can't read. "It's a notice that we haven't been paying taxes for the last four years. They're coming to take you today, Angus," I blurt out.

"Who? Who is taking me today?" he demands through narrowed eyes.

"The palace. The king," I tell him.

"No." Angus's eyes widen. "No, Alex. No, they can't take me!"

Once more, the young man in front of me turns into a little boy. "Please, Alex, please don't let them take me."

I wrap him in my arms. "I won't. I promise. Go anywhere. I'll negotiate with them, but if you're not here, they can't take you."

Angus nods, then exits the back door, his shoulders heaving.

"What did you do, Alex?" my mother says from her bed.

"I'm doing what I can to keep this family together, Mother," I say, catching sight of horses through the window. "They're here," I breathe, my heart pounding in my chest.

"Mr. and Mrs. Mauricio. We are here to collect your taxes," a firm voice calls from outside.

I hide behind the front door, unsure what to do.

"Please don't make this harder for any of us."

I open the door, slowly slipping out to face them.

A huge palace carriage sits outside our home with four horses, two drivers with palace uniforms in the front, and another soldier at the back of the carriage.

"Hello!" the horses neigh. I ignore them, turning to the man in the carriage.

"My name is Sir Andrew. I work for the royal family. We are here to take Angus Mauricio," the man says, stepping out of the carriage. He's wearing a neat black royal uniform. His face has a mustache that makes him look even creepier. His hair is pulled back neatly, exposing his menacing dark eyes. He faces me as if he's ready to strike.

"Please, Sir Andrew. Please don't take my brother," I beg, kneeling in front of him. He ignores me, his men running into the home to find Angus. "He's not here, Sir Andrew. Please, is there anything else we can offer?" I ask, grabbing his arm. But he shoves me hard, and my stomach lurches when I hit the ground.

"Please, Sir Andrew, please, let me offer anything else," I beg, but his men continue to rifle through the house, our things, our property, like it means nothing. My mother yells, and I instantly turn to run to her, but a hand wraps itself around mine, tightening as I move away.

"Do not move," Sir Andrew warns, his voice a threat in itself.

One of his men forces my mother out into the yard. Anger flares through my body at the sight of her being dragged mercilessly across the ground.

"Please, Sir Andrew. Take anything but my brother," I say again. "Don't hurt my mother. Please don't hurt her." I look from Sir Andrew to my mother, who has slumped to the ground.

"We need able-bodied human beings. Your mother is too weak," Sir Andrew retorts.

I pull away from Sir Andrew, eager to take my stand. "Me," I yell impulsively. "I'll serve the palace. Take me."

"No!" my mother yells behind me.

"Please take me instead," I beg, ignoring her. "Please. I'm useful. I can clean; I can help people. I'll do whatever you need me to do. I'll spend years serving you to pay off our debt."

Sir Andrew finally turns to me, his thick dark eyebrows frowning.

"You?" he says again.

"Please," I beg, getting on my knees once more.

"Please, no," my mother cries behind me.

Sir Andrew's beady, evil eyes turn to me, a creepy, wicked smile spreading on his face. "I accept. You will serve the kingdom in exchange for your brother. Serve for five years to pay off your debt."

"I'll do it," I say, tears running down my cheeks.

Suddenly, a body jumps over me, its knuckles connecting with Sir Andrew's face. Sir Andrew's minions instantly grab Angus, pulling him away from their boss.

Sir Andrew chuckles. "So, this is the boy," he says, nodding.

"Please don't take him," I beg.

"He just punched me. That has consequences," Sir Andrew says, patrolling me and Angus.

"Please, take me. Double my years to pay off the damage," I say immediately.

Sir Andrew's ears pique. "Interesting."

"No! No, don't take her! Please!" Angus pleads.

"Hm…But your sister says she'll double her service," Sir Andrew taunts.

I stand, turning back to my brother. "Shut up and take care of Mother," I say, my eyes spilling with every bit of anger I have. He looks at me, just like the little boy version of him used to.

When I turn to Sir Andrew, he doesn't say anything. "Take me. Please take me instead."

Sir Andrew nods. "Take her," he orders.

His palace soldiers proceed to grab my arms and lead me to the back of the carriage. I look back, for only a few moments—just to see my mother and my brother for the last time.

CHAPTER 6

Alex

The palace soldier grabs my arm, shoving me into the back of the carriage. I stumble into it, hitting the floor with my elbow, but I don't have time to adjust. He shoves my knees in, shutting the door behind my legs. I grimace, but I fall forward as soon as the carriage starts moving. My hands hit the floor, and it takes all my strength to push myself up so I can wave at my brother and mother for the last time. Mother's still sitting on the ground, and my brother is perched next to her. He doesn't even know how to make her concoctions. He doesn't know how to take care of our animals.

I sit back on the bench, the weight of what I've just done as heavy as the pain in my elbow. I stare once more at the home I grew up in, the only home I knew, the only people I'd ever known and loved. To my family.

My entire being breaks, and tears stream down my cheeks, so I bend over, eager to hold on while my whole body breaks down. A heavy knock sounds on the wall where the horses are, and I look up to the faces I'll forever remember as the people who took me from my family.

"What?" I glare at them.

But I got no response. Presumably because I didn't deserve one.

"Are you okay?" a little voice says. I jump, turning to face next to me where a tiny mouse sat, its hands enclosed.

"Hello," I manage, feeling the swelling of my eyes already. I pull my long, wavy dark hair into a bun at the top of my head.

"Wow! You heard me and didn't yell when you saw me!" the mouse responds.

I shrug at the tiny animal, not responding to its original question.

Finally, after a while, the mouse asks again, "Are you okay?"

I take a deep sigh, pondering my answer. "As okay as I'll ever be. I don't think I'll ever see my family again," I tell the mouse, looking behind us one more time to see if I can see the house anymore. I can't. All I see now are trees and the King's road.

"My name is Elena," the mouse says.

"Alex," I whisper, the words barely audible above the tremor in my voice.

"It'll be okay, Alex," the mouse squeaks, its tiny whiskers twitching as it scurries towards me and gently places a paw on my leg.

I sniffle. "Will it?"

"Well, it just means you can make the most of your new life," the mouse says.

I look down at it, rolling my eyes. "Is that how easy it is for mice? You move on and make the best of things?"

The mouse shrugs, jumping from where it was, onto my thigh and up the window so I was face to face with it. "We don't have a choice. It happens because we have so many predators. We run for our lives. I don't even know where my family is anymore."

"You don't? Who do you live with now?" I ask.

"By myself. It's easier that way, easier not to get attached. I've been living in this carriage for months, watching that douche collect taxes from people who don't deserve it," the mouse says.

"They've collected from other people, too?" I ask, narrowing my eyes.

"Of course. The palace is struggling, I think." The mouse turns its tiny little eyes onto me. "I don't think it's collected many taxes this year."

I frown, watching the trees pass by. "So, it might not have been my mother's fault? I thought she stopped paying our taxes because she got sick. I didn't get the chance to ask her."

The mouse nods. "Maybe. There's at least eight families that have lost their homes, and we just started collecting."

My thoughts swirl. The palace has never bothered us in the many years we've lived at the farm. We never got any summons, never got visitors. Not one. I've lived there all my life and started taking over household duties as early as ten years old.

"I've never met anyone who could talk to a mouse," the mouse says, turning its tiny head back to me.

I look back at it, shrugging. "I've always been able to talk to animals," I respond. "But I don't know why or how? I discovered it when I was little, and a bird got hurt. We talked. My mother always thought it was weird."

"Are you nervous?" the mouse asks.

"Nervous about what?" I deflect, but I'm only stalling. The only thoughts I have right now are of the palace and how know I won't belong there. I won't fit in with the people of a single color, the people of a certain caliber and status. It feels like the first day of school, only this time, I know what to expect.

"The palace," the mouse responds, and my heart drops. I don't know if I want to say it out aloud. It might make it even realer.

"I think you'll like the prince. He's super pretty," the mouse adds, looking out the window at the trees passing around us.

"You've met him?" I ask.

"I mean, I didn't talk to him, if that's what you're asking. You're the only one I've ever talked to," the mouse responds.

"You might be the only one I'll ever talk to in the palace," I say sadly.

"Oh, I doubt that," the mouse says.

"No one will talk to me, Elena. Look at me. I'm not one of them. I'm an outsider." I point to the mere color of my skin.

"But, Alex," the mouse turns to me, "you can talk to animals. It'll be their loss if they don't."

I look at the tiny creature. "What do you mean?"

It skitters its way from the window back to the bench next to me. "How often do you meet a human who can talk to animals? It's a super rare skill."

I turn to the window, my thoughts swirling as fast as we pass yet more rows of trees.

"I feel like I should tell you, though. You know there are more than just the regular animals in the city, right?" the mouse asks.

"I don't understand. What does that mean?" I rub the back of my ear.

"Dragons, Alex. They have dragons."

CHAPTER 7

Alex

We arrive at the palace hours later.

The palace is huge; our little farm is but a portion of the size of the grounds. Four imposing towers, linked by sturdy stone parapets, each offering a raised platform for watchers to survey the surrounding landscape. The wind whistles through the gaps between the stones. The massive grey stone castle stands in the middle of the courtyard, its huge windows and balconies overlooking the manicured gardens below. Each tower displays vibrant green and yellow flags, their rich colors proclaiming the family's ownership of the palace.

A steady stream of soldiers moves below, and the sounds of their marching and murmured conversations fill the air as they train or pass through. I haven't even seen the entirety of it, like the farm area, the barn, or where the dragons are kept. I hear them, though, the moment we get closer. The growling and rumbling make my chest tighten, and I can even hear them walking around, having conversations loud enough to hear, but not noisy enough to understand. They haul me to a side entrance, where a woman in a simple black dress and white apron hands me a uniform and shoes. The coarse fabric of the uniform feels rough against my skin, and the smell of dust and dampness fills the air.

With a grunt, she pushes me into a tiny, windowless room, the oppressive darkness broken only by the faint light filtering under the door, and tells me to change before meeting my new lady. She also looks at me from top to bottom, as if the idea of someone with olive skin working at the palace is so foreign. I was right then. When I walk into the palace—more like dragged, actually—the only people I see are the ones that look like Serena. Light skin, blonde hair, beautiful blue or green eyes. A stark contrast to who I am—olive skinned, dark hair, dark eyes.

With a loud bang, my door swings open, and there she is again—the woman, her hand holding a waterlogged towel, steam rising from it. She hurls the towel, a damp, heavy weight, that smacks my face just before the door slams shut. I guess I'm supposed to clean myself. I quickly dry myself with another towel, pull on the black dress and white apron, and tie my hair back in a neat ponytail before venturing out to meet my intimidating new boss and the woman who will become the person I serve throughout my time here. Right outside my room, the hallway to the kitchen stretches before me, its dim light barely illuminating the worn carpet under my feet as I carefully make my way toward it.

My eyes widen when the woman with the black dress and white apron appears at the door to the kitchen. She takes one look at me, shaking her head and clicking her tongue. Then she walks towards me, before straightening my dress and my apron. Finally, she takes the tie from my hair, and pulls it straight until strands of my hair are literally snapping out of my head.

"Ow," I mutter.

She clicks her tongue at me, clearly disappointed in everything about me. When she's done looking me over, she sighs deeply, taking a step back to look at me once more.

"This is a bad idea," she mumbles under her breath.

I roll my eyes, which she sees immediately.

"My name is Miranda, I will be your supervisor as you work at the palace. You must be clean and ready by 5:00 am and report for your tasks on a daily basis. Is that understood? Keep your hair straight and proper; this is not the pub," she says, rolling her eyes at me. Like I know what women in pubs actually wear or look like.

When I do the same, she turns to me, bending a little to make sure her face is directly next to mine.

"Keep your eyes fixed and proper. We do not roll our eyes at any royal members, understood?" she snaps, glaring at me.

I nod, feeling out of place. I've never had a boss; I've never had anyone telling me what to do.

"Sadly, for some reason, Sir Andrew insists you be assigned to Dajlia, and I don't understand why. You're..." she mutters, giving me an odd look, "brown, you're inexperienced, and you're brand new to this place. You'll give her a heart attack! Or me, honestly, I highly doubt you'll survive, but who am I to question royalty?" she finishes as she opens a door to get to where we need to be.

I follow her, refusing to say anything as I look through each room we pass. I've never seen anything so grand, so beautiful. So much gold and silver. You wouldn't think they even needed the taxes we allegedly owe. Even the candles are made of silver.

We pass by seven massive rooms and three that are closed. Each room has a huge gold chandelier hanging from the top, accentuated with sconces of light on the sides. Massive tables sit in the middle of comfortable-looking chairs. One table had bowls of fruit that ran from one side to the other. Fruits, something my family and I never had, especially in this abundance. Yet here they are, just sitting uneaten in an empty room.

I follow Miranda through a few more rooms, trying to keep up with her fast pace. After what feels like forever, she finally turns into another wing and knocks on a blue door. She turns quickly to me, snapping, "Stand up straight!" before turning back to the door and knocking again. "It's Miranda, my lady."

The door opens, revealing a bedroom covered in blue glitter. In the middle of the room is a four-poster bed made up with blue silk sheets. A massive window flanks the other wall, where a big blue sofa sits by a gold fireplace and two blue chairs in front of a coffee table. It took us seven years to afford a coffee table. Seven. And this is just one of their bedrooms.

"Come in," a sharp and shrill voice calls out.

Miranda walks in, her head bowed, so I assume I should, too.

A woman wearing blue royal robes sits on the couch. Her hair is silvery ash, floating around her shoulders. Her cheekbones are very pronounced and rosy red, matching her thin lips. Icy blue eyes stare at Miranda and me.

Miranda bows, and I do the same.

"Your handmaid, my lady," Miranda says, stepping aside to show me off. I bow again, not knowing exactly what I'm supposed to do.

The woman on the sofa frowns, her lips tilting to one side. "Why is she…brown?"

My heart flutters in annoyance, but I don't say anything, but Miranda steps in front of me. "This was on the orders of Sir Andrew, my lady, I know not why."

The lady on the sofa gets up, her long dress dragging along the ground as she circles me.

"What's her name?" the lady asks.

"Alex, my lady," I say, but apparently, that was not the right answer.

"I wasn't talking to you," the lady responds quickly, her voice straining my ears. Then, an arm reaches out, and I let out a cry as her palm connects with my cheek.

"Shhh!" Miranda glares at me, but she doesn't move from where she's standing.

"What's her name?" the lady asks again, enunciating carefully.

"Alex," Miranda responds this time.

I hang my head, my cheeks red, shame creeping all the way up to my head.

"You may leave," the lady says, but when I stand, she adds, "Not you."

Right before Miranda leaves, she pulls at my arm. "Do not do anything stupid."

I nod, continuing to bow my head, mostly because I don't know what else to do.

When she leaves, the lady closes the door, then circles me again.

"Do you know who I am?" she finally asks after a long moment of awkward silence.

"No, Ma'am," I respond.

"My lady is the correct answer," the lady wrinkles her nose in displeasure.

"No, my lady," I repeat, not bothering to look up.

"Why are you brown?" she asks, clicking her tongue.

I don't answer. What was I supposed to say? That I was born like that? That my mother is also brown? That we suffer from a "brown" disease?

"My name is Lady Dajlia. I'm the future queen," she says, her beady eyes piercing mine.

I don't know how to respond to that, so I just continue to bow again, keeping my face on the ground this time.

"If you're going to be my handmaid, you need to know the rules," she says.

"Yes, my lady." I swallow.

"Anything I say or do here inside this bedroom is between you and me. If I learn you've told anyone my secrets, I will cut your head off," she says, her face closing on mine. I keep myself from breathing.

"Yes, my lady," I croak.

"You'll respond to every call. You'll do everything I ask in a timely manner. Any delay gets you a slap. Is that understood?"

"Yes, my lady," I say, my body shaking.

"Go get my evening tea," Lady Dajlia orders.

I bow once more, then head out of the room, only to remember that I have no idea how to get back to the kitchen.

CHAPTER 8

Alex

So…I'm lost. I'm at the palace, and I'm lost. How did I not anticipate this happening? I turn a corner. Didn't I come through here already? But then again, the entire fricking hall looks exactly the same as the other side. I continue walking. I'd already chosen this path, so I might as well try. I scan the area, trying to see if there's anything familiar. For a moment, I really wish Miranda hadn't left me, but she could barely stand me either. She doesn't even know me, and yet, she'd already decided I'm not worth it just because I'm…brown.

I keep walking, passing a massive room with a table in it, and then another, and then another, with only tiny variations. Everything just looks the same. I don't understand how people want a massive house only to make every fricking room look the same. What's the point of it? This fricking hallway is so long. How long does a hallway need to be? Jeez. I move on to the next room. This room has a chair and a window, so I enter, looking at the paintings. How do people ever learn their way around this place? I gently ran a finger along the back of the couch, feeling the velvet texture and wondering how much it had cost. Our furniture at home is all giveaways from people around us. My bed was from Serena's grandfather. Angus's bed is from Serena's parents. My mom's bed was given to her by their parents. Furniture is so costly that we barely have anything. But the castle with empty rooms that no one appears to be using is full of beautiful furniture. What's the point of furniture if no one uses it?

"Hey! What do you think you're doing in here?" A soldier frowns at me. At least, he looks like a soldier. He wears a simple white tunic and black pants, but the way his powerful muscles strain against the fabric, combined with his close-cropped hair, hints at a military past. "What the hell are you doing here?" he barks at me again.

"I'm sorry, I'm new," I blurt out, rushing over to him. "Do you know where the kitchen is? I'm lost."

The man has long blond hair tied in a braid behind his back. His eyebrows are thick, his nose is long, but I could get lost in his eyes. They're stunning, a vivid green that evokes the shimmering surface of a calm sea. It takes me a moment to realize I'm staring, mesmerized by his intense gaze, only to see him studying me, too, a slight smile playing on his lips.

"I'm sorry, I'm new," I repeat.

"Are you Quailan?" he asks.

I nod and bow because I don't know how to act around soldiers.

"Why are you…" he trails off, continuing to study me. Then he points across the hallway. "Down that hallway, there are stairs. Go down and turn right."

I nod. "Thank you, uh, uh. Sir. Thank you," I say again, hurrying my way past him to where he'd pointed.

"It's Griffin," he says after me.

I pause, turning. "Sir Griffin," I say, bowing again.

"You don't need to bow to me. It's just Griffin," he protests.

I open my mouth to say something, but think against it. "Sorry, Sir, I–uh–uh–have to go." I turn, running down the hallway and through the stairs.

Did he say left or right? I turn left first, only to find myself in another hallway. Oh shit.

"I said right," a voice says behind me. I freeze, my breath catching in my throat as I slowly turn to see Griffin again. He'd followed me down the stairs. "Do you like getting in trouble?"

Crimson crawls up my neck and spreads across my cheeks, burning. "I didn't plan on this–uh–sir, I just, everything looks the same!" I protest, my eyebrows knitting.

He studies me for a moment, his eyes twinkling, and then his lips tilt up into a slow smile, a low chuckle rumbling in his chest. "Yes, that's clear. What's your name?" he asks.

The two doors behind him burst open, and Miranda steps out, her face etched with a deep, angry frown. The sound echoes in the otherwise silent hallway.

"What the hell are you doing?" She glares at me. "I'm sorry, Sir Griffin, it's her first day." She turns to Griffin for a moment, then ushers me into the kitchen, saying things into my ear, but I'm too distracted as I pass him, hanging my head.

"What the hell took you so long?" Miranda turns on me. "Lady Dajlia has been waiting for hours!"

"You literally introduced me like an hour ago," I blurt out. The words escape before I can stop them, and instantly earn me a stinging slap across my face. Every inch of me wants to say something, but when I see the anger in Miranda's face, the thought dies on my lips.

"First lesson today: You do not get to talk back to me, or I will slap the soul out of you," Miranda snaps, her eyes blazing.

I hang my head lower, nodding slowly.

Miranda turns, grabbing a tray with a teapot and cups on it. She hands it to me. "Take this to her room now. Do not spill it," she hisses at me.

I take the tray, walking carefully through the kitchen, out into the hallway where Griffin had caught me. I go up the stairs and through the hallway, but when I turn, the tray and I hit a hard spot, the chest of a tall, young man wearing a blue royal tunic.

My breath catches at his deep green eyes. His body is built like Griffin, hard and muscular, with thick eyebrows, sharp jaws, and a long nose, just like him. Could they be related? I couldn't escape the pull of his eyes, deep pools that promise mysteries and adventures. Pools that remind me of those clear lakes in Fortuna, lakes my mother, brother, and I used to play in before my mother got sick. Those eyes, so unlike any I'd ever encountered, except Griffin's a moment prior, are now fixed on me. His eyes burn into me as he furiously wipes the spilled tea from his soaked shirt, the damp fabric clinging to his skin. That can't be comfortable, though it reveals the sharp muscles beneath his tunic.

"Oh, shit," I swear under my breath. "I'm—I'm so sorry. I'm—shit." I drop the tray on the ground, trying to help him wipe away the tea, only to realize he's staring at me. He grips my hand hard, his skin clammy as I wipe his chest, the rhythmic rasp of my cloth against his skin a counterpoint to his heavy breathing.

"What do you think you're doing?" he asks, each sarcastic word enunciated viciously from his tongue.

"I'm sorry, I'm sorry," I plead, closing my eyes, waiting for it, waiting for another slap.

"What are you doing?" he asks when nothing happens. His dark green eyes stare me down.

"I–I've been slapped three times today, isn't that the usual punishment?" My eyes widen.

With a tilt of his head and a frown etching itself across his brow, his focus intensifies. "Punishment?"

"Uh–for doing something wrong?" I say.

"Do you not know who I am?" he asks gruffly.

I look down, shaking my head. "I'm sorry, sir, it's my first day. I don't know anyone here."

His eyebrows rise. "You don't know who I am?"

"No, sir. I–uh–I have to bring the tea to Lady Dajlia," I say, stammering. Heat fills my cheeks.

"Okay." The man steps aside, grabbing the tray before handing it back to me. "Please keep an eye ahead of you. Spill more, and Dajlia won't enjoy it."

I nod, accepting the tray. "Thank you, sir. Thank you." I walk away, turning into the hallway for Lady Dajlia's room. When I knock, she yells at me to come in. I place the tea on the coffee table, then step back, waiting for more instructions.

Lady Dajlia smells the tea, then puts it down before approaching me.

"You stupid, stupid girl," she spits as she circles me.

I hang my head, pushing down the anger building in my belly.

"Stupid girl."

I expect it before I feel it—the slap that creates a ringing in my ear.

"I'm sorry, my lady, I'm new here. I—I got lost," I say, keeping my head hung.

"You piss me off," Lady Dajlia says.

And then her leg reaches out, kicking my ribs. I double over for a moment, but I rise slowly, trying to keep the grimace to a minimum.

"Get out of my face," Lady Dajlia growls, and I leave the room, ready to go to my cold, soulless bedroom to cry myself out.

CHAPTER 9

Alex

I don't think I've ever been this humiliated in my whole life. I've never been treated this badly. Never been hit, never been told I was stupid. Throughout my entire existence, my mother has been kind and supportive, and I've never been hated for the color of my skin. Yes, we were looked at, but nothing so blatant as calling me "brown." Eventually, in Fortuna, people just learned to exist with us, learned to realize there were people that looked different. Many years later, we're still being looked at in the village, but at least we're treated with respect. Angus made friends. I had Serena. How am I supposed to survive here if I'm constantly getting beaten up and called stupid? At what point do I break and smack someone, only for me to end up dead? How much of the six years will I actually survive?

When I'd taken my last look back at my family, I thought I'd never see them again because I'll be here for six years. But now I realize it's because I'll die. I knew this was going to kill me from the moment I climbed into the carriage.

"What are you doing?" Miranda's shrill voice cuts through my thoughts.

I get up instantly, knocking off the cups and plates beside me, and stare as they tumble to the marbled floor and break into a billion pieces.

Pink fury paints her cheeks. "What the hell? Pick all of that up and clean it!" Miranda yells, her eyes bulging with anger.

I sigh, nodding. "Yes, ma'am," I say, bending on my knees to start picking up the broken pieces.

I've never been this clumsy before. I've worked with little bottles all my life.

"When you're done with that, make sure you wash these," Miranda says, pointing to the four baskets outside the room filled with shiny silky materials. "They can only be hand-washed, so take them to the washing area by the field. Wash well and make sure you don't ruin the dresses, understood?" she barks at me.

I nod. "Yes, ma'am."

"You ruin one, you pay, understood?" Miranda barks once more.

"Yes, ma'am, I got it," I say absentmindedly. Miranda debates hitting me again. I can see it in her eyes, but eventually, she just turns, rolling her eyes as I continue to pick up the shards of glass and porcelain on the floor. I groan when a piece of it cuts into my finger. I sigh, but I continue to pick up, anyway. After sweeping up the rest of the shards and cleaning the kitchen until it's spotless, I check the laundry room, and as soon as I see the overflowing baskets, I realize this will take my entire day. My chest heaves, but I grab two and start pulling them across the floor. Luckily, I had a vague idea of where the field was; I'd seen it yesterday when I arrived.

I continue pulling the two baskets before running into one of the tall, handsome man I'd run into yesterday. His hair is unkempt this time around, falling behind his shoulders. He wears green pants and a white shirt, looking more relaxed than he had in his uniform yesterday.

"Hello," Griffin says, his eyes boring into mine, a slight smile playing on his lips.

"Uh-hello, sir, can I help you with something?" I ask, lowering my gaze as I pull the baskets out of the door. Then, I come back in, heading for the other two baskets by the kitchen.

"Do you need help?" Griffin asks, frowning as he watches me lug the other two heavy baskets across their marbled floor.

"Uh-uh-from you, sir?" I ask, taking a moment to look at him.

"I mean, there's no one else here, is there?" Griffin says, looking around.

"Uh—I don't think this is in your job description, is it?" I say, tilting my head as I frown at him.

He shakes his head. "It's not, but I'm allowed to ask if you need help, aren't I?" Griffin responds. "Or is there a rule around here that I'm not aware of?" His face breaks into a quiet, teasing smile.

"Are you? I'm new here, so I don't know what the rules are." I shrug, avoiding his gaze as I pull the other two baskets out of the door.

"Oh no, that's definitely clear. Not only have you mentioned it multiple times, but..." Griffin walks to a hidden door in the wall. He pushes, and it clicks open. Griffin pulls out a cart. "How do you think people get so many clothes baskets out at once?"

Frustration flares in my chest, but I nod anyway, between glares, and take the cart from him before pulling it out of the door.

"Again, sir. I'm new." I try to hide the sarcasm in my voice.

"Maybe if you ask, people will actually help," Griffin says, pulling the door open for me. He leans on the door, watching as I put the baskets into the cart.

"Thanks for the help, sir!" I say aloud as I push the cart through the courts and into the field.

When I'm far enough away from him, I sigh a deep breath, feeling a little freer with the fresh air around me. I lead the baskets to the little river with the faucet for washing, ready to get started. Pulling my skirts up, I bend down to open the faucet, watching the waterfall from the basin and into a little river that flows all the way down to the bigger stream below the field. How beautiful. If there's anything working at the palace has given me--it's this. In Cerene, the beauty of Quaila is undeniable: lush green hills rise, crowned with tall trees, their vibrant green contrasting with the colorful wildflowers blooming across the grassy land. I can only imagine the number of herbs this area must have. It's exciting to think about.

I sit on the side of the rock, pulling a few clothes toward me so I can start washing. There's something about doing chores and looking at a beautiful view that fills me with peace. I've always loved that about Fortuna and our home. I always enjoyed getting to do chores in the fields. I hum as I wash a few clothes, the soapy scent filling the air, then carefully hang them on the drying rack, taking extra care to secure each item with a clothespin.

In the corner of my eye, I notice a few wildflowers, their petals a vibrant splash of color against the green. Turning back to the faucet and basin, I promise myself that I'll only look really quickly, and I walk down by the stream, the sound of rushing water filling my ears as I carefully study the plants I see along the way, their vibrant colors and delicate textures captivating me. My fingers brush against the soft petals of small white flowers, their yellow centers bright against the green. I tuck them into my apron, along with several prickly purple blooms, their scent faintly sweet. Finally, I dig up the familiar roots of the white plant; the soil clinging to them, a comforting weight in my hand. I've used it so often I can spot it anywhere now. I smooth the damp leaves, their earthy scent filling my senses, before tucking them gently into my apron.

"What are you doing?" a voice says behind me, and I turn quickly, tucking every other herb in my pockets.

Griffin is standing in front of me, right next to the man I met yesterday—the man I spilled tea on. I swallow hard as my heart sinks into my stomach.

I bow instantly. "Hello, sir."

A deep chuckle, like the rumble of distant thunder, erupts from his chest as he turns to Griffin, a slow smile spreading across his sharp features.

"She has absolutely no idea who I am," he tells Griffin.

A wide grin spreads across Griffin's face, crinkling the corners of his eyes.

"I must be the only handmaid you can't stop visiting sir. I've only been here two days, and I've seen you both twice already." I breathe a weary sigh.

"You really have no clue who this man is?" Griffin asks.

"Why's that so surprising, sir? I've told you multiple times I'm new here," I say, my voice tight with frustration at their relentless teasing. Why bully me? Why harass me? I barely know what this place is right now. How am I supposed to know who they are when they don't; even spend time trying to get to know the other staff?

The man's dark green eyes narrow as a frown creases his face, the corners of his mouth pulling downwards. "I'm the one and only heir to this kingdom."

My face burns with shame as I bow my head. "I'm so, so sorry, uh-sir-uh-Prince-Heir?"

The sound of his loud, unrestrained laughter grates on my nerves. "I've truly never met anyone who didn't recognize who I was and who didn't know how to greet me," he says, shaking his head.

"It's Your Majesty," Griffin offers behind the prince.

"Sorry, Your Majesty," I stammer, my cheeks burning.

"Where are you from and why are you here?" the prince asks, his dark eyebrows drawn together in a frown, his eyes narrowed in thought.

"Fortuna. I'm here because I have to pay off taxes," I mumble, the shame I've been burying deep in me threatening to rise.

"Taxes?" the prince repeats, his head tilting.

"Sir Andrew's doing," Griffin whispers behind him, but I hear him anyway.

I glance up to see the prince and Griffin murmuring to each other, their words barely audible above the gentle rustling of leaves. Suddenly, a deafening roar shatters the morning calm, vibrating through the ground and shaking the very air around me. I look up, my eyes darting around, taking in the vastness of the sky and the surrounding trees for the noise.

"Relax," the prince says. "It's just the dragons."

"I've never seen dragons before," I stammer, my knees weak, and I sink back down, the tremors in my body betraying my composure.

"You're afraid," the prince notices.

"Dragons aren't exactly your regular puppy, Your Majesty," I retort quickly.

He and Griffin laugh, the sound echoing throughout the air, and the blush intensifies on my cheeks. "I have to go finish my chores," I mumble, and with a bow, I walk back to the laundry baskets to finish the rest of the clothes. I watch from the corner of my eye as they talk, the prince's clenched jaw and furrowed brow betraying his anger.

CHAPTER 10

Gabriel

I don't think I've ever seen anyone with that kind of skin before--other than my mother. For some reason, I can't seem to keep my mind off the handmaiden I met last night after coming back from meeting Lady Dajlia. Her beauty is different--unlike anything I've ever seen anywhere I've been. And I've traveled quite a bit. Her skin is beautiful olive, so soft, so unlike mine. I can't seem to get her out of my head. Despite the many girlfriends I've had, none of them had been like her--not in looks, nor in the way she responded to me. My last girlfriend literally tried to barter her way into marrying me just so her family could become royal. That's been my relationships, all sex and power-grabbing, no heart. How could I when every single one of them wants a crown? Would it be too much to want someone to love me for who I am, and not what I am?

My father's office opens as I approach, its big wood double doors creaking as it pushes in.

"Gabriel." His voice echoes through the room, just like I know he likes to hear it. It makes him seem more royal, more ethereal.

"Father," I say, bowing in front of him.

His office is right in front of the castle, with a balcony opening to the main city below us so he can always look out and have his citizens watch him like it's part of a show. My father loves putting on a show. His door is half closed, so I can only see one side. A massive mahogany desk, its polished surface gleaming under the soft light, sits right in front of the doors. Two massive blue velvet armchairs, plush and deep, dominate the space before it, consistent with the castle's luxurious furnishings.

"Have you thought about what I asked of you?" he says, pacing behind his desk. My father has been King for quite a long time. The scars on his right cheek are proof of it. I stare at my father, knowing exactly which features I got from him. Lots of it is more physical, but my heart came from my mother. My father's long blond hair falls to his waist. He hasn't cut it in years. His thick eyebrows are dark and greyish with age, his eyes a jade green, similar to mine. He has a crooked nose from a previous altercation and a short beard and stubble to match his eyebrows. His soon-to-be wife and my soon-to-be stepmother sits on one of the armchairs, her long, white hair cascading down beside her, her legs crossed elegantly, the rich blue of her royal robes pooling on the floor around her. Her gaze, sharp and unwavering, sends a chill down my spine. I gaze at my father instead.

"Which one?" I ask wearily.

"Watch your tone," Lady Dajlia snaps, looking at my father, then back to me.

I sigh at her, then turn back to my father, who's still pacing behind the desk like the weight of the world is on his shoulders.

"I meant your future wife, Gabriel. You don't think you can be single for much longer, do you? If you can't pick one, I'll do it for you," my father drawls, turning to face the open doors, looking out at his kingdom. "We need to make sure that our future is secure, and in order to do that, we need to be allying ourselves with the right people and the right kingdoms."

"Father, you're nowhere near retiring. Why do I have to get married?" I ask, like this isn't the first time we've had this conversation.

"Son," he says, sighing deeply. "Why do you always have to be this difficult?"

"I'm not being difficult. I'd really like to take my time with this. I'd like to actually fall in love, like you did with my mother," I say, looking directly at Lady Dajlia. I knew that'd piss her off. She's always acting like she's my mother, when in reality, she's nowhere near the spark that my mother was, and nowhere near her kindness, her love. The only reason why my father has to marry again is so they can produce a backup heir. Apparently, I'm not enough.

"Son," my father approaches me, planting his hands on my shoulders, "we're trying to build a monarchy here, right? I'll have more kids; you need to have kids. We can build this castle with more children. We want to foster our bloodline and make sure we're producing only the best of the best ."

My jaw tightens. "I don't want to have children. At least not with people I barely know, Father," I protest, sighing.

"Not everyone will have the luxury of marrying someone they know, Gabriel. My marriage to your mother was one-of-a-kind." He shakes his head at me. But there's no warmth, no kindness in his voice, not even when he mentions my mother, whom he claims to have loved deeply. His words feel hollow and cold.

Though his eyes are the color of jade, flecked with darker shades, a cold, hard intensity emanates from them as he stares, seeming almost black in their unwavering focus on me, like chips of polished obsidian. My father, the complete opposite of who my mother was. If my mother was kindness and grace, my father is hardness and evil. How they felt about each other? I wasn't old enough to understand. But more and more lately, I'm realizing the love match I thought they were, can't be the exact truth. For some reason, the kingdom and the palace did a great job of selling their love story, but as I grew up, I realized that my mother might have cried too many times.

That there were too many accidents. Too many coincidences. Too many falls down the stairs. Too many times her eyes were dark and purple, and she'd grimace when I'd hug her. That every time she'd hug me, she'd also cry–maybe because she thought she'd lose me. Or maybe because her body is suffering from unknown bruises. Bruises I never knew about.

"Father, I just need time, please," I plead. For some reason, her face, with its kind, dark eyes and gentle, dimpled smile, appears in my head. As a handmaiden, she'll never be considered to ever become a future queen, and yet here I am considering her. Of all the many beautiful women I've bedded, it's her that appears in my head.

"No, Gabriel. Like I said, you pick one, or I'll do it for you," he demands, his jaw clenching, his eyes burning into me with an intensity that makes my skin crawl.

"Fine." I roll my eyes. "Can I be dismissed?"

My father waves me off, and I bow to him before turning and leaving the room, seething. I'm lucky to be the heir. More often than not, my father can be unhinged, unpredictable, ordering people to do things I could never understand. At this point, I've just learned to go with it.

After all, there's nothing I can do until I take the throne, which won't be for many more years. I find Griffin in the kitchen, with an odd smile on his face.

"Hey," I greet him.

"Hey," Griffin says, nodding towards the door. "Remember the girl you said you met last night? The one with brown skin," he adds, enunciating the color.

"And...?" I say.

"You don't have to hide it from me, Gabriel, I can tell," Griffin says, rolling his eyes.

I chuckle at him. "Where are you headed?"

"Depends. Where are you?" he asks, a sly smile spreading on his face.

I scowl at him, but he follows me when I leave the kitchen and head for the field. There she is, bending by the river, scanning her surroundings. She's wearing the usual handmaiden uniform—a black dress with a white apron—and yet, she looks so different from any handmaid I've ever seen. Her dark, wavy hair falls around her face, framing her dark eyes and thick lashes, and her cute button nose contrasts with the long straight noses most people have around here. But it's her lips I can't pull my eyes away from. They're a natural pink, and in perfect proportion with her delicate, makeup-free features. She smiles as she stares at the surrounding flowers in fascination. Wildflowers are something we constantly overlook because they're of no use to the Kingdom.

"What's she looking at?" I murmur under my breath.

"Beats me," Griffin responds anyway, shrugging.

I walk over, continuing to watch her pick up leaves and flowers around her. But she doesn't even notice me until I'm right behind her.

When she bows, thoughts of her subservience dance in my head, but I push away the tempting fantasy. I can't help thinking how beautiful she looks when she's flushed. How soft her cheeks look, and how I could find freedom from swimming in the depths of her dark eyes. I want to run my hands through her hair to see how soft it is. I blink away the dreams that could never have come true. She could never be mine, regardless of how attracted I am to her. I've never wanted a woman this way just from a first glance.

When she goes back to her chores, I turn to Griffin. "Why are we charging taxes now?"

"Don't look at me, Your Majesty," he says mockingly. "Your father ordered it. Sir Andrew's been doing it to everyone outside of Cerene."

"I don't understand where the sudden change of mind came from," I say thoughtfully, wracking my brain. Why would we suddenly need to cheat people out of money we don't need? "Also, why only outside of Cerene?"

"I mean, because they're the ones that can't question the King? Cerene knows too much and keeps track of too many things. By doing it only to people outside and in rural areas, who's to question him?" Griffin responds, shrugging.

My eyes widen, half watching Griffin and half watching the woman behind him wash the clothes and hang them.

"You know who's behind this, Gabe. It's not exactly the only outrageous thing she's done. Have you even looked at the expenses for their wedding? I'm pretty sure your father's original wedding cost three times less."

I hadn't. I turn to Griffin, my best friend since we were kids. He's grown up at the palace, so he's been my only confidant ever since we were children, and the only person I truly trust in this castle, except for my mother, who passed away almost ten years ago. My mother, the only other person I've ever met with the same skin color as this handmaiden. This kingdom is inherently White, so perhaps that's why I'm so drawn to this stranger. I inherited my father's pale skin rather than my mother's olive tones.

"Do you really think she'd pass on those costs to our people?" I ask, but it's a stupid question. Even I already know the answer. Griffin chuckles, like he already knows what I'm thinking.

"I think you need to talk to your father. The moment they're married, I think we're all done for." Griffin shrugs, sneaking a look behind us at the handmaiden.

I guess I'm not the only one enamored of her. When he turns back to me, he catches me watching him.

"Shut up," he says, rolling his eyes. "She's beautiful."

That, I agree with. "Yes, she is pretty." I glance back at her, my heart singing an unfamiliar song, before adding, "She's different, isn't she?"

"Yes, she is," Griffin responds. "She has the same skin as Queen Estelle."

My heart skips a beat at the sound of my mother's name. It's been years. Years, and yet I'll never forget the day that I found her dead.

CHAPTER 11

Alex

I finish the last basket of laundry and hang the rest around the drying rack. When I turn, I catch a deer drinking from the soapy remains of my wash.

"Hey! Don't drink there!" I say.

The deer looks up at me, surprised, taking a few steps back.

"Don't drink from there," I repeat.

The deer approaches slowly. "Are you...are you a deer, too? Why do you look weird?"

With a chuckle, I squeeze the water from my skirts, the lingering scent of soap and damp earth filling my nostrils. "I'm not a deer. At least, I don't believe so."

The deer, its coat dappled with sunlight, approached closer, its large, gentle eyes gazing up at me. "How come I've never talked to anyone like you before? I mean, I see your kind so often and yet, I've never talked to any of you. In fact, most of you have those big things that kill us."

Kneeling down, I met the deer's gaze—its gentle eyes, wide and alert, reflecting the dappled sunlight filtering through the trees. "I'm sorry. Do they hunt often here?"

"Not here, but around the area, yes. I think I've lost quite a bit of my family," the deer responds.

"Can I pet you?" I ask.

The deer nods. "But only you can."

"Just me. I won't hurt you. I'd like some friends, though. I don't know if anyone here would want to be my friend," I say, petting the deer over her head and behind her ears.

She wriggles, sighing happily. "I think people will want to be your friend. You're nice."

A grin breaks out on my face. "Thank you. I don't think so. Have you seen me?" I doubt it. Only been here two days and I can tell how much the staff and the people I'm serving don't like me.

"What about you?" the deer asks, tilting its head.

"I mean, have you seen people with the same skin?" I ask, pointing to my hand.

"Oh." The deer nods. "You have pretty skin."

I sigh. "Well, I wish everyone else thought so."

"The prince thought so," the deer says in a singsong voice.

I laugh. "The prince? Like the Quaila prince?"

"Yes, he was here a few hours ago. I was watching him and the other soldier talking, and they were talking about you." The deer wags its tail as I pet its lower back.

"Were they? What were they saying?" I ask.

"Well, I didn't hear everything. But the prince said you're pretty," the deer says.

I chuckle. "I'm sure he says that about every other woman in this castle."

The cutest little chortle vibrates from the deer, a sound that makes my heart melt.

"Will you visit me again the next time I'm here?" I ask.

The deer turns to me, its doe eyes warming my chest. "Sure. I'd love to come visit you again. I'll be your friend."

For the first time in the last two days, I actually smile. Like a real smile.

"Who are you talking to?" a voice says behind me.

I turn, jumping to my feet, nearly stumbling over my dress to see the prince once more. My head whirls back to the deer, who's still quietly grazing by the clothesline.

"Sir—Your Majesty," I say, bowing.

The man, nearly two feet taller than I was, circles me, a frown on his face. His dark green eyes study me carefully, boring into mine so intensely I'm the first to blink.

"I asked you—who were you talking to?" he demands, his feet tapping on the ground.

"I mean, there's no one here, Your Majesty," I say, not looking up.

He huffs, his nostrils flaring as he approaches.

"Stop!" I say, stepping back from the heady mix of cedarwood and vanilla that emanates from him as he moves closer, the fragrance both sharp and sweet, filling my senses.

"I heard you talking to someone. Who is it?" he demands.

I shoot a look at the deer now across the field, its eyes nervously on me. My gaze turns back to the absolute prick in front of me, my anger rising. "Okay, just because you're the prince doesn't mean you're allowed to just take up someone else's space. Respect begets respect," I snarl, my glare burning into him, the words heavy with contempt. For a moment, I forget he's the prince and I'm just a handmaid. For a moment, we're just two humans on the same playing field. His eyes widen, and he steps back, silent as he studies me with those green eyes.

"I—I'm sorry. I didn't mean to scare you," he says, his chest heaving with deep breaths.

"Problem with anger, Your Majesty?" I ask sweetly. Internally, I'm slapping myself. Why can't I hold my anger? He rattles me. He gets everything he wants in this life, and I can't control anything in mine. He's the reason that my family is separated. Why I'll probably never see my family again.

His eyes, wide with surprise a moment before, narrow into a deep frown. "That's none of your business," he retorts.

I watch him watching me, appreciating the way his damp shirt clings to his chest, highlighting every muscle, and the way his leg muscles bunch and flex as he stands. I try not to stare at the way his arm muscles, taut and corded, pulse in time with the heavy, ragged rhythm of his breathing.

"Get a good look?" he says, his eyes meeting mine, a knowing smile playing on his lips as he notices my stare.

Heat blooms in my cheeks, and a blush spreads across my face as I stare at him, captivated by the shifting expressions playing across his features. He continues to glare, his dark eyes burning into me like two pools of stagnant, shadowed water.

"I saw you talking to someone. Are you a spy?" he accuses.

The sound of my raucous laugh shatters the quiet, a stark contrast to the somber atmosphere of the previous two days; it's a sound I never expected to come from me, or to experience in this place. Not after all the humiliation and the slaps.

"You think I'm a spy?" I repeat between laughter.

"Are you? You were clearly talking to someone," he says, circling me again.

"Can you stop circling me like I'm prey? It's not helping," I snap.

Again, the prince stops, his eyes blazing with anger. "Stop ordering me around. I'm the prince," he retorts.

"Is that a reminder for me or for you?" I blurt out, the heat rising in my cheeks still further as I wince, wishing I could recoil from my own rudeness. Rudeness that doesn't usually come out. Not the way this man just brought it out. Every part of me wants to punch this man for all the grief he has caused me.

His face darkens. "Answer me, maid. Are you a spy? Who were you talking to?"

"My name is Alex," I mutter, breathing heavily, so I can control my anger.

"Who were you talking to?" he demands again.

I look up at him, my heart pounding, and force myself to take a tentative step closer. "Once again, I said nobody. Am I not allowed to talk to myself? Is that how the palace controls its people? Not allowing them to talk to themselves, especially when they're finally alone and away from the people that keep humiliating her and slapping her for no good reason? Is that it? Just because you're a prince, you feel like you can control how people act and who they can talk to?" I step forward again, his intense gaze locking with mine, a silent challenge passing between us. "You don't own me. You don't control what I do."

A scowl etches itself onto his face as he takes a step back, eyes blazing. "Look at yourself. Apparently, I do," he spits out.

I look at the dress and the apron I'm wearing. Realization dawns, a cold dread creeps into my brain, and a hot, angry fire consumes my body. Then, I glare at him with the most menacing look I can manage, flipping him off before grabbing the empty, clattering laundry baskets and dragging them back to the castle, the cold metal handles biting into my hands.

I hate this castle. I hate this city. I hate the prince.

CHAPTER 12

Alex

"Welcome, welcome!" a voice booms from above the balcony.

I can barely see the king from where I'm standing. The king had called an audience a few hours ago to announce something important. The pungent smell of cleaning product still clings to me as I reluctantly stand and watch the King make his announcement, having been pulled away from cleaning the bathrooms by Miranda. It's a requirement for all workers to be at all announcements, to show support, to cheer. According to Miranda, it is part of our responsibility as palace staff.

I sigh, pressing down on the urge to roll my eyes once more. I'm standing with all the staff--handmaids, cooks, gardeners, cleaners, and I'm not even remotely kidding that we can all probably take up half the amphitheater, a sea of black dresses or shirts and pants and white aprons. We'd look a sight.

I look up, and my heart leaps into my throat, realizing that the king is not alone on the balcony. Beside him stands Lady Dajlia, her silk dress rustling softly in the breeze, which is teasing her flowing hair. A step behind them stands the prince, with his dark eyes, serious expression, and reserved posture. In my twenty-four years, I've never had a boyfriend, never desired one, and have never encountered a man who has captivated my thoughts as intensely as he has. Honestly, I'd prepared to be a spinster, especially after my mother teased me about how little I actually made it out of the house. Angus used to always tell me it was because of my attitude. I was too crass, too rude, too wild for anyone to like or want to be with. Not only did I look the way I did, I didn't act like most women did—eager for men to like them, eager to get married and have kids. I could barely stand myself as a child.

His face tilts, his gaze locks onto mine, and a sudden chill runs down my spine. I know better than to look away, because that would mean defeat. This man may be my boss, but I refuse to make him think he owns me. I'm doing this for my family, but I'd rather die than be owned by a king who thinks he can take everything away from me.

The prince continues to look at me, and I suppress an eye roll. This whole staring contest is becoming so petty. My stare intensifies into a burning glare, my eyes locked on his, unwavering. His face finally relaxes, a strange look chasing away the grim set of his mouth. Is he…is he smiling at me? Heat flushes my face as I break eye contact, my cheeks burning. What the hell does he want from me? Why does he keep doing this? When I look up, his gaze has turned, no longer on me, and for a moment, a sinking feeling grapples me—before I internally slap myself sane. What the hell am I doing?

"Good evening, my people!" the king says from the balcony. I shift uncomfortably, reminding myself that I'm not *his people* and I'm only here because they threatened to take my brother and our home.

"Today is a beautiful day," he continues.

A deafening roar echoes from my left, causing me to lift my gaze to the source of the unsettling sounds. I see a tall, imposing gated fence and a massive barn, but my eyes are drawn to at least three dragons, their roars echoing faintly in the distance. Their long snouts twitch, their eyes glowing red or yellow, and the occasional flap of their enormous wings sends a gust of unnatural wind across the amphitheater. One of the dragons is a massive beast, its dark green scales shimmering in the light as it towers over the others; its yellow breast, eyes, and underwings a striking contrast. The other is a vibrant crimson, its menacing yellow eyes gleaming, and ivory horns jutting aggressively from its face and head, sharp and imposing. The third dragon's bright yellow eyes shine intensely, its rose-red scales shimmering like a thousand polished gems, each catching the last of the sunlight as its ivory chest and horns reflect the flickering torchlight.

My stomach knots.

"Stop fidgeting," a voice behind me says, and I didn't have to look up to know that it is Miranda. I can hear the discontent in her voice. I can feel the disappointment in her gaze.

I'm not fidgeting. I'm shaking.

"Good lord, get yourself together," she sighs deeply.

I don't need to look at her to know she's rolling her eyes. I'm trying, but I can't help it. I raise my hands, watching them tremble, my eyes widening as I look back at the dragons.

The red dragon stirs, and with its movement, a miniature gold dragon, barely bigger than my thumb, becomes visible, nestling between the red and green dragons. I squint, eager to see it more clearly, realizing after a moment that it's a baby dragon. My heart melts a little, looking at the cutest little thing. Obviously, it could still easily blow fire and incinerate you to death. Lovely.

"Our wonderful dragon has a baby dragon!" The king's announcement fades as I turn, my cheeks burning anew at the sight of the prince observing me from across the balcony, his eyes intense. I stare before him, eager to focus on the king, but I can feel his sharp gaze boring into me, a hawk poised to strike.

"To celebrate the birth of our newest fighter, we will be having a ball and a celebration where we can introduce the new member of our kingdom!" the king announces, resulting in a wave of cheers and exhilarated yells.

As everyone turns to face the dragons, the air crackles with anticipation before the green one unleashes a bone-jarring roar that reverberates through the amphitheater, making me jump. Goosebumps prickle my arms; the loud sound raises the hairs on my skin.

"The ball will be in two day's time, and you're all invited! There will be food, drinks, and lots of entertainment," the king continues amidst the celebratory cheers.

The prince is still staring at me.

"That means we have lots of work to do," Miranda whispers behind me. "I hope you know what you're in for."

I ignore the prince and Miranda, turning back to the dragons that I'm so afraid of. I can't hear the words they're saying, but they seem to be having a very intense conversation among themselves. Squinting, I focus on their sounds, trying really hard to get a sense of what their discussion is about. I can tell by the green dragon's furious roars and the clatter of his massive claws that he's upset about something. The smaller red dragon glares, smoke puffing from its nostrils, while its larger counterpart merely scowls, its fiery breath held in check. I think the bigger red dragon is the mother of the golden dragon. There's something about the way she gently nudges it, the soft warmth radiating from her, and the constant, anxious glances she gives it, as if afraid it might vanish if she looks away for even a second.

"Mauricio," Miranda says sternly behind me, and I spin, blinking to get myself back to the present.

"Did you hear what I just said?" Miranda barks.

A hot flush creeps up my neck as I realize the other handmaids' eyes are on me, or perhaps on Miranda's growing fury. "My name?" I offer, grimacing, knowing I'm probably sounding cheeky more than anything. I expect the slap before she even does it.

She clicks her tongue at me. "When are you ever going to be good enough for this job? You daydream, you're slow, you're stupid. I have to spend more time with you just to train you because you come from nowhere important. What am I going to do with you?" she mutters angrily.

I swallow, and my throat tightens further.

"Follow me," she says, and I hang my head as I follow her through the crowd.

Great, one more thing to ruin my experience. Being slapped on the face in front of other people. I can still feel the weight of all the other handmaidens' gazes, burning into me like I'm the world's biggest fool, their silent judgment a heavy cloak.

"Walk faster!" Miranda snarls, her voice tight with impatience as she glances back to see me lagging behind. I speed up slightly, but it's kind of hard with all the people I have to thread through. Miranda, on the other hand, holds some kind of power over everyone else. As soon as she's near, people literally move aside just so she can pass.

"You'll have to do a lot. Besides the fact that you haven't finished cleaning Lady Dajlia's bathroom, you'll also need to make sure that her clothes, jewelry, and her crown are ready for the celebration."

"If she's not queen yet, why does she have a crown?" I ask absentmindedly, forgetting for a moment that she's already pissed at me.

"It's a tiara, dear," Miranda drawls sarcastically, the words laced with a dismissive air. "She doesn't need to be royal to have one."

I scratch my head, blinking at the information. Well, how was I supposed to know that? I didn't even live in Cerene. I barely know who the royal folk are.

Miranda looks at me, the vein in her temple throbbing and betraying her rising blood pressure as she stares at me. "Get out of my sight, Mauricio. If you haven't finished that bathroom within the hour, you will be punished," she threatens, her eyes bulging with anger.

CHAPTER 13

Gabriel

It's fascinating how quickly a celebration can come together. It's like the entire staff knows exactly what they're supposed to be doing and when, just to prepare everyone. Dajlia pushed me to oversee everything (apparently, to show that I'm ready for responsibility). I didn't expect to be constantly bugged to make decisions I've never made in my entire life.

"What kind of flowers should we have?" the gardener asks as I'm walking through the hallway to my father. A few other staff members pass us quickly, each carrying trays.

I look at Griffin for additional input, but he shrugs.

"What kind of flowers do we have?" I ask, sighing as I pause for a moment for the gardener.

He stares at me with wide, disbelieving eyes, as if I've sprouted a second head.

"What?" I ask, trying not to be embarrassed at my lack of knowledge.

"I mean, we're the palace, Your Majesty. We have all sorts of flowers," the gardener responds with a bow.

What were my mother's favorite flowers? "Do we have hydrangeas and peonies?" Those were the most common flowers my mother always had in their bedroom. I can even remember the smell.

"Queen Estelle's favorites," the gardener comments, and I break into a smile. He remembers. At least I'm not the only one who does.

"Yes, my mother's favorites," I say, smiling at him, which he looks surprised about.

"I like that. I'll get on it right away, Prince Gabriel," the gardener says, bowing, then turning to leave. When I turn back to Griffin, he's smiling.

"What?" I ask him.

His smile widens further. "I think that's wonderful, Gabe."

I hide a smile. We don't talk often about my mother, but I do miss her. I knock on the door to my father's room, waiting for him to allow me to enter.

"Gabriel," my father acknowledges as I enter his office.

"Yes, Father." I bow.

"For the celebration, I'd like us to have some of the dragons ready for entertainment. I'd like to be able to stream it out to other kingdoms to show them our power."

"Dragons? You want dragons to entertain us? Father, we can barely control them. The other kingdoms will know that we can't control them!" I protest.

He huffs. "Then learn how, Gabriel. I want to be able to show the dragons during the celebration as a sign that we can."

"But we can't, Father," I say again.

He continues talking like he doesn't hear my protests. "We want to appear strong for our people, strong to other kingdoms, strong enough to be the only kingdom that can actually control dragons. It is step one of my plans."

"Step one for what?" I ask, frowning.

"I'd like you to make sure that we have the green one and the red one ready for entertainment. Is that clear?" my father orders. "With kingdoms like Luntian and their advanced firearms, and Paglaom building their armies, we need to be using our dragons for more. We need to show that we can control them and that there's a benefit to the last five dragons staying loyal to us. That's the only way for us to be able to conquer the other kingdoms."

I'm not sure how I'm supposed to respond to that, but I nod, bowing. "Yes, father."

He waves me away, and I meet Griffin outside the door, who's looking at me with his mouth and his eyes wide open.

"What the hell? How are we supposed to do that?" Griffin asks.

I shrug. "No idea. But what the king wants, I have to get." I start walking towards the exit of the castle, Griffin at my heels.

"Where are we going?" he asks, running to keep up with me.

"Well, I'm going to figure out how the hell we can order these dragons to do something we want," I say. "I'm going to the pen to see if one of the dragon caretakers can help us."

Griffin and I make it out of the castle and onto the dragon field where three of our six dragons are lying, including the new golden one. On the far edge, there's a huge barn where we usually keep their food and water, and where the dragon caretakers live. Towards the cliff there's a massive rock wall, which we used to use to cage the dragons in like animals. Eventually, though, they broke out, and the only reason they're still here is because our dragon caretakers make sure they're fed at all times. They can easily leave whenever they want to, and there's nothing we can do about it. They obviously feel it's easier to remain and be fed than to have to hunt for themselves, but that's the extent of 'control' we have over them.

I lean on the fence by the barn, watching the green dragon clean its own scales. It doesn't look at me, nor does it acknowledge that I'm here. After all, we're royals to people, but nothing to dragons.

"Hello, Your Majesty," Tait says as he comes out of the barn. Tait has been our dragon keeper for as long as I can remember. He's known these dragons since some of them were babies, and he's extremely fond of them. He's also one of the few that actually survived.

"Hello, Tait, how are you?" I ask, keeping my eyes on the dragons.

"I'm well, thank you, Your Majesty," he says, bowing.

"Oh, Tait, you never have to do that. Not to me," I tell him one more time, even though I've told him this multiple times.

"Yes, sir." He smiles, following my gaze to the green dragon. "They're doing well, sir," he adds.

I nod. "I have a dilemma for you, Tait. How do we get the green and the red dragon to be our entertainment for the celebration?" I ask.

Tait starts laughing, but when he sees that I'm serious, he stops. "Your Majesty, these are dragons."

"I know, but my father wants the people to have some kind of entertainment," I say, sighing. Griffin nudges me to see the golden dragon rolling around in the grass, and I can't help smiling.

"They're very protective of the gold one right now," Tait says.

"I'm sure. It's adorable," I say, watching the gold dragon play. "Tait, please help me. At least be nearby to keep them lying down. Nothing fancy, just let people watch them resting and doing nothing. Can we do that at least?"

Tait is quiet for a moment, trying to think as he watches the dragons on the field.

"I suppose I can try, Your Majesty. We'll need twice the food we give them on that day, and I can lure them into a separate pen during the celebration. I'll make sure they're well fed, so all they'll want to do is lie down. Let's hope they're not particularly angry that day," Tait adds after a while.

I beam. "That would be amazing, Tait."

"Also, there's a high chance it won't be the green and the red dragon. I think I can do the smaller red one, and if the big red one is willing, maybe that one. I think the green will be harder, but I can try."

A powerful whoosh of wings slices through the air above us, and I look up to see the smaller red dragon descend to the field, its scales shimmering like rubies in the sunlight, to join its friends.

"That one," Tait says, pointing.

"Please try the green one too, if you can," I add softly, my eyes glued to the miniature red dragon as it settled down, a puff of dust rising from its landing spot, the air filled with the faint scent of smoke and something akin to cinnamon.

"I will, Your Majesty," Tait says, nodding.

I say goodbye to him and thank him before I head back to the castle.

"Your Majesty, we need you to go to the store in Cerene so you can pick out the decorations that you prefer," a lady greets me as soon as I make it to the door. I recognize her as one of the ladies that often help with things like this, but usually, it's Dajlia or my father that she's following around.

"Right now?" I ask.

"Yes, Your Majesty, so they can make sure it's ready on the day," she answers, bowing.

"Why can't they come here?" I demand.

"It's so last minute, Your Majesty," she protests.

I scowl. "Fine."

CHAPTER 14

Alex

I finish cleaning the bathroom, the fresh scent of cleaning products still sharp in the air, within an hour. But before I can brag to Miranda, Lady Dajlia has stopped me at the door of her bathroom, her hand on the doorknob.

"All done?" she drawls.

"Yes, ma'am." I bow to her, keeping my head hung. I really didn't need another slap today.

Lady Dajlia circles the bathroom, her fingers tracing the cool porcelain of the sink, the smooth surface of the bathtub, and the gleaming glass of the shower door, meticulously inspecting my work. "Hm," she murmurs as she walks around. "I need you to go down to the city to pick up my dresses and jewelry for the ball."

"Yes, my Lady Dajlia," I say.

Her face turns serious. "You cannot show anyone those dresses, understood? What I'm wearing on the night of must be revealed at the ball and only at the ball," she continues.

I nod, keeping my eyes on the floor.

"Make sure they have all the dresses ready, and that they're already tailored to my size."

"Yes, my Lady Dajlia." I've learned it's really so much better when I'm not pissing her off. She still treats me like dirt and makes sure I feel stupid, but I'd really rather not get slapped.

"Hm," she murmurs as she exits the bathroom. But before she leaves, she turns one more time to look at me. "I also want my snacks and lunch in my room today. Make sure to get it here on time."

Luckily, I hadn't stood up yet. "Yes, my lady."

She shoots me a final, venomous look before disappearing into her bedroom, the door clicking shut behind her. I leave the bathroom by the servants' entrance, the cool tile under my feet a stark contrast to the warm air of the kitchen, which I could already smell.

"Ma'am, how do I get to Cerene?" I ask Miranda as I open the door.

She glares at me. "If you were from here, this would not be a question you'd have to ask. Waste of my time to be monitoring you constantly," she snaps.

"Yes, ma'am," I bow instantly, peeved that it's also my fault I'm here.

She continues to give me the evil eye before finally referring to the guards to help me get a ride. I head to the guard station.

"Hello," I say to the soldier in the station.

"Who are you?" he barks at me.

"I-I-I work for Lady Dajlia. I need a ride to town," I tell him, frowning, as this is the first time I've ever actually needed to leave the palace.

Narrowing his eyes, he looks at me suspiciously, then finally waves to the men bustling around the horse-drawn carriages. "To town!" he yells. A much nicer carriage, with gleaming brass and polished wood, rushes past, its wheels barely disturbing the dust compared to the others.

"She can come with me," a familiar voice says, and I jump.

"Uh-but Your Majesty, she's just a handmaid," the guard protests.

"Uh-yes, I can just take the regular carriages, Your Majesty," I say, bowing to the prince sitting in the very nice, very royal carriage.

"Don't be silly," he growls. "Get in," he adds, with a look of no negotiation on his face.

He holds out a hand to help me in, but I don't take it. Instead, I hike my dress up, using the step to hoist myself onto the carriage with a large, clumsy leap, nearly tumbling as I reached the top. The wood feels rough beneath my hands. The prince's hand swipes over my back to keep me steady.

"I got it," I protest, and he lets go, the ghost of his hand still a whisper on my back. I settle on the bench in front of him—not a great idea, given the way he's just been staring at me. Pulling my skirts towards me, I sit back, focusing on peering out the window instead of at the handsome man, eager to ignore him. Why is he doing this? Why is he being kind but then suddenly being an ass?

"Where are you going?" he asks.

"Lady Dajlia asked me to get her dresses from the store," I say without turning to him.

"Do you even know what store?" he asks.

Shit. I didn't ask. I assumed there'd be one store for royalty, no? My face flushes at my stupidity, but I don't respond.

"Telia's, Roach," he yells at the driver.

"Is that her tailor?" I ask, finally turning.

"Yes," he says. His eyes are so intense, it's hard to look at him without feeling intimidated.

"Thank you, Your Majesty," I manage, bowing my head.

"You don't need to do that. Not when it's just us," he says.

"Yes, Your Majesty," I say anyway, bowing again.

The corners of his mouth tilt in amusement. "Where are you from?"

"Fortuna, Your Majesty," I say.

"Ah, that's right, you mentioned that before. Are you an only child?" he asks.

"No, Your Majesty," I respond, looking out the window, unable to hide whatever my face is showing. I miss Angus. I miss my mother. I miss Sweet, Virginia, and even Chris. I miss Mouse.

"You miss them," he observes, the hardness on his face softening. I remain silent, my gaze fixed on the winding roads, the distant hum of other horses and carriages a low thrum in the background.

"Tell me about them," he says.

I turn to him. "Your Majesty, I don't think it's appropriate for me to tell my captor about my family."

"Captor," he muses, the corners of his mouth lifting in a thoughtful expression.

"I exchanged myself so they won't take my home and my brother. Sounds a bit like a captor, doesn't it?" I say, my eyes bright with tears that I'd never let fall. Not in front of him.

"I'm sorry," he says.

My jaw drops, and I stare at him, a wave of curiosity washing over me as I study his features. "Do you even know what you're sorry for?"

"That you had to leave your family. That you're burdened with working off a tax you didn't know about," he responds, his eyes sharp and intense, still fixed on me.

"You know, I don't understand you. One minute you think you own me and the next you're being nice. Is this some kind of mind game?" I demand.

He chuckles. "I can be whoever I want to be, whenever I want," he replies.

"Lucky you," I retort, looking away so he doesn't see my expression.

A beat of silence stretches between us. "You know, we're not all bad. Some of us actually want to help," the prince says after a moment of silence. I sigh heavily, just as the carriage stops at presumably Telia's.

"You tell me. Aren't you the prince? If you knew things like this were happening to your people, shouldn't you be doing something about it?" I say, just as the carriage door opens.

He doesn't say anything as I leave the carriage and head for the door.

CHAPTER 15

Gabriel

What happens when a prince is infuriated by a handmaid? They get fired. They get in trouble. Something. Anything.

And yet, nothing happened when she said that to me. Nothing. I didn't know what to say, didn't know what to do. The problem is—she's right. She's absolutely right. What am I waiting for? I should have confronted my father earlier today, yet I avoided it. *Knowingly* avoided it. I'm infuriated, not because she yelled at me, or because she keeps thinking I'm the bad guy. I'm infuriated because she's right, and I've been avoiding this conversation with my father. Let's be honest, my father isn't exactly open to conversation. He's not a diplomatic type of man; he's a do-what-I-say-or-die type of person. I've never had the courage to go against him, never had the balls to say something. Never.

I step out at the shop that handles our décor and turn to Roach. "Make sure you pick her up."

"But, Your Majesty, what about you?" Roach asks, his eyes flitting between me and the royal carriage.

"Send a different carriage down for me. But make sure she's safe and has a way home," I instruct, looking away so I don't reveal any emotions to Roach.

He nods. "Yes, Your Majesty." I watch as the carriage leaves to be by her side.

I enter the bustling shop, the air thick with the scent of old books and polished wood, and a storekeeper immediately approaches me, despite a long queue.

"Hello," a woman with pale skin asks. Her hair is pulled back in a tight bun, and her bright green eyes flash as she greets me with a flirtatious smile at the door.

I nod at her, smiling. But even though her bosom is almost visible through a low-cut dress, she doesn't have the same impact on me as Alex does. I walk past her with the storekeeper, knowing I probably will never think about her again. The storekeeper walks me through the various decorations, pointing out intricately carved wooden elephants and vibrant silk tapestries that feel strangely familiar.

"Has my family used some of these before?" I ask the storekeeper.

He nods. "Yes, Your Majesty. We're the only shop that provides décor."

"Do you remember what kind of décor my mother liked?" I ask.

The storekeeper's eyes widen, his pupils dilating in the dim light of the shop. "Queen Estelle?"

I nod. The storekeeper's gaze softens, his skin crinkling at the corners of his mouth as a warm smile touches his lips. "You miss your mother."

"Yes, I do." I say quietly.

"You know, people may have hated her for her skin, but I always loved her," he says, disappearing into another room. From the open door, the air thickens with the scent of old wood and dust, and the familiar comfort of tapestries long unseen.

"Your mother was extremely kind. She always came here to visit us whenever she needed our services," he says. "She always had a smile on her face, even though everyone outside would look at her weirdly. It's hard when you're so different from everyone else. People hate what they don't understand."

My heart softens, and my eyes sting, so I look around the room instead. Anything to occupy the attention threatening to draw out tears. My gaze lands on the dusty porcelain vases, the crimson tablecloths, the faded tapestries depicting scenes of mythical creatures, the plastic flowers, the worn Persian rugs, and the ornate arches. They were all very much her style, each item a reflection of my mother's vibrant personality and impeccable taste. Simple and elegant.

"Can we use these again?" I say aloud, blinking away tears.

When my mother passed away, my father made sure I didn't cry. He took me to all events, and beat me whenever he saw me shedding a tear. 'Why shed a tear for someone who's dead?' he said. So, I never did. Even up until now.

"I think that's a great idea," the storekeeper says. "I'll pack it up, and we'll be there to set it up before the ball."

"Can you make sure it looks exactly how my mother would've wanted it?" I add.

The storekeeper looks pleased, nodding. "Absolutely, Your Majesty."

I leave the store, not bothering to greet the woman who'd tried to flirt with me earlier. There's no point. Not only is she not on my father's list of eligible brides, but she's also not the handmaid. I continue walking down the bustling main street, the cacophony of sounds and the weight of countless stares heavy on me. Normal for a prince to get stared at—especially since I'm of marrying age and still single, nor have I taken the time to meet any other eligible woman. I don't want to get married. Not yet.

"Hey, what are you doing in town?" a voice says behind me. I don't have to turn to know it's Griffin. He tended to spend most of his free time in town. I thought he was courting someone, but considering the lack of any real commitment after all this time, I doubt it's serious.

"I had to go to the shop to see what decorations we could use for the ball," I say.

"How did it go?" he asks, walking instep beside me.

I shoot him a mischievous smile. "She'll definitely like it."

Griffin bursts out laughing. "Good on you, Gabe. Good on you. It's about time."

I turn to him, frowning. "About time for...?"

Griffin pauses, putting a hand on my shoulder. "Gabe, I didn't mean it."

But I shrug it off. "No, seriously. About time for?"

Griffin hesitates. He lets out a long, weary sigh before turning to me, his eyes darting around nervously, but eventually meeting mine. "Gabe, I've known you for many years. Many years. I've seen you through many events from bad ones to good ones."

"I know, Griff. Nothing that you say to me will break us, I promise," I say, my eyebrows knitting.

"I've seen your relationship with your father. I know what he's done to you," he continues.

I nod as we pass a palace vendor.

"But Gabe, you're scared. You haven't acted against your father, even though you talk so much about it. Even Dajlia, you haven't stood up to. How do you think she made it there so quickly?" Griffin finishes.

My jaw drops, and my first instinct is to assume the worst, feeling a wave of defensiveness wash over me. But this is Griffin. He's right. He's been there through everything with me. If there's anyone I can trust with my life, it's him. I turn to him, but I don't say anything.

"Please don't take it as an attack," he adds, watching me.

"I'm not," I murmur. "I'm just thinking, Griff."

"At some point, you'll fight back. I know it. You're a wonderful prince, and one day you'll be the right king," Griffin adds.

"What if I don't want to be a king?" I ask, sighing.

"Oh, Gabe. There's no one better than you for the job. This kingdom needs you. Needs your heart, your strength," Griffin says.

For a moment, I recognize that my heart sinks. It's true. I've never wanted to be a king. I see it as a responsibility most of the time, as a burden. I wish so much my mother were alive. She'd have helped me through this.

"The girl, the handmaid," I tell him. "She said something to me today."

"Oh, you saw her again?" Griffin asks, nonchalantly.

"She asked me if I should be doing something about it," I say, ignoring his question.

He shrugs. "She's right, Gabe. Of all the people, you're the one who can stop this. You're the one who can fix it."

I kick at the ground, knowing he's right. But for some reason, her voice seems the loudest.

"What is it with you and her, Gabe?" Griffin asks. This time, he's the one with knitted eyebrows .

I sigh, not wanting to answer that in case it makes things real. "I don't know, brother. She just...she got under my skin."

Griffin laughs. "I think there are other things of hers you want under you."

I smack his back. "Griff, I can't even think that way. She's a handmaid. A handmaid, Griff! Imagine the scandal with my father when he finds out that the woman I want is a handmaid."

"Well, maybe she's just what you need," Griffin responds. "I see the way you look at her, Gabe. I've never seen you look at anyone like that before."

I shake my head. He's right, I haven't. Because there's never been anyone like that here before. No one who'd speak to me directly. No one else who'd tell me the truth like she does. None who'd get mad to my face.

She's one of a kind.

CHAPTER 16

Alex

Finally, the day of celebration arrives. I've worked my ass off to get to this date, and honestly, there were moments when I didn't think I'd make it, but here we are. All the palace staff are gathered on the right of the event area, their faces a mixture of anticipation and nervous alertness, ready to spring into action. They're probably worried the dragons will retaliate and breathe fire on us. Unfortunately, they're right in front of me, so I'll be the first to burn if that's the case.

The workers have done an excellent job in such a short amount of time. Massive white tents fill the new area. In the center, a dark chocolate cedarwood stage gleams under the lights, its polished surface reflecting the surrounding room. Blue and white hydrangeas and peonies, arranged in beautiful blue vases, adorn the space, complemented by a blue and white tapestry bearing the Quaila flag, creating an elegant atmosphere. The tents are furnished with numerous round, blue and white tables and chairs, complementing the quaint setting. The tables and aisles showcase still more gorgeous hydrangeas and peonies, their sweet fragrance filling the air. It's perfect.

"Good evening, citizens of Quaila. I'm so excited for all of you to be here! Welcome to our palace!" the king says.

A warm wave of applause and cheers ripples through the audience.

"We are gathered here today to celebrate our baby dragon!" the king says again.

A surge of cheers and applause washes over the arena as the crowd, along with the staff, erupts once more; the sound deafening. I look around at the joyous faces, the festive decorations, and the lively music, and I feel like the only one not celebrating. I mean, what would I celebrate? Yes, I live in this kingdom, but I've never supported them. Yes, I am here, but he's not my king. I turn to the stage where the king is talking. Beside him is Lady Dajlia, but the prince is nowhere to be found. I scan the crowd, looking for his familiar face, but I don't see it. I mentally berate myself again, a wave of frustration washing over me. Why am I searching for him?

Shaking myself, I turn back to the king, who continues to rile the crowd up. He's talking about how the kingdom of Quaila is the most powerful in all the world and how having dragons solidifies that. My gaze turns to Miranda, standing just a few feet from me. She looks just as impressed and just as enamored of the king as the crowd does. Next to me, another handmaid is clapping and cheering as hard as Miranda was.

Am I supposed to be like this? In ten years, will I also be like this and refuse to leave the palace?

I focus my gaze back at the king, where Lady Dajlia is waving and enjoying the attention she's getting. She looks glorious wearing the dress I'd brought to her from Telia's. Well, one of the dresses. Apparently, she had eighteen dresses saved, and I had to lug them all back to the palace. Luckily, the prince's carriage had waited for me, so I actually had a ride back and people to help with the dresses without any of them getting ruined.

"I'd like to present two of our wonderful dragons, on your left!" the king presents, waving his hand. The lights around the smaller pen by the celebration area turn on, lighting the two dragons cooped up in there. One of them is the green dragon I saw the other day. On the ground, the dragon lay with his head directed towards us, the gentle swish of his tail a subtle movement in the stillness. The red dragon is smaller than the one I saw the other day. This one doesn't look as menacing. His snout is smaller, and his tail is a little shorter. It also has ivory horns and chest. The creature perches next to the green dragon, its eyes like chips of gold, watching our every move.

My heart lurches, a tremor running through me as I gaze up at the colossal dragons, their scales shimmering like a thousand emeralds in the moonlight. I've never actually been scared of animals. Never. Mostly because I could always talk to them. But these are massive creatures that have been known to kill without thinking.

The smaller red dragon lets out a growl, a low rumble that vibrates through the very air, making the trees around us tremble. A hush falls over the crowd as everyone watches, fascinated.

"Here are two of our biggest dragons in all of Quaila!" the king bellows.

The smaller dragon lets out another deafening roar, shaking the very ground beneath her feet. "Please help," it says.

I frown, scratching my head. Did I hear that correctly? I focus on the smaller dragon, but he seems to be keeping an eye on us.

The king walks down the stairs leading to the smaller pen. "Make it move," he orders .

I lean over the edge of where I'm standing, only for my heart to beat faster as I recognize the dark hair, the tall, rigid stance.

"Father, they're dragons," the familiar voice of the prince wades through the cheering and clapping for the dragons.

"I don't care," the king says forcefully. "Make it move!"

The prince nods, his footsteps crunching softly on the dry dirt as he walks towards the pen. With wide, intelligent eyes, the smaller dragon watches him carefully, its tiny claws lightly gripping the ground.

Another man stands by the pen. He starts talking to the prince, but I can't hear them beneath the clapping and the whispers.

The smaller dragon lets out another wail, a mournful sound that echoes through the air, more heartbreaking than frightening. "Please help him."

I cock my head. "No."

"What?" Miranda says behind me.

"Nothing." I shake my head, watching the scene before me unfold.

The prince grabs a stick from beside the other man. The other man, his face contorted in anger, looks like he's protesting, but the prince simply ignores him, his expression unchanging.

"Be prepared to run," the prince says, turning to the other man. He turns and pokes the dragon on its massive head with the stick, and a low rumble emanates from deep within its chest.

"No," I mutter. "No, no."

The prince's prod elicits a low growl from the green dragon as it slowly raises its head. The smaller red dragon wails again, its high-pitched cry piercing the silence. "Please help him!" it repeats.

"No," I murmur again, gripping the cold, damp railing. I can barely hear Miranda's hushed whispers telling me to stop fidgeting.

The prince moves to poke the dragon again, this time with more force, eliciting a soft, sickening moan from the dragon that sends shivers down my spine. It's the same wail you'd hear from someone badly hurt.

My hands grip the railing harder, my eyes flitting around me.

The prince continues to poke the dragon. The dragon hums, lifting its head. "I'm hurt. Please don't touch me."

My eyes land on the green dragon, who's begging, pleading for its life.

"Make it move!" the king yells again.

But just before the prince could poke it once more, I launch myself from the balcony, the wind whipping past me as I tumble, hitting the ground hard and scraping my knees. I don't stop.

"No! No, please stop. Please stop; please don't hurt him. He's hurt, he's hurt!" I yell as I run over to the prince, tears streaming down my cheeks.

The smaller red dragon howls. "Please help him!"

The prince looks at me, eyes wide as he stares at me. "What are you doing here?" He glares.

"Please don't hurt him; he's already injured!" I say, practically kneeling in front of him.

"What are you talking about?" he whispers.

"It's hurt, that's why it's not moving!" I repeat.

"What do you mean it's hurt? How do you know?" the prince asks.

"What are you doing, girl?" the king booms from behind me.

"What are you talking about?" The prince pulls my shoulder, his eyes boring into mine.

"I heard them. I heard them say he's hurt,"

CHAPTER 17

Gabriel

"Take her!" My father's voice cracks like thunder, and though I step towards her, his soldiers move with brutal efficiency, seizing her from my grasp and shoving me aside. My eyes bulge, and my head swims.

"Gentle!" I yell at them, my voice cracking with anger as they yank the handmaid along with them.

"Dungeons," I hear my father say, and my eyes widen.

"No!" I yell, turning to him.

He glares at me, his face reddening with barely controlled rage, a low growl rumbling in his chest.

"Dungeons," he repeats, his breath hot and ragged. When I move to follow his soldiers to the dungeons, he grabs my arm.

"Follow her, and I will kill her myself," he threatens.

I stay put for a moment, my foot tapping a nervous rhythm against the cold stone ground as I try to block out her muffled cries as they echo toward me from the direction of the dungeons.

"Stay your course," the king drills at me.

As he strides back to the stage, a triumphant wave to the cheering audience punctuates the silence. "What an emotional night, right? The poor girl must be overwhelmed by the sight of the dragons," he smiles, sparking laughter from the others.

Griffin pulls me aside. "What do we do?"

"I have to wait. Can you make sure she's okay?" I ask.

He nods, then disappears behind the stage. It must be nice to be able to disappear whenever you want.

I step up onto the stage, hearing a number of cheers and bursts of applause as I make it back to my father's side, catching sight of the white projector showing us to other kingdoms. I forget how much my father wanted to show this to other kingdoms. The woman interrupting that was a show of weakness, something my father would never tolerate.

"What the hell was that?" he seethes beneath all the smiling and clapping.

"I don't know, Father," I murmur back.

"You'd better have a good explanation after this. I can't believe you let your *friend* ruin the night," he says. The joyful expression he sustains while muttering his menacing words is impressive.

"She's not my friend," I defend myself, but instantly regret it. This girl has already been a victim of this palace. She will not be victimized again. Ignoring my father's furious glares, I exit the stage, the heavy velvet curtain falling behind me as I make my way to the dank, dimly lit dungeons. Griffin is at the entrance, pacing.

"There you are!" he says. "She won't talk to me."

I enter the dungeons, the musk and cool temperature hitting me instantly as I enter. My gaze turns left and right as I look for her. The soldiers had put her all the way at the end of the dungeon. She sat at the end of the cold, damp cell, her body wracked with sobs, her knees pulled to her chest, head hanging between her legs, and her shoulders shaking.

"Hello," I greet, slowly approaching her. She continues to cry, her chest trembling. She doesn't look up.

"Hello," I say again. "Alex?" I say softly. My heart nearly breaks watching her fall apart like this. "I can help you. Please, talk to me."

"You can't help me," she spits, the words dripping with venom as she glares up at me. Tears stream down her face, reddening her skin, her hair a tangled mess obscuring her puffy eyes. "You can't even help yourself."

"Please. I'm trying to help you, Alex, please," I say, sinking to the cold, damp ground, peering into her dimly lit cell. She goes back to hugging her legs.

"Please. I just want to know how you knew the dragon was hurt," I try again. "I don't want to hurt you, and I will do everything in my power to make sure they don't either. I promise."

She shifts in her seat and looks at me, her eyebrows knitted, like she's wondering why I'm here. To be honest,

I'm wondering, too. I don't even know her but every part of me wants to protect her.

Suddenly, the heavy footfalls and the clang of chains grow louder, and a group of soldiers enters the dungeon, their metal handcuffs glinting in the torchlight.

Alex shrinks back, pressing herself against the cold, rough stone of the cell wall, making herself as small as she can be. Her eyes dart between me and the group of soldiers.

"Wait, hold on, what are you guys doing?" I step forward, my body a barrier between them and her cell, but a soldier's frown and a shove send me tumbling across the aisle as they reach her.

"No!" I yell, trying to get back up quickly to pull the soldiers out of her cell. But I'm overpowered. There are at least eight of them guarding her in the dungeons.

"Stop hurting her!" I yell again as I grab one of them back and land a punch on his face, while another one grabs her forcefully. The soldier I punched lands hard on the ground, and the impact echoes as he hits a nearby wooden bench. I grab another soldier, my knuckles cracking as I punch him again and again until he collapses, groaning.

"Stop hurting her!" I yell again, my voice cracking, and this time, it's Griffin who hauls me out, his hands rough against my arm.

"It's okay, it's okay, they're just bringing her to your father," Griffin whispers as he pulls me away. "It's okay."

I let him pull me, wiping the blood that's dripping down my chin. "They're hurting her," I tell him. I don't even realize tears are streaming down my cheeks. It feels like a sharp, hot knife is twisting and turning inside my chest.

"It's okay, Gabe, we'll protect her," he whispers, his voice barely audible above the rough scrape of her legs on the stone pathway as they drag her from the dank, dark dungeons. My heart hammers against my ribs, mirroring the brutal rhythm of her suffering.

"Please do not hurt her!" I yell after the group of soldiers, but they ignore me, and I follow them blindly to my father's office where they shove her onto the cold, marbled ground. She crumples, blood welling from ragged gashes in her legs, and a furious tide of vengeance washes over me.

My father looks at me the way he used to when I'd cry for my mother. The fury and disappointment in his eyes bring back the shame I used to feel whenever he'd look at me that way as a child. But after a moment, the shame is replaced by a, burning anger that courses through me. Anger that he'd do this to her. Anger that I've let him do this to her. Anger that I can't do anything to stop this. Even in my position, there's nothing I can say or do to convince him otherwise.

"Stop!" he commands, his voice sharp and silencing, and his soldiers immediately back away from her. She sits on her knees in the middle of the room, her head hung, tears streaking her cheeks, and her eyes red. She looks exhausted, like she's this close to giving up. From the corner, Lady Dajlia observes us with a sly smile, her gaze lingering, as though we're providing her with exquisite evening amusement. My father, seething at the back of his large wooden desk, fixes his eyes directly on me, radiating anger.

"How dare you?" he says, each word dripping with controlled fury.

I step forward, placing my body between her and my enraged father. The tension in the air is thick enough to cut with a knife.

"You can't just hurt people, Father, especially people you don't know," I respond firmly.

My father chuckles. "You dare stand between us?"

"Yes, Father. I dare stand between you and a girl who has done nothing wrong," I say.

He steps forward to me, looking me directly in the eye. "You think you can rule without instilling fear. You're wrong." He turns to his soldiers. "Grab him!"

My eyes widen, but I react too late. Five soldiers grab my arms, my legs, my chest, pulling me away from her.

"Relax, I just want to ask her some questions." He looks me over, a sneer on his face.

He bends down, his ringed fingers closing around the neckline of her dress.

"I'm sorry, I'm sorry," she keeps saying over and over.

My father spits in her face. "How dare you, a handmaid, ruin our night?,"

"Stop!" I say firmly.

My father chuckles at me. "If I didn't know any better, Gabriel, I'd say you like her."

"You can't hurt someone just because of one small mistake," I say, willing myself to look him in the eye. "She doesn't deserve it."

He turns back to her, his gaze intense as he studies her small form in his hands; the silence punctuated only by her shallow breathing. "Why, oh why, do you feel like you're worth interrupting an event like this? What makes you think you know and understand these dragons better than I do?"

She doesn't respond for a moment, and then slowly raises her gaze to meet his intense stare.

"I can talk to them."

CHAPTER 18

Gabriel

My jaw drops. My father's eyes bulge, and he drops her, more gently this time. She collapses back onto the cold, hard marble floor, the thud echoing in the silence, making me grimace. The king paces back and forth in front of her, scratching his chin.

"You can talk to dragons?" he repeats quietly.

"I can talk to all animals," she responds, her breathing slowing down. "I don't know why or how, I've just been able to talk to all animals all my life."

My father's eyes flash with a sudden chill that sends a shiver of worry down my spine. "You can talk to animals," he repeats as he paces back and forth.

"Father," I say, but he ignores me. I want to help her up, but the soldiers are still hanging onto me, ready to stop whatever movement I make.

"You can talk to animals," he repeats, a smile crossing his face like he just won a prize.

"Yes, Your Majesty," she says softly from the floor.

My father pumps his hands in celebration as Lady Dajlia and I look at him in confusion.

"What is happening, my dear?" she asks softly from the side, trying to reach for him, but he shoves her away.

"Father," I say again, motioning to the soldiers behind me.

He waves at them, letting me go, and I haul myself onto the floor next to her. She's crying softly, but other than the scratches on her legs, she seems physically fine.

"This is amazing. Can you imagine?" my father says, clearly in his own world.

"Are you okay?" I whisper to her.

She looks up at me, her eyes searching mine, but she doesn't answer.

"Father, we need to get her wounds cleaned," I say to my father, who's still pacing back and forth. "Father!" I say again, louder this time.

His eyes flicker to me, and a look of realization crosses his face as he finally notices her on the floor. His breath hitches as he motions to his soldiers.

"Take her to the special room," he says, then with another look, he adds, "carefully."

The soldiers instantly gather around her to pick her up.

"Father!" I say firmly again. When they take Alex away, I turn to him, my eyes blazing with the anger that's buzzing through my body.

Instead, he grabs my shoulders. "This is amazing, Gabriel, amazing!"

"What's amazing, Father? I don't understand what is going on?" I ask, catching his eye.

He rubs his hands with glee. "Don't you realize, Gabriel? It's been thousands of years since we've had someone who can speak to animals. Thousands of years. Now we can finally control them, really control them," he responds. "Now I don't need to find another way to control them."

"Control who?" I ask. Father squeezes my shoulders.

"The dragons, Gabriel, we can control the dragons," he says.

My heart sinks as his words, which are laced with a cruel sweetness, hang in the air, and his eyes twinkle with a mocking light.

"My dear," Lady Dajlia says behind him.

He turns on her, his voice as sharp as the one he'd used to reprimand Alex earlier. The same venom coated his words. "I don't need you anymore," he says out loud.

Her eyes widen, and a shocked gasp escapes her lips as she stumbles backward, a cold sweat breaking out on her skin.

"Take her," he says to the rest of his soldiers. They grab her as she protests.

"Darling, but darling, I can still be useful!" she yells. "I have lots of connections, and lots of things I can do!" she protests, flailing even with hands on her arms.

"My love, it's you and me, remember. It's you and me, and nothing can stop us from taking the world, nothing!" she calls out again as the soldiers start to drag her out.

"My love, my love please, please, hear me out!" she yells, her voice fading as they take her farther and further from the office.

When it's just the king and me, he faces me. "Thank you, my beloved son, thank you for being such a great advocate. Without you, I might've hurt her, but you fought so hard to be fair and good to her. If I had injured her, she might never be willing to help us. With her, we might actually be able to implement our plans faster than I realize."

I fight to find the words in my spinning mind. "Father, we can't just make her do things for us—she only just found out," I protest.

"Of course, of course, son, we have to be smart about this, okay?" the king says, pacing from one end of the room to another.

Not one part of him feels bad about Dajlia, I realize. Not one. I don't know why he agreed to marry her in the first place, but clearly, Alex's ability to talk to animals weighs more than whatever Dajlia can provide.

"Father, what are we going to do?" I say.

"You know I've always wanted to make sure we're the most powerful kingdom. You know, we're the only kingdom that actually has dragons, and we've worked very hard to get them to stay here. Now we have someone we can use who will help us fully adopt these dragons. Someone who can help us be the most powerful kingdom of all!"

"But Father," I start to argue again.

He doesn't listen, though; he seems to be in a trance, probably imagining a world where he's the most powerful king ever.

"We need to think about this carefully, and we need to make sure that we take the right steps. It's important to the kingdom, the family, and our realm," he continues, pacing around erratically.

I think fast. "Can I go take care of her? Make sure she has a healer, food?" I ask.

"Of course, my son. We have to take care of her. Make sure she's healed and treated well. Go do it. She gets the best care," he says.

I turn to walk out the door, but before I make it out, he speaks again:

"But do not talk to her. Do not talk to her until we figure out what we're going to do. Make sure she gets everything she needs, and that she is bathed and cared for."

My heart sinks.

CHAPTER 19

Alex

Next thing I know, I'm being dragged out of the king's office and then across a few hallways, before I'm shoved into a room. My body falls onto the floor, skidding a little along the wood flooring. The door is closed, and I'm alone at last. After catching my breath, I scan what I realize is a bedroom with a massive four-poster mahogany bed. It looks a lot like Lady Dajlia's room except a little bigger. It has a fireplace on the side, a sofa and two chairs. An armoire stands on the other side with a longer table by the door. I get up, grimacing as I finally feel the impact of scraping my legs across the ground. Pulling my skirts up, I check my knees, noticing instantly how many scrapes and bruises they have, some bleeding, some not.

I move towards the door, pulling at the doorknob to open it. It won't even turn.

"Of course not," I mutter to myself. I frown, walking towards the other room. It's a bathroom, similar to the one in Lady Dajlia's room. Beautiful, porcelain, marble, everything I never had. I turn, smiling to myself, knowing there's a servant's door. But when I pull it, it doesn't budge either. Damn.

Suddenly, the front door opens, and I gasp as a woman in white enters the room. Her blonde hair is tied in a knot at the top of her head. On one hand, she holds a small, black bag.

"Hello," she says.

"Hello." I frown.

"Don't worry, I'm just a healer. I'm here to wrap your cuts and wounds, and make sure you're physically okay," she says, motioning to the sofa.

I walk slowly towards it, keeping a safe distance from her. "Do you... do you know what's going on?" I ask her.

She gives me a sad smile. "I'm sorry, I do not. Prince Gabriel just asked me to make sure your wounds are wrapped and that you're okay physically. I don't know what's happening with you other than this."

I sit on the couch, and she walks towards me, setting her bag down next to her. When she opens it, she takes out a few bottles, a bandage, and some cotton balls.

"Prince Gabriel asked you?" I repeat.

"Yes. He was pretty eager to make sure you were alright," she responds as she pours some of the liquid in the bottle onto the cotton ball.

That man is confusing as hell. One minute he's mean to me; the next he's trying to help me. I turn back to the healer. "Are you new to the palace?"

"No, I'm the healer for the palace," she says, pausing when I grimace at the touch of the cotton ball on my wound.

"Sorry," I murmur.

She smiles, moving on to slowly wipe other wounds on my legs. "It's okay; it's not your fault that it hurts."

"I'm scared," I tell her. I don't know why I did, it just felt right.

She pauses again, looking up at me. "I don't know who you are, but I think you'll be just fine."

I frown. "How do you know that?"

"I've met a lot of people over my time here, and I think you're one of those people."

I stay still and count my breaths for a moment. "What kind of people?" I ask.

When she finishes sanitizing my wounds, she picks up the bandage before she looks at me. "The resilient ones."

I look around me. "I don't know why I'm here. I don't know what they want with me."

She bandages my wounds before she responds, saying, "Good luck to you." When she makes it out the door, I try to follow her, only to be pushed back by two soldiers.

"Ouch," I groan, getting up.

What a kingdom. Not only have I been slapped, called stupid, beaten, but now I'm trapped in a posh bedroom I never asked to be in.

I sit back on the couch, wrapping my head between my legs once more.

The door opens again, and a small, pale woman enters holding a tray of food.

"Hello, my lady," she greets me.

"Oh, um, no, it's just Alex," I say with a weak chuckle.

She approaches, putting the tray on the coffee table. "Of course, my lady," she says, bowing, even though I put a hand out to stop her.

"My lady, Prince Gabriel wants you to eat. I'm also supposed to help you bathe and get ready for bed," she says.

My chest tightens. What's all this about? Though I can't help the warm feeling that floods me at the thought of the prince wanting me to be looked after.

"What's your name?" I ask.

"My name is Katya, my lady," she says, bowing again.

"Please, Katya, when it's just the two of us, please don't bow. It…it makes me feel bad. Please call me Alex," I plead.

Something in her face changes. "I don't want to make you feel bad, my lady."

"Alex," I say again.

She nods awkwardly. "Alex."

I turn to the tray laden with the aroma of freshly baked bread and pastries, the rich scent of red pasta with ground beef, and the sweet fragrance of mangoes, kiwis, and strawberries.

"Will you eat with me?" I ask, grabbing a piece of mango.

"I'm not allowed, my-Alex," she responds, but she eyes the tray hungrily.

I chuckle. "I won't tell anyone. Please. Please eat with me."

She nods, settling on the other side of the coffee table.

"Have you been here long?" I ask her.

She takes a bite of bread. "A few months. My mother works here. So does my sister."

"Do you like it?" I take a bite of the pasta, slurping the last pieces of it.

Katya laughs, watching me. "I've never met a lady who slurps like that."

I grin, enjoying a normal, fun conversation for the first time since arriving here. "I'm not a lady, Katya. I'm just… just Alex," I say, drinking some water.

"Good, good. Prince Gabriel said to make sure you drink water," she comments.

"What's the deal with Prince Gabriel?" I ask.

"He's probably the nicest royal, I think," Katya answers between bites of a fruit and bread.

"You think he's nice?" I repeat.

Her eyes light up. "Oh yes, Alex. Lovely for a royal."

"Am I…am I supposed to sleep in there?" I ask, pointing to the massive bed.

Katya follows my finger. "Of course. Where do you think you're supposed to sleep?"

"I mean…this isn't my bedroom," I tell her.

"Prince Gabriel says it is now." Katya shrugs.

We continue to eat quietly for a while, the comfortable silence punctuated only by the clinking of cutlery, and then Katya leads me to the bathroom. She adjusts the hot and cold water, testing the temperature with her hand until it reaches the ideal warmth.

"Take a bath, Alex it might help you feel better," she says. "I'll prepare your bed and leave you some nice wine before you go to bed."

Dumbfounded, unsure how to process all this luxury, I nod, slipping off my black dress and apron, stepping into the bath, flinching for a moment at the heat before sinking into it, every bunched-up muscle relaxing. I've never had a bath before. We only have a shower at home, but this feels nice.

Katya helps me into new silk clothes. Clothes I've never had. Clothes with materials I could never afford.

"Tomorrow will be a new day, Alex. I'll be back with breakfast," she says.

I don't know how to feel. It's wonderful to be comfortable and looked after, but it doesn't mean I'm not still essentially a prisoner. "That means they're not letting me out tomorrow?" I say wearily.

Katya looks at me sadly. "I'll be back for breakfast."

When she finally leaves, the silence is deafening, and I curl into a ball, letting the tears fall until exhaustion claims me.

Seven days later, I'm still in the bedroom, not able to see anyone but Katya. I appreciate her talking to me, being my friend, the only person who treats me like I'm human. I guess at least I'm getting good food and drink in plentiful supply.

Right after Katya leaves that evening, the door swings ajar, and I stand, my heart thudding, and slowly walk to see if I can get out through the gap. No one appears to be entering, so I pick up my pace, only to be crushed when I see Lady Dajlia at my door, looking like her eyes are about to pop out of her head.

"What did you do? You horrible, horrible woman?" she burst out, pointing her finger at me. "You naughty, naughty girl. I underestimated you. I thought you were an innocent brat, but you're actually a mastermind in all of this, aren't you? Scheming to be his wife so I'm discarded?"

I open my mouth to say something, but nothing comes out.

"What are you all doing?" a familiar voice says outside. "Get her out of there!"

Soldiers burst into the room, their boots thudding on the wooden floor, and they roughly seize her arms. She writhes in their hold, then glares at me, venom in her eyes. "Watch your back, bitch," she says and spits at me. The glob of gross phlegm reaches my cheeks, as I'd turned away a little too late. My body shakes violently.

"Take her out!" a voice growls at my door.

Soldiers drag her out as she spills every curse at me. Prince Gabriel stands at the door as soon as the soldiers are out.

"I'm sorry," he says to me. "I'm so sorry." He looks crestfallen.

I wipe the spit off my cheek. "Do you even know what you're sorry for?"

He enters the room, slowly closing the door behind him. "For everything, Alex. I'm sorry I couldn't protect you. I'm sorry they hurt you. I'm so, so sorry," he says softly as he approaches me, his eyes soft and fearful.

I don't say anything, but I back up.

"And I'm so, so sorry for what I'm about to say," he says, stopping in his tracks when he sees me retreating.

"What is it?" I demand, my heart beating so hard I can hear it.

"You're the new queen, Alex. My father—he wants to marry you," he says, something strange crossing his face as he says it.

My jaw drops. "What?"

"He wants to marry you, Alex," Prince Gabriel repeats, his eyes looking everywhere but mine.

His words slowly catch up to me, but by the time they do, the only thing I see is darkness.

CHAPTER 20

Alex

I have to escape. I have to escape. I'd rather die than marry someone like him. I have to escape. The words came to me when I woke up.

My eyes open slowly, my heart sinking when I realize I'm still in my room, in my bed. When I look down, Prince Gabriel and his sharp jaw sit at the bottom of my bed.

"Alex," he says softly, rubbing my arm.

I pull away from the electricity of his touch.

"Are you okay?" he asks. "I'll send in a healer."

"I'm fine," I murmur.

He frowns, clearly not reassured. "Okay," he pulls back his hand. "I'll let you rest." He leans over the bed, his head close to mine, and for a moment, I'm convinced he's going to kiss me, and my heart ramps up so fast I can barely catch my breath. I try to ignore the stab of disappointment when he pats my head awkwardly instead.

"I'm not a dog," I blurt out, and before I have time to regret my outburst, a peal of laughter escapes from him.

"You're so…so—"

"Clever? Wise?" I'm probably pushing it with the cheekiness. I know he was probably going to say "weird'.

"—Beautiful," he says quietly instead, and my stomach flips. Is he messing with me? Haven't I been through enough this week? He gently brushes the stray strand of hair from my face, and I force myself not to flinch away from the softness of his touch.

I shouldn't be staring back into his eyes; not when they're looking back at mine so intently, but it's hard to rip my gaze away from that mouth. The shadow of stubble on his cheekbone. His lips are closer to mine now. I'd just need to lift my head a few inches, and then…

And then I remember what he told me about his father.

Shit.

"I think you'd better go," I whisper, turning my head away from him.

When the door clicks closed, I jump out of bed, looking for anything that can get me out of this room. After searching for what feels like hours, I flop back down on the couch, pulling my legs into my chest.

The door opens, and Katya enters with a tray. "Oh, my lady," she says, putting down the tray and rushing to my side. "Are you okay?" she asks, wrapping her arms around me. I let her, sinking into me as I cry my eyes out once more.

"Oh, Alex," she whispers as she rubs my back. "Everything happens for a reason."

She pulls away, grabbing the tray and moving it closer to us. "Come eat; it'll make you feel better."

The tray is overflowing with juicy, ripe fruit, fluffy scrambled eggs, crispy bacon, and flaky pastries. I sniffle, moving closer to the tray. My eyes are so swollen I can barely see, and my heart feels shattered. The thought of doing anything makes me want to curl up and disappear. Even the plate of delicious food isn't as attractive as it used to be.

"Don't be like that, Alex; you need to take care of yourself, too," Katya says, watching me stab around my food.

I scowl, but I take a bite of the eggs like they're poison. They're not, of course; they're probably the softest, fluffiest eggs I've ever tasted in my entire life.

But it's a bribe.

In exchange for good food, I have to be a slave to this kingdom, be married to the king, have sex, and be the harbinger of future kings who can also speak to animals. I shudder at the thought of sex with the king. Not only am I not attracted to him, but he's like the devil. And the father of a man I can't stop obsessing over.

"What are you thinking?" Katya asks as I slowly chew and swallow my meal. I've never disliked food. I love eating. Yet, I know I can only eat well if I marry the king. I say that like I actually have a choice. If the king wants to marry you, you marry him. I think about Lady Dajlia and how she was abusing her power. In the week that I'd been working for her, I couldn't even count the number of times she's hit me, spat on me, called me stupid, and more. I shudder to think that could be me.

I don't want to be that; I don't want this power. I don't want this power. My gaze goes back to the girl in front of me.

"I wish I'd never come here," I tell her, my voice breaking.

She smiles sadly. "If only you can get away, right? If only there was something you could do to take down the guards in front, you'd be able to escape and make it out to the woods."

I frown, an idea forming in my head. "What did you say?"

"Well, I was just thinking, if you have two guards at the door and then one time they're not there, then what's stopping you from escaping? To be honest, though, I've never actually been in the woods. I wouldn't know how to survive that." She shrugs, taking a bite out of a slice of bread from the tray.

But I can. I can survive there; I've done it before. I smile at Katya, a plan forming in my head. When she stands to take out our food, I wrap her in my arms, hugging tightly.

"Please know I absolutely appreciate our friendship," I say, squeezing her.

She beams up at me. "We're friends?"

"Of course, Kat. You're the only reason I'm alive today. Do you mind bringing me a teapot with hot water? Don't add the tea yet, though. I'd like to do that myself."

"Of course! Friend," Kat says, grinning happily as she takes the tray and singsongs her way out of my room.

I've been so focused on my own loneliness and unhappiness that I haven't recognized hers. Growing up in the castle—that must be confusing and lonely. She probably didn't have friends to play and grow with as a child. I don't even know if she had her mother and her sister to guide her. How would she when all they focus on is the royal family?

I stand up, my heart pounding with anxiety, and I head for the closest, wishing I'd asked Katya where she put my old clothes. Ransacking the closets, the cabinets, the drawers, I finally find my black dress folded neatly at the bottom of a shelf, tucked away behind all the more beautiful clothes that aren't mine.

"Please, please, please," I murmur as I grab the dress off the shelf with care. Unfolding it in front of me, I reach for the pockets, sighing with relief when my hand touches the leaves and stems of the plants I'd picked up yesterday.

"Yes." I thank the gods silently, placing the stems and leaves in my pockets.

Now, I just have to wait for Katya to send up the hot water, and I can make tea for my guards. I slip into bed, covering my head as I wait for her. I figured the more exhausted I look, the more she'll leave me alone, and I can enact my plan.

A knock sounds on my door, and it opens to Katya bringing in a teapot and cups on a tray. She plants it on the table by the sofa before heading directly to me.

"Do you want me to steep your tea for you?" she asks, patting my foot gently.

"No, I can do it," I say weakly, lifting the blanket above my head. "I just need to rest. Crying really tires me out," I add.

She nods. "I hope you feel better! I'll be back for dinner."

"Thanks, Katya," I say, adding a fake cough.

Her eyes are full of understanding when she looks at me once more, then heads out the door, whistling happily to herself. I don't understand how she can be so chipper.

No time to dawdle. I spring from the bed, my heart hammering, eyes darting around for a tool to crush the leaves and stems into a paste. After scouring the room, my eyes finally land on a dusty old vase in the corner. I take out the flowers, empty the vase and use it to pound the leaves. The closet creaks too much, and the mahogany wood is too noisy, so I end up pounding it with a towel on the floor in the bathroom with the shower on. Once the paste is as ready as I can make it, I steep it in the tea. Now I just have to wait.

I pace around the room, looking around to see if there's anything I could use while I'm in the forest. My stomach lurches at the thought that I should've saved some of the food I had earlier instead of letting it go to waste. I enter the closet, looking for anything that might help to keep me warm in the forest. A beautiful blue coat hangs on one of the coat racks, so I pick it up and throw it over myself. The material is thick and warm, not too heavy, but it's at least two or three sizes too big. Better than nothing. I remove the coat and place it under my blankets before checking the cups again.

They're ready.

I run to the bathroom, shaking my hair and ruffling my cheeks so I look like I just woke up. I cough more, too, trying to practice how I might make it more obvious to the guards that I have no intention of running. Heaving a heavy sigh, I look at myself in the mirror. I look nothing like I used to, I realize. "I got this," I tell myself.

Then I turn, grab the cups from the table and knock on the door.

One of the guards opens it, and I give him a small smile, not so big that he'll think I'm up to something, but enough to make him think I'm nice.

"Hello," I say weakly. "I made some tea, but I don't really want it." I fake a cough. "I'm rather unwell, and the smell of it is making me nauseous. Would you like some tea? I really don't want it going to waste," I add with a little gag as I hand out the tea.

They look at me oddly.

"Please have it; it's such good tea, and I really don't want it going to waste," I plead, adding a little flirty smile. What would I know about flirting? I've never flirted in my entire life.

The guard who opened the door takes the cups. "Okay," he says, shrugging to the other guard. The other one takes the cup, giving me a thankful nod.

"Thanks," he says, smelling before taking a sip. He turns back to me, with a small smile on his face. "This is really good."

"What kind of tea is it?" the other guy asks.

"Family recipe. Always calms me down." I smile. "Thank you for taking it!"

They nod, turning back around as they close the door. A huge grin spreads across my face. Now, I just have to wait. I go back to my bed, burying myself in its warmth for one last time before I brave the forest. I'm not looking forward to it, but it's better than being bred for the king. My feet pull at the coat I buried under the blankets. Once I hear the men drop, I should be ready to go.

It takes maybe about fifteen minutes before a thud sounds outside my door. I grab the coat, throw it over myself and open the door. Both men, big and bulky, lay on the floor, their eyes closed, their chests rising and falling softly. The one on the right was snoring. My grin widens.

"Thanks, Mother," I mutter to myself. My instincts take me to another room where the servants' door leads directly down to the servant's area. No one is around because it's still midday and most servants, handmaids, cleaners are still off doing their chores. I sneak across the hallway, out of the back door, ducking when I see Miranda. She's barking orders at someone, then she stomps her way back into the kitchen. As soon as no one's around, I leap up, running towards the bushes, across the field, and through the forests.

I breathe a sigh of relief when I'm in the next field over, and I fill my lungs with fresh air, darting over to the next cluster of trees, and away from the massive castle that grows smaller and smaller as I get further and further away.

CHAPTER 21

Gabriel

"What are you doing?" I ask Griffin as he races out of the king's office.

"She escaped, Gabe. Your father's asking us to find her," Griffin says immediately.

"Wait for me," I tell him, before entering my father's office. "I'm going with them."

The king sits at his desk, his head down. He takes a single look at me before quickly waving his hand. I dart out the door, catching up with Griffin down the stairs.

"How did she escape?" I ask Griffin.

Griffin's eyes twinkle when he looks at me. "She gave her guards a sleeping tea."

"She did *what*?" But I'm already laughing.

"This is the most entertainment we've had in a long, long time," Griffin says as we make it outside. It's believed she may have escaped through the woods to the fields beyond, and about fifteen of us have been tasked with tracking her down.

"Do not hurt her," I remind the group of soldiers before we separate. "I repeat, do not hurt a hair on her head. If I hear that you have, I will rip your heart out myself. Understood?" My tone is a lot harsher than I ever meant it to be.

Soldiers, and even Griffin, look at me, their eyes wide with surprise. I don't think I've ever spoken to them this way. My father probably has. Griffin pats my chest playfully.

"King Phillip the Second?" he suggests before making his way to the forest.

I scowl at him, then follow them all. He's right, though. I don't know what it is about this woman, but my overprotectiveness has reached another level. I've never felt like this with any woman I've ever dated. Any other woman I've ever met.

"Alex!" the soldier in front of me yells. Soon, multiple voices and multiple yells echo throughout the forest.

"Come on, we have to find her before they do," I say, grabbing Griffin. We know these woods like the back of our hands. We used to play here and get lost in them every day. I lead Griffin through another section of trees, where none of the other soldiers had explored.

"How long was she gone?" I ask Griffin.

"It sounds like it's been at least an hour, but probably more. Her guards are still asleep, so we couldn't ask them any questions yet," Griffin responds.

"Damn," I say, looking around us, wishing, praying, to see a head of dark hair somewhere, anywhere.

Griffin stands beside me, giving me a gentle look. "We'll find her, I promise."

Yet, something in me wishes we wouldn't. There's nothing for her here. Nothing good will come of my father's forcing her to marry him. I shudder at the thought. I'd never want to see that, never want to put her through that kind of pain. I don't even want to think about her becoming my stepmother for a whole other reason.

"She couldn't have gone this far," Griffin says when we make it to our second hour looking for her. Sweat beads down the sides of his face. The weather has been beautiful lately, but it's too hot during these hours.

"I don't know. I don't really know much about her or how much she knows about these forests," I respond, shrugging. "She's from Fortuna. Know anything about Fortuna?"

He chewed his lip. "It's pretty far from here. Lots of forests, lots of open land. I've never been, but there's not a lot of people that live there, so it's not prioritized very much," Griffin says, squinting to see further.

"So, there's definitely a chance she can survive in here?" I say, nodding, as I look up towards the sun. Maybe three hours left with sunlight. Does she know how to make a fire? Hunt? Does she have a coat to keep her warm?

"Alex!" I hear another soldier yelling from afar.

I grab Griffin. "Come on," I say, continuing to speed through the brushes. I don't remember what she was wearing, but she couldn't have made it through wearing a dress with all the tall brush around us. She couldn't have made it through with those cleaning shoes she was wearing. They're thin and not made for walking through terrain.

Pushing aside the brush with my sword, the scent of pine and damp earth fill my nostrils, my eyes scanning our surroundings. Where could she have gone? Could she actually have made it through all of these brush and terrain? Good lords. Could she be hurt when we find her? What if she dies in these woods?

"Gabe, stop thinking so much. We just have to find her," Griffin says to my right.

"How do you know I'm thinking so much?" I scoff at him.

"I can pretty much hear you, Gabe," he says, his voice fading a little as he continues to walk on that side. "Your entire body reeks of all your negative thoughts."

I chuckle. "I'm worried about her."

Griffin looks at me from where he's standing, a little lower on the hill we're coming down on. "You realize, this girl put two guards to sleep and has now been running for a little over two hours now? With the balls to do all of that to the king, I think she can take care of herself."

"Can she? Griff, my family put her through this. She wouldn't have been here had we not implemented fake taxes that we've never actually collected. This is our fault. My fault," I say.

Griffin continues to walk, making it more difficult to talk, so I follow him, slowly coming down the hill, through the bushes and the shrubs.

"This is your father's fault, Gabe. And Lady Dajlia's. It's not yours," Griffin says, looking around him for Alex. "I wish you'd not try to carry the world on your shoulders. You'll have people for that." He looks at me and winks.

I roll my eyes at him. "Easy for you to say, Griff, you're not the heir," I mutter, looking down.

Griffin approaches me, patting my back. "But you know I've got your back, right?"

I stare at him. He's my closest friend. My family at this point. One of the very few people I'd die to protect. "I know." I nod at him.

"Let's go find this girl," he says after a while. I nod, following him down the field.

"Alex!" Griffin calls, echoing throughout the fields.

I turn everywhere, looking for anything, anyone, at this point. We're already so deep in the woods, so far from the palace, that I can't even see the tips of the castle anymore. I don't even hear the other soldiers calling for her now, just Griffin.

We pace through the forest, calling her name.

Griffin approaches me as he sips his water. I do the same. Sweat is pouring down my chest and my forehead. We've been at this for a few hours now, and still nothing. The sun will be down soon.

"Alex!" I call again, my voice coming back to me.

"When do we give up?" Griffin asks.

"I don't know. I don't think my father will ever give up on her. Especially now that he knows about her." I take a few deep breaths.

Griffin turns suddenly. "Gabe," he says slowly and quietly.

I finish drinking, stacking my water bottle on my backpack before racing towards him. My heart skips a beat. The woman lay on the hard-packed ground, her head cushioned by a rough, grey rock. Her face is turned away, but a curtain of long, dark hair cascades next to her, smelling faintly of wood smoke and sunshine. She's wearing a navy coat.

"Is it her?" Griffin asks as he steps through all the wild mushrooms reaching from the damp, humid ground.

"I don't know," I say, approaching her slowly, carefully. It looks like she's breathing from the way her chest is rising and falling softly.

As soon as I reach her and see her face, I know it's her.

"Alex," I say as I run to her side, trying to help her up. Griffin takes to her other side.

She slowly sits up, leaning on the palm of my hand.

"Are you okay?" I ask, scanning her face, resisting the urge to touch her. There's no blood, no bruises, no scratches on her head.

Her eyes, wide with fierce determination, gleam as a slow, sly smile stretches across her face, revealing a hint of mischief. With a sudden burst of energy, she springs up, yanking a muddy mushroom from the ground, its earthy scent filling the air, and hurls it at our faces.

"What are you doing?" I want to ask her, but nothing comes out of my mouth. I try to turn to Griffin, but only my eyes move. A strangled gasp escapes Griffin's lips as he clutches his throat, but no sound emerges. A violent coughing fit seizes me, each cough a tearing spasm in my lungs, leaving me gasping for air that only fuels more coughing.

Alex stands in front of me, eyeing the both of us. "That's for trying to get me to marry your father," she spat out before disappearing from my periphery.

I can't move, and a racking cough tears through my chest, each spasm a fresh wave of agony. Griffin chokes, his face turning red, but no sound escapes his lips, only a desperate, silent struggle.

CHAPTER 22

Gabriel

"Ugh."

My body hurts. It feels like I got stabbed three times and bled out. I rub my body, feeling for any wounds, holes, anything that might explain why I feel the way I feel.

"Ugh," I groan again as I force myself up. My muscles aren't cooperative at the moment, so my body falls back down.

"What the hell?" Griffin's voice next to me sounds.

I grimace as pain shoots up my chest.

"What the hell," Griffin sounds angry, whereas I'm trying to breathe.

I cough again, my lungs burning, blinking rapidly to clear my vision before pushing myself up, my head swimming as I sit up.

"What the hell did she do to us?" Griffin growls. He's half-seated, his upper body bent, a grimace twisting his face as if he's about to be violently sick.

"I don't know. It's these mushrooms. I don't know what they are," I say, gently pulling away from the fungi that had stuck to my skin.

"Ugh," I groan. "Everything hurts."

"I'm going to kill her. I literally will unless you stop me, Gabe." Griffin rubs his neck.

I chuckle. "Sure, Griff. Can you move, though?"

"I will. Eventually," he grumbles.

I scratch my arms, crawling over to grass and sprawling out over it. Perhaps the grass would be better to lay on than the toxic mushrooms.

"Move to the grass. It helps," I mumble to Griffin, feeling the weight of the rock on my chest lessen as I stumble out of the damp, earthy-smelling mushroom field.

Griffin groans as he crawls over next to me, sprawling out on the grass. "Oh, much better. Much better," he murmurs.

We lay on the cool, damp ground, waiting for the strange, swirling effects of the mushroom to wear off, the smell of earth filling our nostrils. I push myself up, the stiffness in my joints easing as I finally feel more like myself. Feeling my legs and arms again, I push myself up, and the world swims back into focus as I look around.

"Did you see where she went?" I ask, bending down to catch my breath.

Griffin laughs. "No, I was too busy being poisoned, Gabe."

I walk further away, eager to make my way out of this stupid field, entering into the thick of the trees again. Griffin follows me.

"Bitch, if I catch you, I'm going to kill you!" Griffin calls out.

I give him a look. "He's just kidding, Alex. We're here to help you!" I yell back out.

Griffin rolls his eyes, but continues to walk around. I do too, separating from him for a little. Suddenly, a figure emerges from the trees, its features obscured by shadow. Her long dark hair frames a face partially hidden by the collar of her navy blue coat.

It's her. My stomach flips.

Her eyebrows are knitted together in a tight frown, and her eyes, narrowed with suspicion, bore into me.

"I'm sorry," she mumbles.

I chuckle, letting my hands fall on my hips. "Why are you here? Didn't you take us down so you could escape?"

"I got worried when you guys fell unconscious. I never meant to hurt you," she explains.

I step toward her, but she doesn't move.

"You know I have to take you in, right?" I say as I step forward again.

She nods. "I deserve the punishment. I hurt the future king. I'm sorry. I've never used that mushroom before, and didn't realize the impact ."

Griffin catches up next to me. "You didn't get that far," he says.

"I got worried," she blurts out, stepping forward once more, her hands tied to her back.

"You got worried?" Griffin laughs. "About me and Gabe? You were worried about *us?*"

She nods, her eyes glistening with unshed tears of regret.

"You threw a mushroom that incapacitated us, but you're worried about us?" Griffin repeats, his voice going up an octave.

"Griff," I warn.

"I told you I'd never used that mushroom before," she says, looking uncertain.

"How do we know you don't have something else just to incapacitate us more?" Griffin asks.

Alex's hands leave her back, empty palms exposed in a gesture so quiet, yet so full of meaning. "Look, if I did actually want to hurt you, I would've run. But I was right here, only five minutes away. I kept checking to make sure you both still had a pulse."

"I don't understand why?" Griffin asks, screwing his face up.

"Like I said, I never meant to hurt you." She glares. "Can we not repeat ourselves? How about you just grab me now and take me back so you can put me into the room and have me marry your blasted father?" The tears finally fall from her eyes, and her voice cracks before taking on a more bitter edge.

"How about he just rapes me, too, and I can produce your future heirs? How about that? Let's do it, let's go," she snarls, instantly moving towards us with her hands in front of her. "Do it," she says again, daring us this time. "I'm already pissed that I felt bad, so let's just get this over with, shall we?"

The click of the handcuffs echoes in the silence as I step closer to secure her wrists. "You know, if only you'd have let me in, let me help you, maybe I could have prevented all this from happening."

She offers me a weary look; her gaze is distant and clouded with fatigue. "Hilarious, Prince. You can't even help yourself."

I yank on her hands, my anger fueling the sharp tug. "Apparently, neither can you."

"Dick," she mutters under her breath.

"Bitch," I mutter under mine.

Griffin laughs beside us. "Let's not go falling in love too quickly, shall we? It might ruin all of our plans."

I shoot him a dark look.

"I'd rather marry your father," she spits, the words laced with venom, her face contorted with rage. My jaw drops, and my heart sinks, but I don't know what to do or feel first. I'm already spiraling. Is that true? Am I no better than my father?

CHAPTER 23

Alex

I'm dragged back to my room by the prince and Griffin. The prince shoves me into my room, and without a single look back at me, he stalks off.

Griffin gives me a kind look. "Can you give the prince a break? He's actually trying to help you, and that's extremely rare in this kingdom."

But I tilt my head at him, my eyes still furrowed. "Oh, I know." I glower. Then, I slam the door in his face.

I'm pissed. I want to scream. But I also want to cry. Right now, my heart's beating so fast I can barely hear my own thoughts, let alone understand what I want to do.

It's not even that they caught me. It's not even that I hurt them. I'm angry at myself for being such a sensitive little bitch who could have easily gotten away if only I hadn't had the heart to feel bad for them. I'd already escaped. I was already out there; none of their soldiers were even on my path; it was just the two of them.

"Never use herbs you don't understand, Alex," my mother used to say. I recognized the mushroom, and I knew it had toxic capabilities if the perpetrator directly inhaled it. I knew it would incapacitate them in some way, I just didn't realize it could potentially take them out for that long. I thought they'd cough, that they wouldn't be able to move, but their losing consciousness was not in that book.

And I wasn't strong enough to keep my promise to my mother, and neither was I strong enough to walk away.

And now here I am, back in the room of death. I slam my hand onto the closet, my hand instantly braving the shooting pain surging up my fingers. Of course, the closet didn't dent. It's too strong for someone like me. God, sometimes I just hate myself. I jump onto the bed, burying myself under the covers.

This was my least favorite thing about myself. My weakness.

The door opens with a knock, but I remain buried. Whoever it is can just do their chore. I don't really want to talk to anyone else.

"Hello," the prince's voice speaks.

I lift the blanket off me. "What, Prince?" I snap. "Haven't had enough of me today?"

He chuckles, but the sound is hollow. He clearly hasn't forgiven me. "Oh, Alex, I've had enough of you today. Definitely. I think I can only take minutes from you on a daily basis, otherwise I might explode."

Grinning, despite myself, I pull the cover back. "Then leave me the fuck alone."

"I will. I just came to bring you this," he says. He's holding a thick blue book.

"What is it?" I demand.

"Come here and see," he orders.

My anger flares again. "Why can't you just tell me? I've had a hell of a day."

"Just come here and see, Sparky," he says, with a roll of his eyes.

"Sparky?" I repeat with a rise of an eyebrow.

"You seem to like blazing through life. At some point, that renders sparks," he says, amusement replacing the anger plastered on his face. "I've been trying to think of a nickname for you. You know, firecracker, maybe, grumpy, and sometimes Sparky." The way his eyes look at me makes me blush.

"Don't call me that," I grumble, but I pull myself off the bed and approach him, reaching out for the book. "What is this?" I ask again.

He hands the big book to me, my hand lowering at the weight of it all. Turning the book, the musty scent of old paper fills my nostrils as I try to read the title.

"*History of the Kingdom of Quaila*," I say aloud. I turn to him, a weary look on my face. "I'm getting a history lesson now? What, my schooling not enough to be queen?" I add sarcastically.

He stares at me with exhaustion on his face. "Just read it. Stop being difficult."

"Fine," I mumble, turning the book open. "Do I have to read the whole book?" I whine.

Prince Gabriel gives me a withering look. "Goodnight, Sparky."

"Don't call me that!" I yell as he disappears behind my door.

A click echoes through the room, and I know I'm locked in for the night. I settle on the sofa, opening the book in my lap. The outline shows:

History of Quaila

- Where the land starts
- The first King and Queen
- The first Castle
- Cerene in the Beginning
- The Quskaha (animal connection)
- Our Dragons

I know some of these already, we're taught them during school. My fingers run across the map of the country, focused mostly on Quaila. A little up north is Luntian, and then you have Paglaom and Dalisay even further up north. Just at the edge of the map were clouds and mist. According to my mother, this was a long-lost kingdom from way before our time, a kingdom that never recovered when the strange mist simply erased it from the map. After all, why learn about a kingdom that's all dead and buried?

My eyes pick up the "Our dragons" subhead, and I flip the book to where that starts. Almost at the very end of the book, the first page of this section is a picture of a massive black dragon with orange eyes and black horns. Its wings are massive, light grey on the inner side, midnight black on the other. I scanned the content. Dragons have always been a part of Quaila. They like it here because there's a lot of food, and because the king and queen have always kept them safe.

There used to be other types of dragons who hunted and killed them.

There are other kingdoms that preferred to hunt and kill them, but Quaila has always been different, mostly because of Quskahas.

Quskaha? I blink. I don't think I've ever heard of that word before picking up this book. I flip back to the section on "Quskaha." I flip back through the book again, making it to the dragon section, then flip back a few more pages so I can start the section.

Quskaha (animal connection) are a rare species. They are human, but they share a connection with all beings. As a result, they are able to talk to all animals, including dragons, which makes them invaluable to the kingdom. This power is passed down through bloodline, but it has been known to skip generations unless fate deems it necessary to change or empower a situation. No one knows when or why the power is bestowed. Quskahas are primarily born in Quaila.

What the hell? My bloodline? What for? Why me? What did I do to deserve a curse like this? Did my mother know? Was I born in Quaila? I know I wasn't. At least, that's what my mother told me. So how can I be a Quskaha if I wasn't born here?

Quskahas are extremely loyal to dragons and most animals in the kingdom.

Loyal to dragons? I can barely stand to be near one!

Quskahas are very rare, appearing once in many lifetimes. Here are the known Quskahas and their existence:

- Teryn Malina Y7000 BC
- Saoirse Fell Y2000 BC
- Philippa Dargan Y100 AC
- Twaila Canan Y2000 AC

I gulp. It is Y55000 after Cerene. This was how we dictated our years, before and after Cerene, because Cerene was the beginning of all civilization. When Cerene started getting built, that was the start of our learning, our growth. We built nicer houses, nicer carriages, a school was built, and the palace got bigger. But the true question is: why was there no one between me and Twaila? Why did the prince give this to me? Is he trying to tell me something? Am I supposed to be doing something for this kingdom? I wanted only to save my brother. I only wanted to keep our home.

I don't want to be this.

For the first time since I found out I could speak to animals, I feel like it's a curse. I've always loved being able to speak—to do it. When we first found Mouse, I enjoyed being able to understand her and know when she's pissed or what she's angry about. I loved being able to talk to Chris and Virginia, and I've always thought it was a gift. Now it's something that wants to haunt me to my deathbed. Great. I slam the book shut before tossing it onto the chair, then I slip into bed, pulling the blanket over me. Maybe that will help protect me from the weight of this responsibility.

Damn that prince.

CHAPTER 24

Gabriel

"My son!" my father says, beaming with excitement when I enter his office. He hasn't been this happy in a while.

"Father," I greet, bowing.

"I'm so grateful to you, my son. So grateful. Had you never met that woman, we would not be in this position. I can't believe we've found a Quskaha in this lifetime. It'll be my greatest pleasure to have her as my wife," he says as he paces behind his desk.

My anger flares, but I force myself to push it back down. "Father, you know she's not just going to agree to be married, right? You can't just force someone to be your wife.

She's literally from the woods of Quaila, and they have their own customs," I try.

My father frowns.

"Please, Father, we need to be smart about this. She'll run again if we just force her to do something. This has to be her doing, her choice, otherwise, her loyalty won't be to us," I continue. I can't stand the thought of him being anywhere near her, let alone being bound by marriage to her. "She's already so distrustful of us, what with the way that we charged the taxes and took her away from her family. How we threatened to take her brother."

My father hums, turning his back on me to look out his door. For once, Lady Dajlia isn't here to color his decisions.

"This has to be her choice. Our forcing her to marry into our family won't get us anywhere with her. Please trust me on this, Father; I've spent a little time with her. I know her well enough to realize how stubborn and difficult she's going to make this for us," I plead, taking a step towards him.

"What an interesting argument, my son," he says, his back still turned to me.

"Please, Father, this is me trying to protect our kingdom. I want to use her skills for us, but I don't want to turn her away from us—because she can just as easily turn these dragons away from *us*. We need her on our side, and we need her to want to be on our side." I take a few more steps forward until I'm by his side.

He nods, sneaking a look at me. "You're growing up so fast, my son; one day you'll be a great leader," he says.

The comment alone makes my heart burst with happiness. My father's never been one to compliment anyone. This is probably the first time he's ever acknowledged me as his heir in any meaningful way.

"Just not today. I know what I'll do with her," he says, and my heart sinks as the mischievous glint in his eyes returns.

"Father," I try again, a deep sigh heaving from my chest.

"I'll take your advice into consideration. Can you bring her here? We need to talk about a few things," my father says.

I heave another sigh and nod, slipping out of my father's room to head straight for hers. I'm not exactly excited to see her. We've had a few not-so-great moments, and what she said to me the other day really messed my head up.

My heart beats fast as soon as I catch sight of her door. The soldiers in front of it nod at me, then make way for me to enter. I knock twice, then let myself in. She was sitting on her couch, with the book I handed her yesterday on her lap. She doesn't look up.

"Is my presence needed somewhere, Prince?" she drawls.

"Actually, yes." I clear my throat, standing awkwardly at her door.

She finally lifts her face, her eyes meeting mine. "What do you need?"

"Get dressed; my father wants to see you," I order firmly to cover my nerves.

"Hm, must be nice to just order people around, huh? That get you going?" she snaps at me.

"If you don't get up and get dressed, I'll dress you myself," I growl, stepping forward.

She stands up, giving me a haughty look. "Wouldn't you like that?"

I'm in front of her in seconds, and her eyes widen. My heart is trying to beat itself out of my chest. "What if I say I would? Is that what you want?" I murmur, my gaze feasting on her beautiful eyes, the delicate rise of her nose, the plumpness of her lips. She freezes, her breath a tickle on my neck as she slowly breathes in and out. She smells wonderful, like fresh linen with hints of lemon. I can see the rise and fall of her breasts, telling me her breaths are coming just as quick as mine are.

When she finally moves, she slips out from under me, shooting her tongue out at me.

"Ooh, real mature," I say after her as she heads for the closet. She flips me off before disappearing into the room.

"So…what do I wear for an audience with your father?" she asks from the closet.

I move towards it, freezing the instant I catch sight of her naked back. When she turns, she sees me, and her face turns red. I spin around quickly.

"Uh…just anything nice," I finally respond, unable to hide the twitch between my legs.

"Super clear, Your Highness. Super clear," she says, her voice dripping with sarcasm as she pushes the door closed with a sharp click.

Gods, this woman is irritating. Irritated, however, was not the way my body felt. I shift uncomfortably as the hardness tents in my pants. I take a deep breath, moving closer to the door, where I should've just stayed this entire time.

When she is finally out of the closet, my breath hitches. She's wearing a long green linen dress that goes to her ankles. The dress had a V-back, revealing the gentle slope of her smooth back.

"So?" she asks, turning to me.

I swallow. I'm so fucked. "You look beautiful," I manage, my face paling as I take in her breathtaking beauty, her eyes sparkling like stars, her hair framing her face like a goddess.

She shoves a black coat around her shoulders, then slowly steps up to me, slipping her arm around mine. "Take me to my husband, dick," she whispers.

I roll my eyes at her. "You know I won't let that happen, right?"

Her eyes light up mockingly. "Ooh, protection from the prince? How will I ever thank you?"

I sigh. "Why must you be so difficult?"

"Bet your life was easy peasy before me, wasn't it?" she whispers into my ear.

"Yes. Yes, it was," I agree as I lead her to my father's office.

The moment we get closer to my father's office, her fingers tighten around my arm, and she tenses. I pat her hand, looking at her encouragingly.

"I'm here, Sparky," I say with a smile. She gives me a look.

We enter my father's office. He smiles at us from behind his desk, though there's a darkness in his eyes. "Welcome, welcome!" He skirts around his desk, meeting Alex on the other side.

"Hello, my dear," he says, grabbing her arm and wrapping his around it. "I hope my son has treated you well?"

She continues to grip my arm, tightening it as the king draws closer to her.

"Y-y-yes," she mutters, looking up at him, speechless. She doesn't let go of my arm until my father pulls her away.

"My dear, you have a very important mission in life. As a Quskaha, you are our hope, our future," my father says.

She looks down, her eyes unable to meet his.

"We want you to be happy. We want you to have a choice. So, I will give you one," my father says.

She looks up instantly, her eyes searching his. So do I. I didn't know he'd made his decision already.

"Father," I say, but he lifts a hand up to stop me.

He smiles at her. "I have no idea why or what happened before, but my son seems to be extremely protective of you." He shoots me a look.

She turns to me, frowning, like she doesn't believe him.

"But I am overprotective of our kingdom, my people, my realm, and my son," he says, turning back to her.

She takes a long breath. "I never wanted to be here, Your Highness. All I wanted was to make sure we don't lose our home and that my brother gets to live," she says. "I'm happy to go back home, and you'll never have to deal with me or my family again."

The king chuckles and shakes his head. "Oh, but darling, you have been chosen by fate! Does that not make you want to serve?" my father says. The way the king's eyes twinkle when she shakes her head is unnerving; and the mischievous light makes my skin crawl.

"Well, all right, then. I'll give you a choice," my father says, turning back around to his view.

Alex stays where she was, her head bowed.

"Your first choice. You go through three tasks. If you win, you serve the country, and I give your family a second chance. No taxes, no serving, except for you. You'll serve as the Quskaha of Quaila," he says, not turning around.

Her eyes widen, but she finally looks up at him. "What if I lose?"

My father turns to her, his eyes gleaming. "Well, then you die."

Her eyes widen even further, her breasts rising and falling in a panicked rhythm in tune with my own. "What's my second choice?"

His face contorted into a creepy, sly smile, the corners of his mouth curling upwards in a way that makes my stomach churn.

"I'll kill your entire family while you watch."

"Father!" I protest, but he holds up a hand once more. "Father, you can't do this!" I beg, despite the hand he's holding up.

Tears stream down her face, and I fight the urge to rush to her side, my heart aching for her. I turn back to my father. "Father, please."

He frowns at me. "Maybe I'll kill my heir, too, as you watch."

My eyes bulge in horror, my throat constricting at the chilling implications of his words as a cold dread washes over me. "I-I'm your son," I stammer.

"No," a small voice comes from the girl to my left. Her cheeks are stained, but she's wiped her tears away already. "No, I'll do the tasks."

"Alex," my voice fades as I gulp. She doesn't meet my eye.

"I'll do the tasks," she repeats, looking up at my father. "I'll do it. Please don't kill my family," she adds, her voice cracking with the unshed tears pooling in her eyes.

My father looks at her in triumph, then gives me a chilling look. Goosebumps rise across my spine. "Yes, you will."

CHAPTER 25

Alex

"Your task will be in a week," the king says before dismissing us from his office.

"I don't even know who you are anymore," the prince snarls at his father before opening the door. His voice shakes, but it ascends to a mighty shout before we leave. "This isn't about the kingdom, or anyone apart from you, and your lust for power. You're pure evil. I don't know why I ever looked up to you."

I glance at the king, wincing and expecting a retaliation, but all I can see in his eyes is glee. He's pleased he got under his son's skin, I realize.

As soon as we're outside, the prince grabs my arm, hauling me back into my room. I don't say anything, and neither does he. When we enter my room, he releases my arm, and the door clicks shut behind him. He paces back and forth in my foyer, his footsteps echoing on the hardwood floor. I stare at him, a strange numbness washing over me as I struggle to decipher my feelings. Am I angry? Am I terrified? Am I sad?

He moves toward me, his mouth opening to say something, but I push him away with all my might, my hands firm against his chest.

"What the hell?" he says, his arms raised.

"You were supposed to protect me! You were supposed to help me!" I say, tears running down my cheeks involuntarily.

He closes his eyes, then goes back to pacing. "I know," he mumbles.

I frown, snatching up the ornate vase from the nightstand—its delicate carvings, a testament to its exorbitant price, only fueling my anger. Why do people with more just get to take? Spinning on my heel, I hurled the vase at the doorframe, the ceramic whistling through the air. Only, I'd slightly misjudged the angle, and he has to duck to avoid being blasted by it. The vase crashes behind him, showering him with shards of pottery and a cloud of dust. He stands, glaring at me.

"What the hell?" he yells at me.

"Oops," I said, the sarcasm dripping from my voice as I snatch up the other vase; its delicate floral pattern strangely fragile in my hand. Let him think I did that on purpose. Maybe he'll think twice about leading me to his father next time.

"You better not throw that at me, bitch," he growls.

"Stop telling me what to do!" I yell back, throwing yet another expensive vase at his head.

He growls, stepping forward. "Feel better?"

I frown. "No," I lie. I *do* feel better. It wasn't going to change my situation, but throwing something was exhilarating.

The look on his face changed. "Do it again."

"What?" I ask, my eyebrows knitting even more.

"Just throw another fucking vase," he orders, rolling his eyes.

I stomp into the bathroom, snatching the porcelain vase from the counter, its smooth coolness against my skin, and hurl it at the mirror above my dressing table. He ducks instinctively, though it goes nowhere near him this time, and a grin spreads across his face as his eyes light up with mischief.

"Again," he orders.

"Shut up," I yell, but I throw the plate that was under the vase against the far wall. My chest is heaving, but the feeling of control has me ramped up.

"Again," he says.

I grab the bottle on my nightstand, throwing it across the room. Suddenly, I don't feel so exhilarated anymore. Tears pool in my eyes as I stare at him. All I see when I look at him are all the lost opportunities. All the things I lost just because his family are incredibly selfish and would rather their people died than have themselves lose out on things. If I do nothing, my brother will die. My mother will die.

And if I do, I'm going to die.

I swallow hard, tears streaming down my face.

And yet, when he approaches, I crumble, my tears soaking his crisp white tunic, the scent of him mixing with the salty tang of my own tears. His strong arms encircle me, the muscles taut as he pulls me tightly against him.

His voice, thick with remorse, whispers, "I'm so sorry, so sorry," against my hair; each word a rough caress against my ear as I cry on his chest, my sobs muffled by his tunic.

When I wake up the next morning, I'm in my bed, alone. I don't know how I made it to bed last night; I don't even remember the rest of the night. But the door opens, and Katya comes in with a tray full of breakfast.

"Good morning, Alex!" she says as soon as the door is closed.

"Hello," I manage, pushing the blankets off of me.

"You must've had a rough night," Katya says, noticing my swollen face. I run into the bathroom to see just how bad it is, grimacing when I see my reflection.

"Don't worry, I'll help you fix it after breakfast and before you go on your trip with the prince," Katya says. I look back at her.

"What trip?" I ask.

Katya shrugs. "I'm supposed to dress you and take you to him after."

"Where are we going?" I ask, dropping into the chair beside her.

"I don't know." She hands me a fork. "He asked me to make sure you eat plenty."

I roll my eyes, stabbing at the eggs. "He needs to stop ordering me around," I mumble, taking a bite.

A soft chuckle escapes her lips as she watches me take a small bite.

"I think you're supposed to eat more than that," she says, nibbling some of the toast. I stab at the eggs once more, each bite feeling like I'm exchanging my soul.

"Are you excited?" she asks, munching on some fruit.

"I don't know what we're doing or where we're going. Kind of hard to be excited when I'm not sure what's happening," I respond, thinking about the night before. He took care of me. He let me cry on him the entire time, and not once did he talk. Somehow I made it back to bed, and he never took advantage of me.

When I've eaten at least half of breakfast, Katya helps me bathe, then dresses me in riding attire from my closet of clothes that aren't mine. The smell of fresh leather fills the air as she grabs the new boots from my closet and helps me tie them.

"Why do I have to wear these, Kat?" I whine, watching my reflection in the mirror. She'd braided my hair behind my back and added a short, white coat over my black pants and white shirt. I look nothing like myself.

"Ready?" Katya asks. I nod. She knocks and the door opens.

"She's with me," she tells the soldiers standing outside my door. I smirk a little, realizing they'd changed my guards.

Following Katya, I walk down the dimly lit hallway, the air growing colder with each step, then down the steep stairs and out the large, imposing double doors.

"Where are we going?" I ask, struggling to follow Katya's small but quick steps.

She doesn't answer. We pass through the amphitheater until I'm led to a barn.

Prince Gabriel stands outside, looking as handsome as ever, his dark green eyes easily catching me from afar. His gaze is intense, following my every move.

"What?" I snap as soon as I make it within hearing distance. His mere presence makes me so angry.

He smirks, his eyes plastered on me. I shudder.

"Your Majesty." Katya bows. The prince gives a curt nod, and she turns, her footsteps echoing slightly on the stone path as she heads back to the castle.

"What am I doing here, Prince?" I say the last word like it's venom.

"Come with me," he grunts, turning into the stable. A man emerges from one of the four stalls, leading two magnificent horses—a striking chestnut beauty and a smaller, elegant palomino dappled with black. The rhythmic clip-clop of their hooves on the cobblestones echoes on the quiet street.

"Can you ride?" he asks, turning back to me.

I didn't hear him. Instead, I pet the horse, feeling its warm, muscular body beneath my hand. "Hello," I say softly to the creature.

"Hello, my name is Queen," the chestnut horse whinnied, its coat gleaming in the sunlight.

Next to Queen, a black and white horse with a calm demeanor nudges closer and says, "I'm Betty."

"Hello, you beauties," I sing, and their manes sway gently in the breeze as they turn their heads to look at me.

"I guess you can," Prince Gabriel says. "This is--"

"Queen and Betty, yeah, I know," I finish for him.

"They told you?" he asks, a small tilt in the corner of his mouth.

I nod, looking up at Betty to pet her. "Beautiful," I murmur.

"Very beautiful," he agrees, a smile playing on his lips as his eyes, however, are fixed on me, not the horses. Heat blooms in my cheeks as I wince and quickly avert my gaze, hoping he doesn't notice.

"What are we doing here?" I demand.

"I got permission to take you out for a ride," he says, mounting Queen.

I mount Betty. "We'll have fun, won't we?" I say to Betty.

The prince continues to ride, and I follow him. We ride onto a beautiful trail, the scent of pine filling the air as dogwood blossoms paint the edges of the path in shades of white and pink. A fresh breeze carries the sweet scent of lilacs and jasmine blooming profusely along the trail, filling the air.

"This is beautiful," I whisper, the words escaping my lips, as I'm mesmerized by the scenery before me.

His smile is strained, a mere twitch of the mouth that doesn't reach the icy glint in his eyes. "It was my mother's favorite trail. She used to take me down here all the time."

I look up at him, the sunlight catching the subtle shift in his expression. He's never talked about his mother before.

"How did she die?" I ask, unsure if he'll answer, but I study his face for a moment, wanting to see his true reaction. He was quiet for a moment, the only sound the gentle clip-clop of our horses' hooves on the trail. "She had a heart attack," he says, a flicker of something unreadable in his eyes before he looks away.

"A heart attack?" I repeat.

"Extremely healthy woman, a random heart attack. Odd, right?" he adds a moment later.

"I'm sorry," I say. His face has a quiet sadness I haven't seen before in him. His dark eyes lighten a bit in the sun. We continue to ride, shooting random looks at each other every now and again. "Do you know what the first task will be about?" I ask after a while. He shakes his head, sighing deeply. "What do I do?"

"Griffin and I are working on it, but we don't know what it is," he says. "We'll let you know as soon as we have anything."

"Prince, why are you doing this?" was my next question.

"Doing what, Sparky?" A slow smirk stretches across his face, his eyes crinkling at the corners.

"Why are you being nice to me? Why are you trying to help me?" I ask, sneaking a look at his face. He seems so calm and at peace—a stark contrast to his agitated state of the last few weeks; his eyes are tranquil, his breathing even.

"You can call me Gabriel, you know. Or Gabe. Especially if it's just us," he responds.

I lift my head. "And you can call me Alex, but Sparky is what always seems to come out of your mouth," I point out with a sarcastic grin.

His laughter fills the air—a genuine, booming sound that resonates with unexpected warmth inside my chest. "Fair enough."

My heart skips a beat. Did he have to be so beautiful?

"You didn't answer my question," I remind him, turning away to hide the flushing in my cheeks.

He laughs again. "Why do you seem so adamant not to trust me?"

This time I laugh. "Are you kidding? Is that even a serious question?"

The smile on his face grows. "I like that," he says.

"What?" I ask, frowning.

"And…it's gone," he smirks.

As we round a bend, the trail plunges into shadow; the dense trees block out most of the sunlight, creating an almost eerie quiet.

"This isn't where you kill me, is it?" I say, my eyes darkening at the trail.

He laughs again. "You really have serious trust issues, don't you? I've tried so hard to get you to trust me, and I've helped you multiple times, *and* got into trouble for it, yet you still can't seem to believe anything I say."

I study him for a bit, trying to see if I can make out the evil or the good in him. I want to trust him; I really do. But sometimes, when I think of everything that happened to me, I blame him.

"Prince, your family did this to me," I start.

He sighs, the pain in his eyes unmistakable. It was gone again so quickly, that I might've been imagining it. "I'm going to help you. Griffin and I, we promise we'll help you as much as we can. We'll train you, make sure you're ready for whatever my father is planning. We'll help you if you let us," he says after a while.

My brow furrows. "But that's what I don't understand. Why would you help me? What are you hiding?" I ask.

"I'm not hiding anything," he says, laughing.

His laugh puts a smile on my face. "Yes, that's totally convincing."

His face turns more serious, and he chews his lip. "I want to help you because we did this to you," he says, looking me in the eye.

I hum. "I don't believe it," I mutter.

"Why? Do you really think we're that bad?" he says, turning to me.

"I know your family never gave a shit. Otherwise, people in Fortuna, outside of Cerene, wouldn't be suffering, but we are. We couldn't afford to put Angus through school. Can you imagine how that must be like for him?" I explain.

"But that's why I'm here, Sparky. I'm here to help you. If once upon a time, my family didn't do anything, then at least I can help now. I want to," the prince answers, clicking his tongue.

His horse speeds up, and I frown.

"I'll let you help me, Prince. But I don't trust you," I call after him.

He rolls his eyes as he turns around. "You know what? If it has to be like this, then I'll earn your trust."

Shaking my head, I click my tongue just like he had, and Betty speeds up in response. "You can try," I respond with a chuckle.

The prince winks at me. "I definitely will." He continues to ride, and I follow.

"Where are we going?" I yell behind him. He doesn't answer, just continues to run through the trails. I speed up a little behind him. At the end of the clearing, Betty and I stop next to Queen and the prince. My mouth drops.

Water cascades down the side of the mountain in levels, dropping to a single pool at the end of the trail. On the other side of the trail is a river, roaring with powerful water. Each side of the water is filled with beautiful red and yellow canna lilies and blue and purple water forget-me-nots. Pink and purple wisteria climb the sides of the waterfalls, hiking all the way to the top of the mountain. Vibrant green moss glints in the sunlight peeking through the lattice skies beyond the tree cover.

I pat Betty's head, swinging my leg over to one side where the prince offers his hand. I frown initially, but take his hand anyway, jumping off. My feet land on the ground, but his hands surround my waist to steady me, capturing a portion of my bare skin. The skin beneath his touch electrifies me, and I flinch, stepping away. A snicker escapes from him as he hums, but I ignore him, moving towards the edge of the pool where I can feel the mist of the waterfall on my face.

"Beautiful," I breathe, staring at the scenery in front of me.

"One of my mother's favorite places. We used to have lunch here all the time," the prince adds, and I feel his presence next to me.

I bend down, removing the boots from my feet.

"What are you doing?" he asks, eyebrows knitting.

I toss the boot away from the water before moving onto the next one. Once I'm barefoot, I fold my pants up as high as I can before carefully walking through the mossy, slippery ground to get to the edge of the waterfall. The water is cool and refreshing—a beautiful counter to the humidity at this time of the day.

"Careful!" the prince calls behind me.

I turn back, and he's still where he was standing moments ago. "You coming?" I tease. His face changes, relaxing a little as a smile spreads across his face. He bends to pull off his own boots, and I turn back around, walking across a few more wet rocks before reaching for a higher ledge and gripping onto it. I leverage my knees to get up higher, grimacing when I hit my shin on the rock. But I make it up higher anyway, and even though the rock is damp, I sit on it with my feet out by the waterfall. My pants are already wet from the mist. My gaze turns to the prince, who's stepping across a path of rocks. He slips on one, his back hitting the wet moss with a groan. I laugh, and he scowls at me before pulling himself up, skipping a few smaller rocks to make it next to the ledge.

"Having fun?" He smirks.

I chuckle. "I am, actually," I respond, holding out a hand to help him up. He takes it but doesn't really need much to make it up the ledge. He takes the seat next to me, his hair dripping wet from when he fell earlier.

"It's been a while since I've climbed this," he says, looking ahead of us. "Griffin and I used to play here so often.

"It's so beautiful," I breathe.

"It's called the Estella Falls," he says. "Because my mother would come here every day right after she got married to my father just to plant around it. These flowers— they were hers."

I turn to him, watching the grief in his eyes, the sadness on his face. "You miss her."

"I do. She was wonderful. The only other person I'd ever seen with the same skin color as you," he says, pointing at me.

I frown. "Was she from here, too?"

"I don't think so. She was from the kingdom of Dalisay; she married my father to join their families. Why?" he asks, tossing a small stone into the pool below us. The rock sinks, creating ripples across the pool, breaking through the regular patterns of the waterfall.

I shrug. "I actually have no idea where we're from," I respond thoughtfully. "My parents always just said we traveled a lot before ending up in Fortuna. I've never seen anyone with skin like ours. It makes me curious."

He leans closer. "Is that important to you? Knowing where you're from?" he asks.

I kick my legs. "Wouldn't it be for most people? If you grew up in a place where no one looks like you? It didn't use to matter this much when I lived in Fortuna, as I didn't see a lot of people. I didn't have people staring me down or calling me names as often as I do here. I didn't have people judging me just because I have brown skin, and I've never had people slap me just because of it. Here, in the short time I've been here, I've been called that multiple times."

"Oh, ignore them. That's what my mother always did. She ignored all the negative comments and just did what she thought was right. The people who knew her loved her." He shrugs. "Sometimes, that's what matters most."

"I don't even have people who love me here, Prince. I'm all alone here," I say, shaking my head.

The prince reaches out to grab my hand and looks at me. "No, you're not."

And somehow, in the middle of nowhere, a spark is lit. And I want to believe him.

CHAPTER 26

Gabriel

"Why are you such a dick?" she asks as we run through the trail. Day two of her training, and we've been doing a mixture of running exercises and fighting. After all, if I know my father, the tasks will be all about figuring out someone's strength. Griffin has been training her to fight, while I've been running miles with her at least three times a day.

I smirk, letting her keep up after I'd sped up. "Just so you know, I don't enjoy torturing you, Sparky. It's not exactly my favorite pastime."

She humphs, but continues to run. I hear her breathing speeding up.

"You need to keep your breathing calm, Sparky," I tell her as she passes me.

"Why can't I do this by myself again?" she mutters under her breath.

I turn to her, smirking. "Uh, because the last time you escaped you tried to paralyze the heir of this kingdom?"

She rolls her eyes. "I should've just escaped," she sighs heavily.

"Yes," I agree, running backwards so I can see her face. "You should've."

A sly smile stretches across her face, a glint of mischief in her eye as she subtly extends her foot to trip me. My feet fly out from under me, sending me sprawling on the hard ground as she speeds past me.

"Bitch," I murmur under my breath, smiling as I watch her make it to the end of the trail.

She turns to me, flips me off, sticks out her tongue, and starts walking back to the castle.

Gods, this woman. I get up and race toward her, catching up to her within minutes. After all, I've been trained all my life.

"Dick," she mutters under her breath. I burst out laughing.

"You're a joy to be around, you know that?" I say, barely containing my laughter.

She rolls her eyes at me. Then, her head turns as she pauses in her steps. "Prince, why did you give me that book?"

"What book?" I frown, almost forgetting that I'd given her one. "Oh, the history book?"

"Yes. Why give it to me?" she asks, her dark eyes boring into mine. Katya had put her in tight leggings and a tank top, and her hair was pulled into a bun behind her head. We'd been exercising the entire day, and sweat glistened down her forehead. She looked more beautiful than ever.

"I don't know." I shrug. "I guess I figured you'd want to know who you are."

She sighs. "Well. That's shit."

I laugh again. "It's shit knowing who you are?"

"I'm not whatever that thing is. I'm no Quskaha. Sure, I can speak to animals, but I'm terrified of dragons!" she explains, shuddering.

I let the words sink in. It isn't going to be easy to convince her. "I think you just haven't been around them much. Maybe we should go there at some point," I suggest.

Her eyes widen. "You don't think he'll have me talk to a dragon, do you?" she asks, turning to grab my arms.

I feel her fear with just that one touch. I pat her hands gently.

"I don't know, Sparky. My father's a lot of things," I say. Which means it's highly likely. "We'll go to the dragon field tomorrow."

She looks down, and it seems to take forever for her to get her words out. "Do you expect something out of me?" she asks softly. "Am I supposed to give you something in return for your help?"

"I don't expect anything out of you, Sparky," I respond.

"Lies," she spits out, then stomps off. I grimace before following her.

"Sparky--"

"Don't call me that!" she yells, turning around.

"Alex," I start again, "I don't, I promise. All I know is that I want you to survive." I'm telling the truth. But before I chicken out, I continue, "I don't know exactly what you are to me yet." I pause for her reaction: eyebrows knitted, her lips tense, and she backs away.

"I don't know what you are to me yet," I repeat. "I just–I just know I should help you."

"I don't know what that means," she mumbles, looking down.

"It's okay," I tell her kindly. "I don't know what it means, either."

She looks me in the eyes like she's searching for something. Then she turns around and heads back into her room.

I stare at the place she left for a moment, hoping something would tell me what to do.

"Convenient," a voice says behind me. I turn, and Griffin stands in his workout clothes, black pants and a blank tank top. His forehead was slick with sweat, and his shirt was soaked through in patches, clinging to his back.

"Couldn't shower yet?" I chuckle at him.

"Nah. I like to impress the women around me, you know. They need something pretty to look at," Griffin responds, shrugging carelessly, then flexes his muscles.

I laugh. "Yeah? How's that going for you?"

His eyes widen mockingly. "Very productive."

"Good for you," I say, shooting him a weary look.

"I'd tell you to do the same, but it looks like you're only doing it for one person," he says.

I pause. "Okay?" I frown at him.

"You know you have to be careful, right? Your father can't find out about this." His eyebrow is raised, but his tone is careful. "The things your father would do to her if he knew."

I continue walking, turning my head away from him. "There's nothing to tell, Griff, nothing."

"You can't lie to me, Gabe," he says.

He's right. I can't. If anyone knows me better than I know myself, it's Griffin.

CHAPTER 27

Gabriel

"Punch," Griffin says.

Alex extends her arms, hitting the pad on Griffin's hand with her fist.

"I said, punch! Punch like you mean it!" Griffin encourages. Alex's eyes darken as she punches the pad. "What did I just say? Punch like you mean it! Use that anger!"

Alex frowns, but she continues punching harder and harder.

"Don't lose your stance, Sparky," I say from the sidelines.

She shoots me a look, then turns back to Griffin. "Well, now I'm furious," she seethes, her knuckles white as she hits the soft, yielding pad.

Griffin sneaks a look at me, winking. I roll my eyes. I wasn't supposed to be watching, but after being excused by my father, I ended up here after all. Training has done her well, truly, but she was already strong, fast, and quick to learn.

I turn back to them, fighting. We're in the castle's gym, a massive workout room with a pool, a sauna, a basketball court, and a punching bag with durable mats. It also has an archery and an area for weights, something only royals have access to, whereas the soldiers get to train in a bigger area, outside the castle. Griffin takes her here every day, helping her learn how to fight. I'm certain my father's tasks will require some sort of strength training in preparation for a fight, so that he can entertain his people.

Despite the fact that she's punching that pad like a maniac right now, she seems a little more comfortable with Griff. Maybe not being the future heir makes him more approachable? She even seems to be more relaxed, even though he's technically teaching her how to fight.

Griffin pauses, grabbing a bottle of water, and hands it to her. Their voices are quieter now, harder for me to hear from the sidelines.

When she laughs at something he says, I revel in the sound of her genuine, unadulterated laughter; it's like music to my ears. It does things to my insides; to my chest. I think I'd like to hear it more, but being only two days away from the first task, I don't know if I'll ever hear it again. I watch her face carefully, studying the dimple forming at the edge of her cheek as she smiles, and the dip in her eyes. The pink glow forming on her cheeks. I don't think I've ever seen anything more beautiful.

I force myself to turn around, eager to hide any other emotion that might be showing on my face right now. Griffin's right, I can't do this. I can't show my father that she means anything to me. I don't even want to think about what he would do to her. She's already so close to becoming his wife, so close to everything she said the other day. The idea of her being raped by my father just so he can have his spare heir turns my blood to lava in my veins.

"Gabe?" Griffin says behind me.

"Yeah, what's up?" I ask, turning back to them, forcing down all the angry emotions threatening to come out. He frowns the instant he sees my face, but he sneaks a look at Alex and drops whatever he was about to say.

"Ready for the next training session?" he asks instead.

Alex groans next to him. She wipes her neck and shoulders with a white towel, but comes over to sit by me, looking at me with those beautiful dark eyes. "Do we have to?"

I mock her whining. "Yes, we have to."

She sticks her tongue out at me. "Dick," she mutters under her breath. Then, with a final bounce, she leaps from the boxing ring and heads out, the squeak of her shoes fading into the distance. "Well? Are we going to see those dragons or not?"

A smile spreads across my face as Griffin and I follow her out of the castle.

"Tell me about the dragons," she says, pausing at the entrance so I can lead us to the dragon's barn.

"We have six. Some of them don't really stick around, but we see them flying around every now and again. The green one is usually here," I tell her as we continue to walk to the field. I can see him lying on the ground from here, so I point to him. She shudders.

"There's the red one," I add, pointing to the massive red dragon lying beside him.

"And there's the baby," I gesture toward the much smaller one rolling on the grass.

She frowns, hesitating. "Do they have names?"

I shake my head. "Maybe Tait has one for them, but we've never been able to name a dragon. How can we? None of us knows who they truly are."

Her frown turns into a glare when she turns back to me. "You want me to name them?" she demands.

I gaze back at her, a chuckle slowly erupting from me.

"No, Sparky," I respond.

She scowls.

"I want you to ask them if they have names."

Her eyes widen, but she smirks. "How about we just get there first, huh? I've never been this close to a dragon. Who takes care of them?"

"We have a few dragonkeepers. Tait gives them their food and cleans their field. He's the one that helped with bringing the two dragons to the pen for the celebration," I tell her, pointing to the further-out field where a man's cutting the grass with a machete.

"Have…h-have they ever killed anyone?" she asks, her voice shaking.

"Of course, they're dragons, Sparky; they'll kill anyone who gets in their way." I chuckle.

She hesitates again, like she's stuck in place.

Griffin crashes into her back, and she falls over. Without thinking, I step in front of her, grabbing her waist to steady her.

"Griff!" I say, glaring at him.

He scowls. "I wasn't the one who just randomly stopped on a hill," he says sarcastically, glancing at Alex.

She rolls her eyes at him and stares back at the large fenced field in front of us. She swallows.

"Are you okay?" Griffin asks her. She nods. Her eyebrows are knitted when she turns to me.

"Do I have to?" she asks.

She's shaking. Her eyes are full of fear, and her face is pleading. For a moment I want to tell her to just turn back, but this is my father, and there's no better way to help someone over their fear than exposing them to the source.

I grab her hand, and she jumps but doesn't pull away. "Come on," I encourage her. "It won't take long, I promise."

She lets me drag her closer to the pen, and I feel her grip getting tighter and heavier the closer we get.

Her eyes stare at them, and her legs tremble as hard as her hands, so I wrap my arms around her shoulders

"What are you doing?" she mumbles.

I don't answer her as we slowly walk toward the fence.

"Prince," she protests slowly.

Suddenly, the green dragon stands and growls. The grip on my arm becomes a vice. When I turn, Alex's eyes are closed. Griffin runs forward, catching her unconscious body before it falls to the ground. He eyes me nervously.

"What are we going to do?"

I bite my lip. "Hope my father doesn't have a challenge involving dragons?"

CHAPTER 28

Alex

It's getting late. The prince was supposed to pick me up half an hour ago for the task, and he still hasn't made it here. I'm pacing around my room, tapping the riding boots I'm wearing. Katya has dressed me in a green tunic with black pants, and I have this weird, black, canvas vest on with multiple pockets. She braided my hair down my back, which I actually like. The boots I'm wearing, according to Katya, help with long walks and have ample support. I've never worn anything like it, and the riding boots I wore a few days ago feel a little different.

I continue pacing, taking a drink of the water bottle Katya had left with me. Where is he? Why isn't he here with me? He promised he'd be here to help, yet here I am alone, and late for my first task. I can't even imagine how angry the king would be if he thinks I'm not coming.

My door bursts open, and the prince enters, his face pale, sweat trickling down the sides of his face. He's wearing the same green tunic and black pants, with a dark coat around him. He looks as if he's about to vomit.

"What the hell, Prince? Where have you been?" I yell.

He turns to me, his eyes wide.

"I'm so sorry, Alex, I'm so sorry. I tried to stop it. I tried to get him to change his mind, but he wouldn't. I'm so sorry," he rambles, his voice frantic.

I frown, turning to him, my heart thudding faster than ever. "What are you talking about?"

His voice cracks. "I'm sorry, Alex. The task. He wants you to ride a d-dragon."

I freeze. No. No, no, that can't be right. No, I back up slowly until I hit a wall. I can't breathe. I can't move. I can't see. Tears stream down my face as I imagine the many ways a dragon can kill me. The majestic roar it gave out yesterday. The amount of fire it can breathe out. How big it is.

"Hey, hey," a faraway voice says.

I can't move. My entire world is frozen. Thoughts swirl in and out of my brain, but I can't understand them. I try so hard to find them, place them, but nothing happens.

A hand touches my knee. "Breathe, Sparky, breathe with me," he says.

I follow his voice, breathing in and out as he does, my vision returning when the prince kneels in front of me. His hand is on my knee, the other one on my cheek. I focus on his dark green eyes, and breathe in, out. In and out.

Finally, he asks. "Are you okay?"

I gulp. "How do I ride a dragon?"

He tilts his head, and I know he'd do this in my place in a heartbeat if he could. "You just gotta try, Sparky. Talk to them, and ask them if they'd give you a chance. Talk to them," he repeats, eyeing me.

My eyes widen as the door bursts open with three soldiers. My heart stalls. The prince takes my cheek, turning me back to face him.

"You've got this, Sparky. You can do this," he says to me.

The soldiers grab my arms, helping me up as I nod at the prince.

"Hey! Be gentle with her," he snaps at one of the soldiers at my side.

I stay silent as they hold on to me, leading me to wherever I need to be. My head turns back to the prince, who's following us. This might be the last time I see him. My stomach twists, and the tears threaten to fall, but the prince just gives me an encouraging nod and mouths: "You've got this!"

The soldiers take me out the back door, where I know the staff have been creating a designated area for this. I saw it when we were training in the gym a few days ago, since the gym is located at the back of the castle. Today, it looks beautiful. The massive arena is round, made of stone, and painted with Quaila's colors.

Rows of seats curve in delicate waves, but don't actually start until they're practically at mid-height of the arena. They're tiered, probably for the commoners and the people the king wants to impress. The center is a field of green grass, mimicking the dragon's field, large enough for two dragons to be there, sprawling out on the grass. I shudder the instant I see them. I feel sick at the thought that people are actually there to watch me. Watch me what? Die?

I hear them chanting something, but I don't quite understand the words. I'm brought inside the arena, and the chanting and the stomping get louder and harder, vibrating throughout the arena. The more I try to listen to the chanting, the more I realize they're saying "Quskaha". I swallow hard. I'm *not* a Quskaha.

I'm not.

How could I be? I've barely been able to stay awake in front of a dragon. The only time I've actually been around one without fainting was the day that they were hurting the green dragon.

The day everything went to hell.

"Ah, there's our Quskaha," the king says as we step into the main viewing area, where his knights and advisors are.

I feel every pair of eyes on me as I'm brought in front of the king.

"Our Quskaha, everyone!" he booms throughout the arena, and cheers reverberate throughout the space. Then he turns back to me, a mischievous glint in his eyes. "Are you ready to prove your worth, Quskaha?" he says only to me.

I shudder. "Your Majesty–" I start to protest, but he cuts me off.

"Remember, it's this or your entire family dies," he warns, his voice a chilling whisper against the roar of the cheering crowd behind him.

"Yes, Your Majesty," I gulp.

"Are you ready?" he booms to everyone again. Then, just to me, he adds, "You better be ready to prove your worth, child. There's no going back now." Laughter erupts from his mouth, but his eyes display a storm.

"Yes, Your Majesty," is the only thing I can say.

He looks at me once more with disdain, then turns to his soldiers. "Take her down."

I glance around for the prince, but he's nowhere to be found. The soldiers nod, then proceed to grab me and walk me back down, and I struggle to catch up. Eventually, I just lift my feet, and they're strong enough to carry me down. A soldier looks at me warily, and I roll my eyes.

"Then slow down," I mutter to him.

The soldiers take me to an arch-like entry area with steel cell bars, preventing anything in the center from coming in. They shove me inside, then exit the door. It slams behind them. I get up, pushing at the handles, but nothing gives way. A loud clinking reverberates around me, and the steel cell bars open from the ground up. I shudder.

It's time.

The cell doors open, and I step out slowly. There aren't two dragons; there are three. The massive green one that was hurt the other day is here, then there's the smaller red dragon, and the bigger red one. The moment I step out of the entryway, their gaze goes to me. I walk slowly, flanking the sides of the arena as far as I can from them, my heart pounding. I already regret fainting at the dragon field the other day. This would be so much easier if I already knew them and they knew me. But they don't. All they see is food, right here where I'm standing.

I swallow hard, continuing to walk the sides of the arena.

"Who are you?" the red one growls.

"I-I-I'm Alex," I yell back.

Instantly, all three dragons get up on their hind legs, their massive snouts closing the distance between me and them within moments.

"How the hell are you talking to us?" the green dragon says.

"It's a trick," the massive red dragon says just next to him.

"N-N-No, please, it's not a trick!" I say immediately, but I'm too late.

The green dragon backs up with a roar, and when it steps forward, it opens its mouth, and searing orange flames burst out.

I run.

CHAPTER 29

Gabriel

I hold my breath, the acrid smell of sulfur singeing my nostrils as I watch the green dragon open its mouth and breathe a hot torrent of fire exactly where she'd been.

No. No. The wall, where she'd stood just moments before, was now a blackened ruin, the stone crumbling to ash. My throat feels dry as I swallow hard, fighting back the rage that threatens to consume me.

But Griffin nudges my elbow, pointing to Alex running wildly on the sides, her braid flying behind her like a dark, streaming ribbon. I breathe out a slow sigh of relief, my grip tightening on the railing until my knuckles whiten with the pressure. She looks so scared.

"You've got to help her, Gabe," Griffin pleads, his hand touching my elbow.

My breath shakes, but I walk over to my father on the other side of the viewing area.

"I hope she dies," someone says above us.

"Really? I think she'll survive," another says. "Want to bet on it?"

My mouth dries, but before I can even react, the familiar husky tone of my father's voice speaks up. "I think she'll die, too," he says. Then he turns back to Alex in the center of the arena. "Die, Quskaha! Die!"

My jaw drops as laughter surrounds us. I turn back to Griffin to see a thin line plastered on his lips. My father is such a dick. When my mother died, he put me through so much just to make sure I was like him, and Griffin told me so many times how much of an arsehole my father is. I knew he was difficult.

But this side of him is beyond evil. I remember the many times I found my mother crying because of him. I never believed it because, well--he is the king. Kings are supposed to be kind, fair, strong, and understanding. But my father is just…a bully.

I make my way to my father. "Father, please, you have to help her. Get her out of here," I plead.

His eyes bury into mine, his expression going from laughter, to curiosity, to fury.

"Father, please," I repeat.

"Careful, son. I'd wonder if you're in love with this little thing. I mean, for sure she's a different kind of beauty, but there are better ways for her to use her mouth," he says.

His entire group of advisors laughs.

Anger heats my body, but I push it down. "Father, please. I'm just trying to save one of our people from getting hurt unnecessarily," I beg again.

He and his advisors laugh.

"Father--"

He stands up, approaching me fast. "You don't get to make the decision on our people," he says. "They are not your people. They are mine." His eyes bore into mine. "*My* people."

"I'm your heir," I say, blinking rapidly.

He breathes a frustrated breath. "We'll see about that."

I ignore the comment. "Father," I implore. "We can't be hurting people like this."

His expression turns into a glare as his eyebrows knit and cheeks tense. "When she proves herself worthy, then she's one of our people," he responds.

Anger wraps around my jaw, and I click my tongue without saying anything.

"Son, you and your weak heart will be the death of me. Strengthen your heart, then you may yet become my heir ," he whispers into my ear. Then he struts back to his seat and laughs harder at Alex's pain.

My father has always loved making me feel like the throne won't be mine, making sure I never felt like I was enough. My mother has always told me to ignore it, that I'll be a great leader, and that I'll make a great king.

He beat me multiple times, but I've never forgotten her voice. I'll always live my life for her. But to become a great leader, I need to be one. And to be one, my father has to die.

I grit my teeth, walking back to Griffin.

"What did he say?" Griffin asks softly, moving closer so we keep our conversation to ourselves.

"He wouldn't do it. He says he won't until she survives," I tell him, seething. "He threatened my position again. Griff, what do I do?"

Griffin stiffens by my side, shooting my father a look before he turns back to me. "You tell me, Gabe. What do we do?"

I stand back up, hanging onto the rail as I watch Alex escape the dragon's fire.

"I have to stand up to him eventually, Griff. The question is how? I have to take the throne eventually, otherwise who knows what he could do to us?" I whisper low.

Everything I'm saying is treason. Thinking it is treason. Thinking of overpowering the king is treason.

"He will kill her. He will use her," I say to Griffin.

Griffin nods, his eyebrows furrowing. "Gabe, you know I'm on your side. You tell me what to do and I'll do it."

Never have I been this determined to take the throne. I've never wanted it this much. But if it means protecting her, I'll take it. I'll do anything if it means saving her.

CHAPTER 30

Alex

"Please, please don't kill me. I'm not tricking you," I say as I run for the umpteenth time. "Please," I say again. Sweat is pouring down my forehead and cheeks. My heart is pounding. Thank goodness for the running training we did the last few days, though I never suspected it would help prepare me to run from fire. I think a part of my hair got singed because there's an acrid smell of burning hair, and my scalp feels warm. A part of my leg is burned already; I can see the angry red skin peeking out from the torn fabric on my calf, throbbing with a dull pain. I scratched my arm when I rolled on the ground earlier, trying to get away from the heat of a dragon's breath.

"I've been able to talk to animals all my life," I say aloud.

The green dragon unleashed another torrent of fire, and I ran, the searing heat scorching my elbow, making me grimace.

"For pity's sakes, Ciri, can you stop being such a dick?" the big, red dragon says, turning to the green dragon. "You're burning her."

"Well, maybe she needs to stop lying to us," the green dragon retorts.

"I'm not, I promise I'm not lying," I plead. "I've been able to talk to animals all my life."

The green dragon roars, a sound like splitting thunder, then pulls back. Smoke curls from its nostrils as it gets ready to blow again.

"Please, please, I'm not lying!" I cry as I scramble away.

"Prove it," the green dragon spat out. How the fuck was I supposed to do that?

"Ciri, I swear to God, if you blow fire again, I'm going to kick you," the enormous red dragon says.

The green dragon sinks to the ground, a low rumble vibrating through the earth as it exhales a cloud of steam and smoke. "Suit yourself. She's the one who couldn't help us last week when I was injured."

"Ciri, is it?" I plead. "Please, please. I wanted only to make sure they didn't hurt you. I-I-I've never seen animals like you guys before. Please, I don't know why I can speak to animals, I really don't!" I step forward.

With a low growl rumbling in its chest, the green dragon eyes me suspiciously, its head remaining fixed on the earth.

"How did you get hurt the other day? What was wrong?" I ask.

His eyes narrowed, the pupils shrinking to pinpricks as he focused on me. "How did you know I was hurt?" he asks.

"The other dragon asked to help you. He was crying out, and I heard him. I tried to get the prince to stop poking you," I say quickly.

"The other dragon asked to help you. He was crying out, and I heard him. I tried to get the prince to stop poking you," I say quickly.

The green dragon's slitted eyes narrow, and the intensity of his gaze sends a chill down my spine. I can feel the heat radiating from his nostrils. He moves his large claw and turns to the smaller red dragon as if to confirm.

He huffs angrily and marches to me so aggressively that I retreat in fear. Behind him, I hear faint shrieks, screams, and breaths being held.

"How would they know? That prince couldn't even tell I was hurt," he breathes directly to my face. My entire body shakes again, but I hold my ground.

"She was trying to prevent the prince from hurting you even more," Dimonyaga adds.

"I was hurt when Malakas and I were flying through the forests. Something was shooting at us," the green dragon huffs again. "I couldn't move for three days."

"Did-does the palace not do anything to help...you know...heal you?" I ask, my brows furrowing.

"Please, I promise I'm not trying to hurt you. The king is making me do this, and I'm only trying to save my family. Please. I have a brother, and my mother is sick, and I don't want them to die. He threatened to kill them both. Please," I beg once more.

The massive dragon steps up a little, lowering its snout towards me. "Who is threatening to kill your family?"

"The king. Please, please don't hurt me." A fresh portion of sweat beads on my brow as the red dragon's fiery breath washes over me. Its breath, a rancid odor of stale sweat and something else I can't place, assaults my nostrils.

"Hm…you're like Twaila," the red dragon says again as it lifts its head.

"T-Twaila, yes! The last Quskaha!" I say, momentarily thanking the prince in my head for that history book. "Wait, how do you know about her?" I ask, looking up again.

"We met her, of course," the green dragon says lazily, huffing out a breath.

"You've met her? How old are you?" I ask, lifting my gaze to the red dragon.

The massive red dragon laughs. "Definitely years and years older than you, human."

"My name is Alex," I gulp, a nervous tremor running through me.

"Alex, huh? Are you the new Quskaha, then?" the red dragon asks.

"I-I guess. I don't know what that means, though," I say, hanging my head. "I just wanted to protect the people I love."

"My name is Tuliikaarme," the large red dragon says. "I'd shake your hand, but I might kill you."

My face breaks into a cautious smile. "I understand. Tuliikaarme," I repeat.

"You can call me Tulii," the red dragon says, then points to the smaller red dragon beside him. "This one is Dimonyaga,"

"You can call me Dimon. Or Yaga. Or Dimonyaga," the smaller red dragon quips, stepping forward so I see him more clearly. "I like sheep." His face brightens. "But you're not sheep."

"No, I'm not," I say, my eyes widening in alarm as I stumble backward, a cold sweat breaking out on my skin.

The massive red dragon turns to the smaller one. "We don't eat our friends. Remember our conversation yesterday? And this one," she says, pointing to me with her claw, "she's our friend. Or at least, we want her to be."

"I want to be your friend, too," I mumble, breathing a sigh of relief.

The red dragon turns to the green one lying on the ground. "This one is Cirianiel. Or Ciri, as we call him."

The green dragon huffs wearily. "I'm over this conversation already," he says.

I kneel. "Please don't kill me. I promise I'm just trying to save my family."

"Oh, Alex, you don't need to do that," the red dragon says. "We're not your lords. We're your partners. Please get up."

I stand up hesitantly. "I wasn't lying when I said I want to be your friend. I'll do everything in my power to make sure they do nothing to you."

The three dragons are quiet for a moment.

"But right now, it sounds like you need our help more," Tuliikaarme says, blinking her yellow eyes at me.

"What does he want you to do?" Cirianiel adds, finally getting up. I swallow hard as I crane my neck to look at him. He's almost as big as the red dragon, except his neck is a little longer. His yellow eyes blink.

"He wants me to ride you," I mumble.

"Sweetheart, you'll have to keep your voice loud, otherwise we'll need to lean closer to hear you, and I don't think you'd like that." Tuliikaarme chuckles.

"He wants me to ride you," I say loudly this time.

The smaller red dragon, Dimonyaga starts laughing. "You're going to ride us? Look how small you are! I can eat you in a single bite."

"Dimon, we've talked about this," Tuliikaarme says, sighing.

The smaller red dragon stops laughing and walks towards me. "Can you even ride?"

I shake my head. "I've never ridden a dragon before."

This time, it's the bigger green dragon that laughs. "Your king wants to control us so badly that he sends a Quskaha who can't even ride?"

"I don't want to control you," I say loud enough for them to hear. "I'm asking for your help, so they don't kill my family. Please help me."

"We haven't had a Quskaha in years," Tuliikaarme says, his eyes narrowed in thought.

The green dragon huffs in agreement. "I wonder what Malakas would think about her?"

"Who's Malakas?" I ask, rubbing my aching shoulder.

"You don't know who Malakas is?" Cirianiel asks, his eyes narrowing even more.

I shake my head. "I was taken from Fortuna, from my family. We never got the same education as the people here had. I didn't see dragons until I got here."

"Their family has some weird agenda, don't they?" Tuliikaarme says, turning to the king high above the arena. "If only I didn't like this place, I'd scorch him right now," Tuliikaarme growls.

"Please don't. I don't want people to get hurt, Tulii; most of them don't deserve this," I plead, finding myself walking towards the dragon.

"So, which of us is she going to ride?" Tuliikaarme asks, turning back to me and the other dragons.

"Me, me!" Dimonyaga says, his eyes lighting up.

Tuliikaarme looks at him warily. "Not you, Dimon, not until I can trust you not to eat her."

"Fine, but you'll have to hold on tight," Cirianiel says.

"I don't know how to ride a dragon," I repeat, hanging my head.

"Then, you'll learn," Tuliikaarme says. The green dragon steps towards me, then as he gets a little closer, he bends his head, the claw by his head acting as stairs to get up on his head.

"What do I do?" I say nervously.

"You climb up, silly; how else do you think you're supposed to get on his head?" Dimon says, giggling. Tuliikaarme also looks at me, waving a massive foot at Cirianiel's claws.

"Okay," I say, unable to keep my voice from shaking.

"Don't be nervous. Cirianiel will take care of you," Tuliikaarme adds, as I scramble up Cirianiel's claws and up his head. His skin is scaly, but he has lots of horns to hold on to.

"Climb all the way to the base of his neck. There will be a softer area between his spikes that you can sit on. Hold on to the spikes very carefully when he flies, okay?" Tuliikaarme advises as I make it up his head, then shuffle toward the base of his neck.

"Comfy?" Cirianiel asks, his voice booming towards his back.

"Will—will I be okay?" I stammer, my face heating.

"Take care of her, Ciri." Tuliikaarme laughs. I turn to her, and my heart pounds.

With a low growl, Cirianiel takes off, his wings flapping next to me. I scream, holding onto his spikes for dear life as I close my eyes. As he rises into the sky, my stomach drops, a terrifying plunge mirroring his ascent.

"Human, you can't close your eyes. Not during a moment like this. You'll miss it," Cirianiel's voice sounds. "Open them, human. Open your eyes and see the beauty of this kingdom."

I continue to hold tight, unwilling to let go, but slowly, I open my eyes. My breath hitches. I'm in the air. Blue skies surround us, and small clouds circle us every now and again. Birds squeak and chirp loudly in the air. But below us is what Cirianiel was talking about.

Below us are beautiful green hills, towering over the sides of the valley of Cerene. Beautiful mountains with blue-green lakes, different types of trees surrounding them. The castle stands taller than any other building, and I can see the little stream where I met the deer, and where the water flows into a bigger river. It's hard to glimpse beyond the tall trees, but I catch sight of that mushroom field where I threw the mushrooms at the prince and Griffin.

I chuckle to myself.

"Cirianiel, is this your daily view?" I breathe.

"Yes, it is," he says proudly as we fly through more hills and lakes.

"This is beautiful. I've never seen anything so stunning. Thank you for taking me. I owe you my life and my family's life," I say, continuing to marvel all around me.

"It's Ciri," the green dragon beneath me says.

"What?"

"You can call me Ciri," he responds.

"Ciri," I repeat, breathing a sigh, the clean, fresh air a welcome to my lungs.

A roar so loud it vibrates throughout ground, echoes through the kingdom, causing me to look up and spot the vast, dark shapes of wings in the distance.

"That's Malakas," Ciri says, pointing with his claws.

"Malakas," I repeat slowly, my throat closing.

"He's the strongest and the oldest of all of us," Cirianiel says. "You'll meet him eventually, probably. We haven't had a Quskaha in a while."

"But, Ciri," I ask, frowning. "What does a Quskaha do?"

Cirianiel's laugh reverberates through his body. "Are you asking me what you should do?"

"I-I mean, yes? What did Twaila do?"

"Oh, Alex," Cirianiel sighs. "When you've done your research, come back to me and ask me that question."

I frown. "Okay."

"Every Quskaha has a path, but it varies depending on the time, the kingdom, the players around you. You need to be careful, Quskaha. You're going to be wanted, simply because you can talk to us. We'll protect you as much as we can, but you need to protect yourself as well," Cirianiel says.

I nod, my stomach lurching again when Cirianiel drops a significant height.

"You ready for real life?" Cirianiel asks.

"Not really," I say honestly. "But I guess I need to go back."

Cirianiel nods. "Such is life, Quskaha."

"Alex, please, Ciri," I beg.

Cirianiel drops again and then makes a turn to drop even lower. When he lands back on the grass field, applause takes over the entire arena. Yells and screams of "Quskaha!" sound throughout.

"Ciri," I say, turning to him as I slide down his claw.

"Yes, Alex?" Cirianiel says, his eyes narrowing into slits.

"Thank you for taking care of me," I tell him.

He stands as soon as I'm off its claw, and a massive growl announces me--not to the people here, but to the dragons nearby. Then, it turns back to me, its snout closing in on my space. I pet its nose, feeling the breeze coming out of its mouth.

"Take care of yourself, Alex. Remember our conversation," he says. Then it opens its yellow eyes to me. "I'm sorry I hurt you."

I smile. "I understand why. You were just trying to protect your family," I tell him.

The dragon pulls away, and with the flap of its wings, lifts off the ground and flies away.

Tuli nods at me, then does the same, Dimon right behind her.

Then, it was just me in the arena, where hundreds of people surround me, clapping and cheering my success. I look for the only face that matters. When the steel gates open and he comes out, without even thinking about it, I slip into his arms, enjoying the feeling of his muscles tightening around me.

CHAPTER 31

Gabriel

"How do you feel?" I ask her as she slips into my arms. I can't even explain the feeling I have when she does this on her own. No quips, no sarcastic comments, no excuses. Her head lies on my chest, and all I want to do is keep her there where she is safe and I can see her always.

"I need your help," she murmurs, looking up at me, her eyes drooping.

"Anything, Sparky," I say.

"Please carry me," she says, my eyebrows knitting as soon as her legs give out from under her. I bend slightly, the heat from her scorched calf searing through my hands as I support her weight under her legs. Her skin is still red and inflamed. A grimace twists her face as my fingers graze her burned skin. I shift my hold, carefully lifting her by her hamstrings instead. Her arms circle my neck, her soft breath warm against my skin as she closes her eyes, her head nestled against my chest. Quickly, I turn with her in my arms to where Griffin stands, silhouetted against the entryway of the steel gates, his eyebrows furrowed in a frown.

"She's hurt. We need to get her a healer," I say as soon as I'm within hearing distance.

"I'll grab a healer," he says. "Take her to her room." He disappears quickly.

I do what he says, carrying her to her room where I set her down gently on her bed, instantly telling the soldiers by her door to grab Katya, her handmaiden. The smell of smoke fills my nostrils as I unzip her boots, the charred leather a testament to the fire, slowly freeing her feet from the damaged footwear. She lets out a soft groan, her face contorted in pain as I carefully pull off her sodden boot. I move onto the other boot, untying it slowly. Katya's eyes bulge when she enters the room and spots the burn on Alex's leg.

"Help me dress her," I say, looking up quickly from the boot I'm trying to take off.

Katya nods, and with a rustle of clothes, she disappears into her closet to grab a pair of shorts and a shirt for Alex.

I finally pull out the other boot, scanning her other leg for further injuries. Some scrapes, a smaller burn, but that's it. I ease off her socks, my eyes widening when I realize that parts of them have stuck to her skin. Katya removes her vest, Alex groaning as it is lifted.

"Your Majesty, I'm removing her shirt next," she says, slowly slipping off Alex's tunic from above her head. I catch a glimpse of her olive skin and turn to give her some privacy.

"Good to see you're honorable, prince," the weak girl on the bed rasps.

"I'm glad to see you haven't lost your humor, Sparky," I say, a smile spreading across my face.

"No, just a bit of skin." She laughs. "Just kidding, just kidding, it's a lot of skin." I gulp.

"You're okay to turn, prince. I'll need help with her pants," Katya says.

I spin around to see Alex wearing a midnight blue shirt, and my stomach tightens when I see her nipples peeking through the thin material.

"She'll need plenty of rest," Katya says when she catches me watching her. "We have to remove her pants, but I think some fibers from the fabric might stick to her."

I nod, grabbing a pocket knife from my pockets. "Hold her," I say to Katya.

Laughter comes from Alex, her body writhing in pain. "As if," she mutters.

Katya hops onto the soft bed beside Alex and drapes her arms across her legs.

I place a hand on her hips and carefully slice through the fabric with the knife, starting from her hips and moving down to her calves. I hand the knife to Katya for her to do the other side. I grip Alex's legs, my fingers sinking into her skin; the raw feeling of her vulnerability is a heavy, agonizing pressure in my chest.

Alex fidgets as we get closer and closer to her calves.

"Angus, I'm sorry, buddy," she says, and I realize she's hallucinating.

We lift her up as Katya pulls the pieces of her pants off, and I turn away from her as Katya deals with her underwear and puts on her shorts.

"She's also got burns on her side and her arms, Your Majesty," Katya says.

"Go get food and something to drink. Check on the healer," I say, turning back to Alex.

The heavy oak door creaks open, and Griffin strides in, followed by one of our healers, whose robes smell faintly of herbs. The healers, heads bowed in respect, silently part to allow me to move aside so they can attend to Alex.

"How is she?" Griffin asks.

"She's hallucinating, I think. She was calling out for someone named Angus earlier," I say, shooting Griffin a look.

He frowns. "Who's that?" he asks.

I shake my head. "No idea."

"Do you think she has a boyfriend?" Griffin wonders aloud.

"It's my brother, dummy," Alex's voice comes through, and a pillow whizzes by us.

"Missed," Griffin retorts, a faint blush warming his pale cheeks.

"Stop moving," one of the healers says.

"She has a bigger burn on her right leg, a smaller one on her left, a burn on her back and another one on her elbow," I tell the healer.

"Can you hold her down?" one of them eyes me and Griffin.

Katya climbs over the rumpled sheets and grips Alex's arms, her fingers tightening around her biceps. I lean over her bed, carefully holding her other leg, feeling the warmth of her skin through the thin cotton sheets.

"It hurts, it hurts," she says, murmuring, as she tries to wriggle from our grip.

"It's okay, Sparky, it's okay," I murmur to her, looking at her.

She breaks free from Katya's grasp, writhing and groaning as the healers try to help, so I jump onto the bed and signal for Kat to hold her legs tighter.

We switch places so I'm by Kat's head. Rather than restraining Alex, I position myself beneath her, wrapping my legs around her while cradling her upper body between my legs and resting her head on my chest. I hold her close, feeling the warmth of her body against mine as she cries silently into my arm.

"It's okay, it's okay," I murmur to her as the healers clean her wound. "Hold on to me, okay?" My whisper is barely audible above the hiss of the antiseptic, as her burned skin is cleaned, and her fingers dig into my arm. With a shudder, she writhes again, her fingers digging into my arm, leaving crescent-shaped marks on my skin.

"It hurts, it hurts," she groans, tears welling in her eyes as her face contorts in pain.

"Can we hurry this up, please?" I demand.

"Your Majesty, we need to clean it properly before treating it; otherwise, it's going to scar," the healer says.

I remain silent, my grip on Alex tightening when they scrape the burned skin away. She starts screaming, her arms and legs flailing, her body a convulsive mess.

"It's okay, Sparky, it's okay," I whisper. "It's almost done, almost done," I say, pulling her close, the scent of her hair filling my senses, while ignoring Griffin's obvious displeasure.

"It's true; it's almost done," the healer repeats. "Grab the fish skin," she orders Katya.

Katya carefully carries the white icebox to the healer, who lifts the lid to reveal the pale fish skin inside. The healer gently places it on Alex's wounds.

"Keep this on her for at least twenty-four hours. I'll come back to replace it. We need this on her for at least seven days. We'll see how it is then, and decide how much more we need to do. She needs to rest now, but remember, she also needs to eat and drink enough water," the healer says after placing the last fish skin on her other leg.

I nod. Alex is already asleep, tears brimming in her eyes, her breaths shallow and ragged. "Let's let her rest for a bit, but bring up food and water maybe in two hours?" I say to Katya, who nods and bows, then exits the room.

Griffin and I remain.

He looks at me, a knowing expression on his face. "You're so fucked," he says.

I nod, pushing the hair from her face as I watch her sleep. "I am."

CHAPTER 32

Gabriel

"You've been summoned, Prince Gabriel," one of the soldiers says as they knock and enter the room. I wave them away, and they hesitate at the door.

"I'll be right there," I growl.

They nod and exit the door, and I roll my eyes before staring at Griffin across the room. "Will you stay with her?" I ask.

He nods. She hasn't awoken in almost two days now, just occasional moments where she'd ask for water, but otherwise, nothing concrete. I slip out of the bed as quietly and gently as I can.

"I'll be back," I whisper to her. She only groans in response. "Can-can-can you let me know if she wakes?"

Griffin sighs. "Of course, brother."

I know what the sigh is all about. I haven't left her side, not since the healers were here the first time around. The healers looked shocked to see me still here when they came to change her fish skins at the twenty-four and forty-eight-hour marks. Griffin is worried the king will realize I have some sort of attachment to her, and he'll take it out on her.

I shouldn't be here.

Yet there's no other place I want to be. I know there'll be consequences. But I'd rather deal with them than leave her to heal on her own. Griffin has also been there most of the two days, taking over whenever I'm called for duty. He thinks I don't see it, but I know he cares for her—I see it every time he asks. To what extent? I'm not sure.

I reach my father's office, taking a deep breath before entering.

"Gabriel," he greets me when the doors open and I enter. "How is our Quskaha doing?"

My eyebrows knit. This can't be good. "She's doing well, my king."

"Good, you didn't deny it," the king says, turning to his view once again.

"Deny what, Father?" I ask, my heart beating twice as fast.

"Deny that you've been by her side the last few days," he says in a tone I've heard before.

"Of course, Father. We took her from her family for taxes we've never charged before, then put her through tasks she didn't ask for. The reason she's hurt is because of us," I respond without a beat. I already know there's a chance I'm going to get punished today. I used to get so nervous, so scared whenever he used this tone.

Now, I just feel prepared.

"You made us appear weak," he says in the same low voice. "By begging for her case right then and there in front of other people, you made our kingdom appear weak. What would our advisors think of us now? I can't even fathom how weak we must seem to my knights. We do not beg for handmaids!" he growls, finally turning around.

It takes me a moment to fix my composure. "She's not just a handmaid, Father," I remind him.

This angers him even more. His face contorts, his eyes narrow to slits, and his jaw clenches tightly.

"Maybe so. But, Father, you said before that she will save our kingdom. She can't do that if she's dead," I add.

His lips press into a thin, pale line.

"If this girl dies, we lose our only chance of controlling the dragons. The only chance. Did you see the way she talked to the dragons? The way she got them to take her on? Where else would we find someone who can do that?" I continue.

His eyes narrow. "Careful, son. I'd think you were in love with her or something."

"No, Father, I'm doing this for the good of the kingdom. For the good of our future. Without her, we won't be able to control the dragons," I say, focusing on keeping an even tone that doesn't show my frustration.

"I don't like relying on anyone for the future of Quaila, let alone a handmaiden," he mutters.

I nod, hoping I looked sympathetic to his plight. "There's nothing we can do about that. We just need to learn to respect her, especially if we want her to serve this kingdom," I respond quickly.

My father's eyes darken. He walks past the desk over to meet me. "Are you saying I'm not respecting her?"

I swallow, thinking fast. "Not if you're going to put her in harm's way like this just to prove her worth. Isn't the first task enough? She's already been through so much!"

I expect the punch that comes from him. The blow lands hard against my right cheek, the force intensified by the weight of his royal ring, its edges digging in with agonizing pressure. When I get up, his face tightens once more at my expression. His knuckles whiten, and he punches me again, this time hitting my cheek with a sickening thud and bursting the right side of my lip. A metallic tang fills my mouth and nostrils.

"So weak. So much like your mother," he murmurs, his breath hot on my face before another punch sends me sprawling onto the cold, hard floor.

"You can punch me all you like, Father. It doesn't change our scenario," I tell him wearily. I know I'm treading a very thin line. My father expects me to act a certain way, especially in front of him, and even when we're alone.

He studies me carefully as I haul myself off the floor. I wipe the blood from my mouth.

"You cannot be seen in her room at all times, Gabriel. Not when you're to be betrothed to the Luntian princess," he announces.

"What?" I respond, before catching myself.

"You took too long to decide, so I've signed a match with you and the daughter of Luntian king, allowing for a good partnership throughout these lands," my father says, a glint in his eyes telling me he thinks he's won. "Can you imagine? With their advanced weaponry and our dragons, we'll be unstoppable."

I let out a hollow laugh to avoid sobbing. "Okay, then." I have no choice. My father will always go with whichever kingdom he prefers. Even if I have the illusion of choice, I'd bet that he'd never actually go with anything I wanted.

"Okay, you'll stay away from her rooms?" the king says, looking back at me.

"Yes, Father. I was only trying to help her. We're not… intimate," I stammer, a blush burning my cheeks as the image of her naked form floods my mind.

He chuckles. "Good. We don't need another scandal in this kingdom," he spits out at me.

I bow. "Yes, Your Majesty." No, we wouldn't want that. The last time we had a scandal was before I was born, but I still remember the reactions my mother had every time it was talked about. I don't know what it was about, but I know the palace worked very hard to cover it up. The mere mention of any "scandal" just made my mother and everyone around her walk on eggshells. After all, as the palace, we write history the way we want it.

"Good, good. Now, the second task will be similar. It will involve dragons again, so she needs to be prepared," the king continues.

"Father–" I begin.

"She has their trust already, Gabriel. If she still gets hurt this time around, it's of her own doing," the king retorts quickly before I say anything else. He turns around and sits at his desk.

"We'll see how she does with ordering them around," he mumbles to himself.

"Father––" I start again.

His eyes land on me. "I did not ask for your opinion, Gabriel, did you hear me ask?"

"No, Your Majesty," I say, resigned.

"Then you may go," the king waves me away. "Clean yourself up," he barks, a final triumphant glance lingering on the bleeding gashes he'd carved into my face.

CHAPTER 33

Alex

I wake up groggy and sick, groaning as I move.

"Hey, are you okay?" a different voice asks, my heart sinking a little when I realize it's not the voice that's been waking me whenever I come to. My gaze moves up to the tall man sitting at my hips, creating a dip larger than what I make. Griffin.

"Are you okay?" he asks again.

"Water," I manage, and he grabs the bottle on my nightstand. I take a good sip, letting the cool water coat the dryness in my throat. That feels good.

I graze my elbow across my bare stomach, feeling something slimy.

"What the…" I say as I bend my head to look at it. A pale, scaly thing sticks to my burned elbow.

"Fish skin," Griffin explains when he sees me looking at it. I grimace, putting my elbow back down. "What do you need? Think you could manage some food? You haven't eaten in two days since the tasks."

I frown, turning to him. "What happened?"

His eyebrows knit. "You don't remember?"

I rack my brain, too tired to think. "It's hazy."

He hums. "You were burned during the tasks. You won it, though. Gabe carried you here, and a healer put fish skin on your burns. It helps with scarring."

"The prince carried me?" I repeat, scratching the back of my neck.

He nods. "How do you feel?" His arms reach over me to feel my forehead. I'm so surprised by the gesture that I swipe it away. "The fever is gone," he adds.

"I had a fever? Uh…hungry, I think," I repeat. "Can you help me up?"

He nods, pulling all of my pillows behind me, then grabs my back and under my legs to stack me against the pillows. I blush, realizing my legs are sweaty.

"Let me get you something to eat. What are you hungry for?" he asks, making his way to the door.

"Whatever you want," I respond.

He nods, grinning, then steps out the door to pass on my order to the staff. When he returns, I ask, "Have you been here a while?" I sip more water. It helps with talking. I feel like I haven't drunk water in days.

"Yes, the prince and I have been here the entire time," he responds.

My eyes widen. "The prince, too? Why?"

He chuckles. "He barely left your side, Alex."

I roll my eyes, raising a hand to feel my wild hair and frowning when I find it in a mess on top of my head.

"Katya tied it when she came to clean you up, but you roll around quite a bit in your sleep," Griffin explains with an amused look.

I glare at him. "You watched me sleep?"

Griffin laughs. "Alex, you literally fainted after the tasks, you have really bad burns all over your body, and you screamed your life out when the healers cleaned your wounds. We were worried. Sue us for being concerned about you."

I study him carefully, watching the way his jaw moves as he laughs, the way his cheek rises with every movement, and how his eyes dip and gleam while laughing.

"You didn't have to take care of me; I'm just a handmaid," I respond.

"Not to Gabe, you're not," he replies even quicker. "He didn't get any sleep at all as you snored and drooled on his chest the first night," he teases.

I swipe at my mouth, removing any remains of drool. "What a confusing man."

He laughs. "What are you so confused about, Alex?"

I screw up my face. "I don't understand why he spent his time here," I murmur, odd feelings fluttering in my stomach--feelings I've never felt before. Feelings I don't understand.

"Oh, Alex, you're so naïve." He chuckles, standing up when we hear the door open, and Katya comes in with a tray of food. My anger flares, a hot flush creeping up my neck and staining my cheeks crimson.

Katya places the tray beside me. "I got you your favorites, A-uh-Al-uh, my lady," she says, stammering when she catches Griffin watching her.

"It's okay, Kat, he's harmless," I say, turning to the tray.

The tray is filled with food—a bowl of what looks like chicken noodle soup, pastries and bread, crackers, and some fruit. I grab a piece of mango and start to chew on it, motioning for Katya to have some. She shakes her head shyly, her eyes darting to Griffin.

"For goodness' sakes, just have some," I say, rolling my eyes and pushing it towards them.

Griffin dismisses Katya, and she leaves, bowing awkwardly to me. "Alex, you need to eat, okay? You've gone without food for at least forty-eight hours already. You need to eat," he adds as soon as she's out the door. "Your handmaid is fed just fine."

"You realize I was a handmaid for a few weeks when I arrived here, right? Handmaids are not fed just fine; they're fed at specific times and only of a certain quality. If we miss that time due to the chores we're doing, which happens often, we don't get anything until the next meal," I tell him hotly.

His face drops. "Well, we'll figure that out later. You just have to eat right now, okay?"

"Why? So you can fatten me up and then feed me to the dragons next? Or is it so I produce acceptable heirs?" I say sarcastically, the words dripping out of my mouth.

Griffin laughs, a deep, booming sound that shakes his chest, his eyes lighting up like I'm the funniest person in the world. "Just eat," he orders.

I roll my eyes, but I bend to take a sip of the soup. It was good, so I pull it closer, taking a few more substantial bites.

"Happy?" I shoot at him after I'd eaten a bit.

He nods. "Ecstatic. So would the prince be," he adds, and my cheeks turn red again.

The door opens, and my heart lurches, seeing the prince enter. He walks towards the center of the room to face me.

"I'm glad you're doing well," he says robotically.

I frown, turning to Griffin.

"I just heard that the second task will require you to ask the dragons to follow your orders. The king wants to see how much you can get them to do your bidding," the prince croaks.

"Wait–what does that mean?" I ask, but the prince is already turning around, headed for the door. I swallow hard, turning to Griffin, my eyes wide. "What did I do?"

He puts a hand up, then exits the door to follow the prince.

See? Confusing. One minute he's hot, then next freezing cold. I've been asleep for two days, and he's just switched off like a light. The door opens again, and Griffin comes back in before sitting at the end of my bed. He motions for me to continue eating.

"Confusing," I tell him as I take another bite of a piece of bread.

"Gabe and I grew up together," he starts. "When his mother died over ten years ago, his father tried to train him to become like him."

I frown. "I don't know what that means."

"Every time he showed emotion, was sad about his mother, and every time he cried, he got beat up by his father and their soldiers. This was when he was fifteen years old, Alex," Griffin says.

"His–his father beat him up?" I repeat, frowning, biting into another piece of bread.

"As heir, he's not allowed to do certain things, Alex—including taking care of you," Griffin finishes.

My chest tightens, but I try to hide my dismay.

"Why?" I ask, keeping my voice even.

"Because he's heir, and heirs have their own requirements." He shrugs.

"You mean it's because I'm a handmaid. Or is it because I'm 'brown'?" I ask, rolling my eyes.

His face turns grave. "All of the above, plus the fact that you're a Quskaha," Griffin responds. "Even I'm not allowed to be here, but he said he'll make sure no one knows."

"Why aren't you allowed to be here?" I snap, sitting up.

He laughs. "Because I'm not in the same league as you are, Alex. You're special to the kingdom. I'm just a regular soldier."

I sigh. So, I'm not special enough to be with the prince, but also too special for someone like Griffin? Got it.

"Do you want to take a bath?" Griffin asks.

"No," I grumble. But he pours me a bath, anyway.

CHAPTER 34

Gabriel

Four days later, I tell Griffin to take her training. She's nowhere near ready, but the tasks are only a week from today. I've managed to avoid her room at all costs, instead getting all of my updates from Griffin or Katya. Then, at night, right when the soldiers make a change, I slip in quickly to check on her for a mere few minutes before I have to leave. I miss her smile. I miss her snarky retorts. I even miss the glares. I've been extra moody, knowing Griffin's getting all of that instead. I enter the gym, knowing they'd be here, at least trying.

Every instinct in me wants to go to the boxing ring because I can already hear her. But my brain turns, entering the viewing area instead. I gulp the moment I see her. No matter how she dresses, I can see the anguish in her eyes. Her hair is braided behind her, and she has new scars on her cheeks. The fish skin healing her burns are bandaged to her legs, arms, and back. She's wearing blue pants that cling to her every curve, doing things to me that no other woman has ever done. I wonder if she even realizes how beautiful she looks. I know how much she's hated being different, yet that only adds to her beauty. My gaze turns to Griffin. His frown has been on almost permanently these days, probably from all his worry about how my father will react to my feelings for her—or maybe the fact that he wants to hide his from me. Griffin's not exactly a one-woman type of man, but I've never seen him give this much attention to anyone. And he's dated and had sex with pretty much every eligible woman in the entirety of Cerene.

My eyes go back to her as she tries to do what Griffin asks her to do. He has a pad on his hand, and she's supposed to punch at it, but every time she reaches out her arm, she grimaces. Griffin steps forward, patting her back and whispering something in her ear. My chest constricts, and anger rises, but I'm forced to push it down and remind myself that I'll be married soon, and not to her. When Griffin backs up, his pads are up again. She takes her stance, then turns and tries a kick, only in the middle of it, she bends over and then collapses to the ground.

Anger rises in me. She can't do this. She's clearly not ready. I turn, my face burning with anger at my father. He has to push this back. She can barely walk, barely talk, yet he's forcing her to do this. As I climb up the stairs, I realize why.

He wants her to fail.

Considering how much he wants to control dragons, you'd think he'd try a little more. I burst into my father's office, ready to speak my mind, but the moment I see him and his advisors, I swallow hard--my fear of him overpowers every drive I have.

"Yes, Gabriel?" he says, turning to me, his eyes like lasers getting ready to cut me in half.

I pull myself together. "I have to speak with you about the tasks," I announce, trying to hide the embarrassment at crashing his meeting.

The advisors study me, then turn their eyes back to their king. A smirk appears on the king's face. "You dare disrupt my meeting," he says. It wasn't a question, just a statement of my bad behavior.

"Yes, Your Majesty. It's important," I say. For sure, this will have consequences, but I don't care.

The king frowns. "More important than this meeting? Than the future of this kingdom?"

I know I'm playing with fire when I say, "Yes, Your Majesty."

His frown turns into a glare. Then it softens, and he looks back at his advisors. "Give me a moment with my son, will you? Apparently, his needs are more than the needs of the kingdom."

I remember that line from many years ago. It made me feel guilty back then, and it reminds me of a time when I instantly told him I was good to wait. My head was bleeding from an accident, but of course, it wasn't that important. Not as important as the needs of the kingdom.

The advisors nod at him, then stand to bow before exiting the office. When they've all left and the door is closed, the king turns his glare back on me.

"What do you want?" he demands, his voice booming throughout the room.

"We need to talk about the tasks," I say again.

His eyes flick to me with venom. "What about the tasks?"

"We have to postpone it. She's not yet better. She needs time to heal," I respond, taking a slight step towards him. "Please, Father, you can't do this to her. She's still struggling to stand up. She won't be able to protect herself against the dragons."

My father laughs, but it's hollow. "This is what you came to me for? This is what I disrupted a meeting for the kingdom for? Your handmaid, the handmaid who can talk to animals?"

"Yes, Father, this is important," I insist. "She is the future of Quaila. You can't do this to her."

His eyes narrow at me. "What part of her is the future of Quaila?"

"She can talk to the dragons, Father. She can control them for us," I say, suddenly confused. Hadn't he been saying all this time that she is the future? That this is what she would do for us? Isn't that what the tasks are supposed to prove? "Please, Father, please move the tasks. She needs more time."

The king walks, his pace slow and deliberate as he takes steps towards me. Then, he circles me slowly, studying me carefully. He hums.

"Can she use her legs?" he asks.

"Yes, but--"

"Can she use her arms and hands?" he asks.

"Yes, but--"

"Then she's fine. I don't understand why she'd need time," he says, turning from me.

I blink rapidly in frustration. "Father, she got burned by a dragon," I try again.

"But she can stand?"

"Yes, Father, but not for very long," I respond.

"Then she can do it. If she really is the Quskaha, then she can tell them not to hurt her," the king says, turning around to face the view outside his balcony once more.

"Father, you know dragons aren't like this. They're unpredictable. If she's in trouble, she'll have no way of defending herself," I protest.

The king laughs. "Well, that's not really our problem, is it?"

My eyes widen. "Father, you can't just feed her to the dragons; she's not food!"

The king turns back to me, his eyes narrowed. "What is this really about, Gabriel?"

"It's about protecting our future. Making sure she's alive to help us. It's about keeping our people safe!" I blurt out.

He frowns, tucking his arms into his sides. "Is it really? Is that really all?" he urges.

"Yes, Father," I lie. "We need to protect her as the only Quskaha in our time."

He plants himself directly in front of me, his gaze unwavering and intense, so close I can feel his breath on my face.

My father loves a good power trip. He loves reminding me that I'm a nobody next to him. That I'm no one until he officially stands down or passes.

"I think you're getting too close," he says after a while. "I think the time you and that girl have spent has made you weak. I think she's a liability to us because of that, and because she's the only one who can control the dragons."

"Fath--" I begin, but sputter instead when his fist connects with my face. It hasn't healed since the last time he punched me.

"I thought making you bleed would be enough to change you. I thought the punishment we put you through years ago rewired your brain successfully. But I was wrong," he spits out, disgust written on his face. "You're just as weak, as useless as your mother."

"He waves a hand, and his soldiers barge through the door, taking me with them. "Father!"

He says nothing. His eyes are ice-cold, even as his soldiers drag me away.

CHAPTER 35

Alex

I wake up with a jolt, the room coming into view slowly. My eyes blink, a form appearing at the edge of my feet.

"Griff?" I say weakly as the form solidifies itself.

"So, he's also been visiting you," a voice says, and I jolt up, my eyes widening. "No, that will not do. I'll have to punish him, too."

I recoil, pulling my sheets up around me, backing to the furthest corner of the bed. The king smirks, the scar on his face moving with his cheeks. I look around me for anyone, anything. But it's just me. I swallow, my heart pounding in my chest.

"What do you want?" I demand.

The king stands. "Don't worry, child, I'm just here to talk."

I'm aware I'm wearing sleep clothes under the sheets, so I pull the bedding higher, trying to feel safer and less exposed.

His eyes flick to me slowly, like he's amused. "Child, you don't need to hide yourself from me. I have no desire to look at you. You are…" he pauses, looking me up and down. "A handmaid, after all," he drawls. "Some genes just aren't meant to mix, you know. Poor people, and people with bad…everything."

I raise an eyebrow. "You think my genes aren't good enough?"

"Oh, you poor thing. Sometimes, some people are just stupid. And it shows. Why do you think I don't want to marry you either, girl? You're…you." He stares through me as if I'm insignificant.

"Get out," I respond, pointing to the door. My voice shakes. Am I really asking the king to leave? Who does that?

The king's eyes glimmer in the light, but his expression sends chills down my spine.

"You may be the Quskaha. But I will not rely on anyone for this kingdom, not even you. Especially not you," the king says with venom. "You dirty brown bitch."

My mouth opens to say something, but he beats me to it.

"I'm the smartest, greatest king that's ever lived. And I will do everything in my power to make sure everyone knows that. You either get in line, or else," the king states, then turns.

"Or else what?" I demand.

He smirks and leaves the room.

CHAPTER 36

Gabriel

"Mother?" I say, blinking rapidly, as I slump against the wall, my head lolling back. I must be delirious already. I don't know how long I've been in here, but it feels like days. My father's soldiers have taken turns beating me up, pounding my face, my back, chest, stomach, feet and more. My father's only guideline was not to break my legs, because they're necessary for serving. The tang is back in my mouth, but I'm fairly certain it's everywhere. The liquid dripping from my forehead isn't just sweat; it's blood, and it's dripping from my ears, too. A sharp pain keeps shooting between my eyes, and there's a throbbing pain coming from my cheeks, lips, and forehead. My stomach is cramping in more ways than one. I don't even know if I can stand.

"My love," the ghost of my mother says as she bends in front of me. I'm clearly dreaming. No matter how many times I've been punched, kicked, and smacked, I know my mother's gone. It's etched into me, the loss of the only person who believed I'd be a good king. The only person who's ever loved me unconditionally.

"What are you doing here, Mother?" I ask, the words blurry. My eardrums must be busted, too. I mean to say something, only to hear it come out differently every time. My skin tingles at her touch.

"My love," she says again, and I taste the salt of my tears when I look at her face. She was so beautiful. I remember my father telling her she should see a healer to see if they could lighten her skin a little.

"Mother," I say, my entire body breaking into sobs.

"Oh, my love," she says again, putting her hand on mine. My face crunches as I turn my hand to hold hers. It's so real I can almost feel her. I've missed her so much. "How the hell did we get here, huh?" she says, and I chuckle.

"Mother, I've missed you," I say, more tears mixing with the taste of tang.

"Oh, but I'm always here, my son," she says softly, pointing to my chest. "I'm always here, my love, especially for you."

I'm wracked with sobs, and I force my hand to rise so I can touch her face, but all I feel is air.

She places her hand over mine. "I'm so proud of you. So, *so* proud of you."

"Why?" I say between sobs. "I haven't done anything to make you proud."

She frowns. "Gabriel, you stood up for yourself. You stood up for a girl you barely knew. You stood up for your people." She walks over to sit by me, and I lean my head on her shoulders. "I am so proud of you for doing what you think is right. I'm so proud of you for trying to defend someone, even though you knew how your father would react."

"And yet, I'm here, Mother," I respond wearily.

"Oh, my love, getting beat up isn't a sign of weakness. Sometimes, especially for princes, it's important to know when to back up, but most importantly when to keep fighting. You are my smart little one. You know what's right and what's wrong. Yes, the path will be hard, but I know you, my son, and you are the cleverest, bravest person I know. You're braver than I am, cleverer and smarter. You can do this," Mother reassures me as she squeezes my hand.

"Mother, she could get hurt if Father finds out about this," I sigh, my head pounding even more.

"She really is special to you, isn't she?" Mother teases, kissing my forehead. "I wish I could've been there to witness your first love."

"I don't know how to protect her," I admit, swallowing hard.

But she turns to me, squeezing my hand tight. "My love, yes, you do. You know how to protect her; you're just afraid of the consequences. That was my fault. I never got to protect you from the influence of your father. But I know you, my child. You are brave. You are wonderful. And you will become the king that this kingdom never had."

"How do you know, Mother?" I sob, already feeling the weight of my head.

"I know, because you'll make the right decisions for love and for the kingdom," my mother continues, holding my hand.

"What if the decisions for love don't match the ones for kingdom?" I question, chewing my lip.

"How could it not, if she's the key to the kingdom?" Mother responds.

I frown, turning to look at her. "She's the key to the kingdom? What does that mean?"

"Oh, my love. Know that love and the kingdom are the same. Know that love will always get you to the right places. It didn't for me, but it will for you," she squeezes my hand.

"Mother--"

"Be brave, my son. Be honest. Be smart," she looks me in the eye. "Follow your heart, my wonderful son. I'm so sorry I left you, but you've already paved your path. You just need to follow it, do you understand?"

When I blink again, she's gone. I cry into the quiet until my next set of soldiers arrives.

"Are you ready to follow your father's orders?" the soldier asks, kicking me in the stomach.

"Are you ready to be a man?" the other soldier asks, his fist connecting with my face.

I remember my mother's words. With all the energy I have left, and all the strength I can muster, I kick one of them in the groin and use my other leg to kick the other soldier's shins. I push myself off the ground to stand in front of them.

"I am the heir to this kingdom," I declare. "Tell my father that when you see him next."

I kick the second one in the groin again, pulling a heavy punch onto his face that knocks him out. With the first soldier, I only have to punch once in the face before he's knocked out. I huff a response, then exit the cell, locking it behind me. My entire body hurts; I can barely feel anything. I'm sure I've lost quite a bit of blood. I just need to find someone, someone I trust. I walk out of the dungeons and into the castle, leaving a trail of blood in my wake. When I stop to rest on the stairs, a staff member comes to ask me if I'm okay.

"Griffin," I manage, bending to catch my heavy head. She runs off to find him.

When I open my eyes again, I'm back in my own bed.

CHAPTER 37

Alex

It's been at least a week since I've seen the prince, a few days since the king came into my room, and days since Griffin disappeared on me, too. I told him about the king, and Griffin doubled my guards, but I highly doubt the guards would prevent the king from entering.

My only company is Katya, and I can't even go anywhere to train or run without Griffin or the prince. So much for training me. The second task starts tomorrow. How could I possibly succeed without training? At least Griffin had dropped a few more history books for me to read; otherwise,

I'd go batshit in this room with nothing to do but wait for the inevitable.

My door swings open, and I look up from the book I was reading. My heart skips a beat.

It's the prince. But he looks different. He has bruises around both eyes, welts on his lips and cheeks, and a bandage over his nose.

"What the hell?" I blurt out.

"It doesn't hurt that much," he says.

"Liar," I accuse, frowning as I get off the sofa and cross the distance between us.

"I'm fine, Alex, really," he says, stepping away, but I don't listen.

I grab his arm to steady him, watching his reaction as I lift his shirt.

"I mean, would you like to take me to dinner first?" he teases, then he grimaces, and my jaw drops. His chest is all bandaged up, but any patch of skin without a bandage showcases a scar.

"Prince," I breathe slowly.

"It's okay, I have healers," he manages, his cheeks turning red.

But I turn anyway, heading for the bathroom where yesterday I had asked Katya to bring me certain herbs so I can help myself heal.

"Take your shirt off," I order, disappearing into the bathroom to grab the salve I've made with Katya's help.

"Again, maybe dinner first?" he teases, stepping into the room.

"Ooh fun," I say sarcastically. "Or you know, maybe you can just remove your shirt so I can put this on you and stop being so difficult," I add, emphasizing the last words.

He winces as he lifts his arms to remove his shirt. "Uh. I might need help," he says, so I grab the salve, then pull him to the sofa before moving the fabric over his arms.

"This is not a good idea," he mutters.

"Or maybe it is." I lift the fabric of my pants to show that some of my burns had already started scarring. "My mother taught me how to make things to speed up healing," I tell him as I gently and slowly remove the bandages attached to his body. I swallow hard, my throat dry, seeing the powerful sculpture of his chest, the sinewy cords directing my gaze between his legs, but I push down any unsettling emotions that arise. My goal right now is to help him heal.

"How did you get these wounds?" I ask, sneaking a peek at him. His eyes are on me, and a blush creeps up my neck as I feel his intense gaze. There's an unnerving depth to his stare; his eyes seem to pierce through me, making my skin crawl with a strange sense of being completely known.

His hand reaches across, pushing a strand of my hair back. Goosebumps rise along my spine at the simple touch. My eyes meet his, and I swallow, nerves creeping along my neck and chest.

"You're so beautiful," he says, his hand cupping my cheeks.

I swallow again. "No other woman around to tell that to, I'm guessing?" I tease, hiding the feelings I don't understand.

He smirks. "None as beautiful as you," he responds, his eyes boring into me as I lower my gaze to pull away the final bandages off his chest.

"Turn," I order, and he does.

"I love it when you tell me what to do," he says.

I chuckle. "Do you? Want to lie to me a little more?" I pull a bandage off gently, gasping at the large lacerations on his back. "Prince…" I breathe again. I see him gulp.

"That's what happens with birch rods." His eyes darken and glisten with unshed tears, and a furious rage ignites within me at the thought of anyone causing him such pain. I want to unleash a dragon's fiery wrath upon every single one of them.

"Prince, who did this to you?" I breathe softly as I pull the last bandage to reveal another cleaned and stitched wound.

I look up at the anger, pain, and hurt on his face. When a single tear drops, I let go of the bandage, moving toward him to pull him into me. He hesitates at first, but as my arms tighten around him, his arms encircle me, tightening around my waist. I swallow hard, feeling him break apart in my arms, his tears wetting my shoulders, his body shaking with each sob.

We're two different people from two entirely different worlds. Yet, here we are comforting each other in a moment I'd never expected. I tighten my hold on him, pretending for a moment that this is real, like I could actually have him. Like I's not a nobody from the middle of nowhere, with no title, no money, nothing to offer this world but the fact that I can speak to dragons.

When his shaking stops, I let go, moving to grab more salve from the table. I open it, grabbing a good amount with my fingers.

"Alex…" he starts.

I turn to him, my heart already sinking. "I know. I get it." I turn him around, quietly spreading the salve as gently as I can across his wounds. I let a few tears escape before composing myself and turning him around so I can put the salve on the wounds on his chest.

"Ugh," he groans at the touch.

I scowl at him. "Stop being such a baby," I scold.

He laughs at that, grimacing as his body vibrates with his laughter.

"You should put something cold on that," I tell him as I point to the bruises on his face.

"I did. I just took it off to come see you," he says.

I grab his shirt and open it at the neckline to pull it through his head. "Thanks," he mutters as I help him put his shirt back on.

"Make sure to keep that on for at least twenty-four hours. If I survive this next challenge, I'll put more on, so it heals evenly," I tell him.

"You know you don't have to do this." He turns to me.

I nod. "I know. But you also didn't have to help me these past few weeks," I respond, shrugging. "Despite what your father might say, we normal people actually like to help."

He chuckles. "Do you now?"

I widen my eyes mockingly. "Of course, prince. We normal people rely on each other. Must be an uncommon thing for rich folks."

He laughs. "I didn't have anyone outside of Griffin who's helped me just because. We pay everyone in this castle. Everyone is required to help me."

"That's obvious, Prince. But I'm not your staff, nor am I even from here." I shrug. "Everyone in Cerene is so different from the people in Fortuna."

"Do you miss it?" he asks, watching my reaction.

"Of course. But the moment I can get out of your family's hold, they'll be my first step." I turn so he doesn't see the emotions written on my face.

"You're one of a kind, Sparky," he says, standing up to leave.

"I think you just need to get out more, Prince," I sigh.

He turns back to me, his eyebrows knitted, questions lying beneath his eyes. He hums, then opens his mouth to say something, but nothing came out.

"Your father came to visit me," I start, looking away to hide the fear and shame.

He frowns, a hand coming to touch my arm. "Are you okay?"

"I am," I say, but somehow, even I'm not convinced.

"What did he say?" The prince's grip on me tightens.

"Just…he told me I wasn't worth it. He told me why he's making me do these trials. For someone who was married to your mother, you'd think he didn't have anything against the color of my skin, but apparently, he does," I press my lips together, sealing words I don't want to say.

His hands rise to caress my cheeks gently, thoughts swirling in those beautiful dark green eyes. But instead of saying something, he slips a white envelope into my hand, then whirls back around to the door.

"I'm sorry about my father, Sparky. I'll make sure your door is watched at all times. Good luck with the task," he says right before he leaves.

I stare at the door, frowning, deciphering his actions. I've never been in a relationship, but I sure can understand why it's so hard. How are you supposed to understand how people feel? How do you know what they are thinking?

I look down at my lap, where the white envelope lies. I turn it over to read my name, my heart thudding instantly when I recognize the handwriting. Ripping the envelope open, I pull out the piece of paper. Tears stream down my cheeks. My hands shake as I read the letter.

My dear Alexandra,

I'm sorry for what happened. I'm sorry you have to bear the burden of past sins. But I know there is no one stronger than you, who can do whatever it takes to do the right thing. You have always had the heart and the strength to step out of your comfort zone. I know without a doubt that you'll find your way.

Know that I'll always love you.

Mother

I crawl into my bed, vision blurring, my heart hurting, waiting, hoping, praying for the world to disappear for just one moment.

CHAPTER 38

Alex

My heart pounds as the door opens to let in the soldiers who are taking me to the task. I'm wearing similar boots to the ones I was wearing during the first task: brown sturdy boots that reach my knees. Under that is a pair of tight-knit black pants with several pockets down the sides. I wear a white tunic this time, with a black padded vest that gives me some protection from the wind. The vest is fire resistant, and so are my pants, according to Katya. She's been working with the prince and the royal tailor to find some clothes that might protect me from fire. My hair is braided and rolled at the top of my head like a crown. I'm better today; I can walk, maybe even run a little. I don't know how fast, but I'm hoping since this is the second task, that I won't have to worry so much about being burned. After all, the dragons and I have an understanding now.

The soldiers grab my arms, leading me out of my room. Griffin and the prince stand outside, waiting for the soldiers. Griffin is wearing his soldier uniform, his hair braided down the back of his head. The prince is wearing a white tunic and black pants, with a long black coat over his body. I sneak a look at his chest, wondering if the salve is still there.

"What are you guys doing here?" I ask, frowning.

"Escorting you, clearly," the prince responds, shaking his head.

I roll my eyes. "Yes, sure, because two soldiers aren't enough. I'll absolutely get lost at some point," I add sarcastically, gesturing at the arms wrapped around my own.

"Of course, we wouldn't put it past you to poison us again, Sparky," the prince says, and Griffin bursts out laughing.

I glare at them. "I didn't poison you," I defend myself. "I just temporarily paralyzed you." But I sigh in defeat, letting myself get pushed to the arena. The arena is bigger this time, curved like a crescent moon towards the swamp area, and the rows of seats are much higher, as if dragons can't just fly to blow the entire arena out. I'm dragged to the inside of the arena, pulled to the top viewing area where the king and his advisors and knights sit once more.

"Gabriel," the king greets the prince as he skips steps to beat me and the soldiers to the top. Rage flares inside of me when I think about what he did to the prince, and as I catch sight of the way he's glaring at his son, my heart constricts.

How easy would it be for him to inflict the same damage on me? My family?

"Hello, Quskaha," he greets me with a hollow smile. "I hope you're doing well."

"Do you?" I respond, unable to control my big mouth.

From the corner of my eye, I see his jaw drop, and the king chuckles. "Has the prince been putting stuff in your head?" he adds.

"He didn't have to, Your Majesty; I saw it all for myself," I counter, staring into his eyes. No, I'm not about to back down. After all, how much more can he punish me?

"Oh, Quskaha, you can't be that naïve?" he says, smirking, and his advisors laugh behind him.

I smile sweetly. "No, Your Majesty, I'm just observant."

A flicker of hate, sharp and sudden like a viper's strike, crosses his eyes, then vanishes as swiftly. "The prince and I will talk about whatever it is you think about me."

I frown. "Maybe you should be talking to me about it instead, Your Majesty. After all, isn't this between you and me?"

The prince's eyes bulge. "She doesn't mean that, Father," he says, but the king and I ignore him.

"How about we don't keep your advisors waiting?" I say instead, keeping my eyes on the king. "After all, my death would be so exhilarating."

"Alex," Griffin warns beside me. I didn't even realize he was here yet.

But the king doesn't take his eyes off me, either. His eyes narrow, then he turns, a fake smile on his face. "She's right, isn't she? Let's not keep the people waiting," he says, and everyone behind me celebrates with loud cheers and clapping.

"What's my task today, Your Majesty?" I ask confidently.

He turns to me, a sly smirk playing on his lips, his eyes twinkling mischievously. Then he turns to his people. After all, he must play the game correctly.

"Today's challenge for the Quskaha is to ride a dragon and get the dragon to breathe fire on that old barn over there," he says, pointing to a brown barn barely visible where we are.

I frown. "That barn?" I ask again.

"Yes, Quskaha, think you can do that?" the king responds, not a part of him looking concerned.

"Is there anyone in that barn?" I ask, unable to hide the concern in my voice.

The king lets out a laugh, a chilling, empty sound that sends shivers down my spine. "Wow, child, do you really think that badly of me?" he says mockingly, encouraging his peers to cheer and laugh with him. "Of course not!"

I turn to the prince, his worried gaze meeting mine, concern etched into every line of his face.

"Promise me there are no humans or animals in that barn," I insist.

The king laughs again. "You think you can command the king to do something?"

My gaze doesn't waver. "Promise me. I won't do it unless you do."

The king's intense gaze bores into me. "Of course, Quskaha, there's no one in that barn." His voice is steady and firm.

I swallow hard, then turn to the soldiers beside me. "Let's do it."

The king's smile, as thin and cold as winter ice, sends a chill down my spine as I descend the stairs, my soldiers at my heels, the prince and Griffin at my side.

"Are you sure you can do this, Sparky?" the prince asks.

"Are you okay enough to go to the dragons? How are your legs?" Griffin adds.

I ignore them, and sprint down the stairs on my own. I remember the path to the entry point and follow that in my head. When I enter the arched door to the steel gates, I stop, Griffin and the prince right beside me.

"I'm fine. I can do this," I tell them, my eyes burning into them.

Griffin nods, turning to leave. "Good luck, nightmare," he adds as he leaves.

I shoot him a face. "Nice, because Alex isn't my real name," I shoot back sarcastically.

Griffin laughs as he exits the door. I turn back to the prince. "I'm fine," I repeat.

He swallows hard, like he has plenty to say, but none of it comes out. "Fuck, you're so beautiful when you're like that," he finally rasps.

I frown. "Like what?"

"When you're angry," he teases, a smile playing on his lips.

I roll my eyes. "I hate your kingdom. I hate your father."

His face sobers. "Good luck, Sparky," he says, his warm hand enveloping mine, and a jolt of electricity sparks between us. "Come back…to me," he says, the last words barely audible against the steel bars rising in front of me.

My eyes narrow at him. "I don't need you," I declare.

My chest warms. The smile on his face grows wider. "But I need you," he finishes, slipping his hands in his pockets before turning to leave.

"Prince," I call out before he disappears through the arched door.

He stops and turns, that boyish smile still on his face.

"What does that mean?" I ask, my eyes narrowed in question.

"How about you survive this one, and I'll tell you?" he says, a tilt in his mouth.

I glare back. "Dick."

"Bitch," he responds with a smile, right before he disappears through the door.

I watch the door closing in behind him, my heart skipping a beat. I hate that he has such an impact on me. I hate that I don't understand how I feel. When I turn to the dragons, I clear my head. I don't need the prince for this.

I can do it myself.

CHAPTER 39

Alex

"Hello, Quskaha," the green dragon greets me. "How are you feeling? We haven't seen you since the first task. Too busy for dragons?"

"Ciri, can you stop antagonizing for maybe a second of your entire life?" the bigger red dragon interrupts as it walks over to me.

"After all, you were the one that hurt her," Dimonyaga says from behind the bigger red dragon.

The green one huffs in response, putting its head close to me as if smelling me.

"Why do you smell aroused, Quskaha?" Cirianiel asks, and I turn red, my jaw dropping.

Tuliikaarme laughs so hard, the sound rumbles through the arena. Thank God only I can hear what they're saying.

"Do you have to be so direct, Ciri?" I say, chuckling as I turn to hide the blush.

"Oh, it's the prince, is it?" Cirianiel snorts, lifting its head to look for the prince in the rows of people.

"Stop embarrassing her," Tuliikaarme laughs. "Look at her; she's so embarrassed."

"It must be hard to know what it all means, isn't it?" Dimonyaga says, approaching me. He nudges me gently, but it's strong enough to push me over.

"Oops," Dimonyaga says. "Sorry. I don't really know my strength yet."

I laugh, pushing up off the ground.

"Careful, Dimonyaga, you have to be careful with her. She's like a twig you can break when you sit down," Cirianiel adds, laughing.

"Ouch. I'm glad you guys are in a good mood," I respond. "I'm feeling better, Ciri, thanks for asking."

Cirianiel nods, her snout nudging me for pets, and I do so, his eyes closing in contentment as I rub the front of his nose.

"So, what's today's challenge, Alex? What are they making you do?" Tuliikaarme asks.

I turn to the bigger red dragon, scratching my ear. "They want me to ask you to blow fire on something."

They look at each other for a moment. "Huh. That king of yours really has some weird shit, doesn't he? I wonder what he's planning," Tuliikaarme comments thoughtfully.

Suddenly, I hear screaming and the flapping of wings above us, and a large black dragon hovers just above us.

"Uh, you better move, Quskaha, Malakas doesn't care where he lands," Cirianiel comments, his gaze on the sky, too.

"Get under my wing, Quskaha," Tuliikaarme orders, and I do what she says, cowering under her wings. The world vibrates, the arena shakes, and people scream as the massive black dragon lands, skidding right in front of us. A wave of dust blows around me.

"Malakas," Tuliikaarme greets as he flaps his wings once more, before getting up on his hind legs.

"Hello." The black dragon really is massive, towering even over Tuliikaarme, and his head, when stretched, reaches all the way up to the top of the arena. His horns are black, his spikes are black, even his underwing and belly are black. Of all the dragons I've seen, he's the only one that seems to be of one pure color. Except his eyes. His eyes are red, different from the yellow that Tuliikaarme, Dimonyaga, and Cirianiel have. He hums, his neck stretching to smell me under Tuliikaarme's wing.

"This is the new Quskaha?" he asks. When Tuliikaarme nods, he moves closer, his face approaching me. "Doesn't look like much." He huffs.

I'm not sure how to take that, so I just stare.

"Be nice, Malakas. Nobody needs your foul mood," Cirianiel says from Tuliikaarme's other side, my heart beaming with pride. Even Cirianiel is defending me. That means I have some sort of trust or connection with them-- however little it might be right now.

The black dragon huffs.

"Hello," I say, stepping out of Tuliikaarme's wings. "I'm not much. But I need your help."

He laughs, sparks of orange flickering from his mouth. "Humans. Always thinking we owe them."

Red creeps up my neck and onto my cheeks. "I don't want to ask you, but they will kill my brother and my mother if I don't do what they ask. I know you don't owe me anything."

Malakas approaches me quickly, his breath huffing, and I'm tossed backwards. "Oops," he says, not really sorry for it.

"Please," I plead, getting back up on my feet.

"I'll do it," Cirianiel offers, stepping forward, but Malakas' wings flap, the wind forcing him to step back a little.

"No," Malakas growls. "I'll do it."

My heart skips a beat.

"Or I can do it!" Dimonyaga offers, stepping up beside Cirianiel.

Malakas only gives him a wary look before he turns, looking disappointed. "I just wanted to make you happy."

I approach Dimonyaga, and pet his snout as he lowers his face to me. "One day. You make me happy either way."

The smaller red dragon's eyes widen, but fire sneaks out of his mouth. I duck, barely missing the fire he blew.

"Dimonyaga!" Tulii scolds. "You almost burned her!"

"I-I'm sorry, I didn't mean it," Dimonyaga says, pouting. I stand, petting his snout again.

"How about you learn control, and I learn how to fly? Eventually, you and I can work together."

The small dragon lights up. "Okay!"

Malakas steps forward, its snout and claw stretched out so I can climb it. "Hope you can fly, Quskaha."

"Malakas, you better take care of her," Tuliikaarme warns.

I climb up his claw and snout, then find a spot on his neck to ride, holding onto his spikes.

"I'll be fine," I say to Tuliikaarme, who nods.

Malakas gives a loud roar as he lifts up off the ground, breaking into a portion of the arena by using it as a stepladder.

"Can I blow fire on them?" he asks as his snout is level with the king's row of people.

My eyes widen. "No! There are innocent people in there, Malakas!" I point out quickly. The dragon lifts up more, a vibration coming from its body.

"Relax, Quskaha, I was kidding. Mostly," he responds as we fly above the arena.

"It's Alex," I say loudly.

"A Quskaha who refuses to be called Quskaha," Malakas observes. We're above now, flying above the castle.

"I don't know what Quskaha really means, Malakas," I tell him.

The dragon huffs. "A Quskaha who doesn't know her history."

"I didn't grow up here. I've started learning though!" I protest.

"A Quskaha who didn't grow up here," Malakas comments.

"That's the barn they want me to ask you to blow up." I point to the barn just below us. The barn is massive and made out of wood, with the roof shaped like a gambrel. A small window pokes light into the barn almost at the peak of the roof. A few sash windows line the sides, but it looks dark right now, like someone's painted or covered the windows from the inside. The fast-flowing river borders the barn on three sides.

Malakas huffs. "A Quskaha asking to blow fire on something that doesn't need it."

"I don't ask lightly, Malakas. The king has some sort of agenda towards me, and I don't like it either. But if I don't, he'll kill my brother and mother," I protest.

"A Quskaha with a conscience," Malakas huffs.

"Do you know the history of dragons in this kingdom, Quskaha, and why we're here?" the dragon asks, once more flying above the castle before it turns.

I blush. "I don't."

"A Quskaha who doesn't lie, even if it could mean death. Good for you," Malakas says.

"I haven't gotten to those books yet, Malakas. I'm still learning," I say.

Malakas hums. "If I do this for you, I need you to do a favor for me," he says.

My heart thuds in my chest. "I don't know if I can, but I'll certainly try."

Malakas dips suddenly, and I scream. He hums. "You really should fly more, Quskaha, isn't that your purpose?"

My jaw tightens at the criticism. "I just started, Malakas, I didn't even know I was anything until just a few weeks ago!" I protest, holding onto his spike for dear life.

Malakas hums. "A Quskaha who didn't know she was a Quskaha. How fascinating."

"What can I do for you, Malakas? You said you wanted a favour in exchange for helping me. Just remember, I'm only human."

Malakas flies over the barn once more. "In the deeper dungeons of this kingdom, there's a larger cave. Our friend, Kidlat, has been tied there for thousands of years. Thousands of years, Quskaha. He doesn't deserve it. You need to let him out. Will you do that for me?" Malakas says. "Will you help us?"

My head swims. How barbaric for someone to be bound for thousands of years. What could that do to a creature's psyche? "I-I-I didn't know that. Why did they tie him up?" I ask.

"Why do you think we're here? They tied him up to keep us tied to this kingdom. There's a reason why we're here. We want our family back, Quskaha," Malakas says.

Anger flares throughout my body. How dare they keep that a secret from me? How dare they do that to the dragons?

"Read your history, Quskaha. It's all in there. We need you to bridge the gap between humans and us," Malakas adds.

"I'm sorry, Malakas, I didn't know," I respond, a part of my heart feeling heavy. It makes sense, though, that they know what it is to desperately want to keep their family safe and give them their freedom. I know that more than anyone.

"Will you help us, Quskaha?" Malakas says as we take another turn.

"I'll try my best, Malakas. I'll do it. I'll help you," I promise him.

Malakas speeds up, dipping up and down the kingdom, and then he twirls up high, shooting for the heavens. I hold on tight, closing my eyes.

"Quskaha, don't close your eyes. This is the best part," Malakas reminds me.

Where have I heard that before?

CHAPTER 40

Alex

I marvel at the view of the entire kingdom, the beautiful green lands, the hills, and the trees. When Malakas gives me a signal, he turns, sending me upside down as I hold on to his spikes, and I hug my knees tightly around Malakas's ridge.

"Get ready for the fun part," Malakas says as he continues to roll in the air, my stomach doing the exact same thing.

"Hold on!" Malakas yells as he increases his speed, his wings barely flapping as he rolls through the air.

I don't speak. I'm afraid if I do, I'll lose my teeth. Instead, I tighten my hold on his spike, praying I don't fall.

"Oh, Quskaha, you have a lot to learn!" Malakas yells at me.

"Well, I'd really like to learn it all, you know, and maybe not dying before I get the chance would be kind of nice."

Malakas laughs. "Aha, the talent of sarcasm. Twaila had it too."

"Yes, it's in my blood," I respond dryly, finally able to come up for air with Malakas straightening up.

"Ready, Quskaha?" Malakas says again.

"Are you actually doing it this time?" I respond, barely peeking out.

"Probably. Maybe. Who knows?" The dragon shoots up into the air, then opens his wings, free-falling. "Whee."

I scream. When Malakas straightens, he's laughing at me. I roll my eyes.

"Can we just get on with it?" I argue loudly.

"Okay, Quskaha, as you asked," the dragon says, rolling his red eyes at me. "Ready?"

"I was ready three times ago!"

"You're funny," Malakas responds. Then, he speeds up, flying downwards directly towards the barn. He stops suddenly and pulls his head back. With a single blow, his entire body vibrating, his jaw opens, fire breathing in a single concentrated flow, directly into the barn below us. Fire catches instantly, and my heart sinks.

Distant but loud human screams fill the air as fire takes over the entire barn, spreading fast.

"Quskaha, there are people in there," Malakas says as he drives us back up. "Did you know this?"

My entire body shakes. My vision blurs. Anger takes over. "No, Malakas, I did not know this. I wouldn't have done it had I known there were people there."

"What do you want to do?" Malakas asks.

"Put me down. I'm going to have a word with the king," I say, my vision blurring from tears or anger, probably both.

Malakas nods as he makes a wide turn. Then he flies down, speeding as he does, only to stop mere moments from hitting the ground. When I slide off of Malakas, I turn, patting its snout gently. "Thank you, Malakas. I'll look for your friend, and I'll do what I can," I whisper to him. Then, I stomp my way back into the arena. Cheers and applause ring out through the arena, but I don't care.

The arched door opens immediately, and the prince and Griffin are right inside, but I ignore them, heading straight upstairs to where I know the king is.

"Alex, Alex," the prince takes two steps to keep up with me.

When we make it to a level floor, I spin on him, my anger flaring more than ever before. He steps back, his eyes widening.

"Did you know?" I demand.

"Know what? Know what, Sparky?" he asks in a gentle tone as he reaches for my hand.

I shove his hand away. "Did you know that there were people inside the barn?"

He looks stunned. "What? No, no, there could't have been."

Tears pool in my eyes, threatening to spill, but I won't let them. "I heard the screams, Prince. I heard the screams." I whirl on him again, heading up a few more staircases up to where the king is laughing and cheering with his advisors. The king waves the soldiers away.

"Congratulations, Quskaha!" he says, raising his hands.

The people behind him erupt in cheers and applause.

But I didn't care about the applause. I didn't care about the cheers. I stare him down, my eyes so hot I could probably shoot lasers from them.

"You knew," I accuse, "You *knew*!"

"Knew what, Quskaha?" the king says, not even fazed by my accusations.

"You knew there were people in that barn!" I shriek, my voice louder than ever. I fight hard not to release the tears threatening to pool in my eyes. People whisper, their eyebrows frowning. "Your king knew there were people in there and had me murder them," I yell up at them. "Your king did that!" I repeat scathingly.

The king's eyes narrow, and he waves his soldiers to take me away. When the soldiers ask where to, his eyes glint mischievously at me. "The dungeons."

The king approaches me with a menacing stare. "Say one more thing, and I will kill your brother and mother. Angus, right?"

My eyes widen, and I reach up to punch him before a soldier pulls my hand off.

"Take her and make sure she understands the repercussions of her actions," the king tells the soldiers. They grab my arms and drag me down the stairs so carelessly my knees scrape the edge of each step.

When the prince and Gabriel try to follow, the king waves a hand to summon soldiers to prevent them from leaving the area.

I'm dragged to the dungeons mercilessly, my legs scraping the ground. They throw me into the cell, and I stumble, hitting my head on the bench. I groan at the impact, a throbbing pain starting in my head. But they're not done. The soldier comes in, smacking my face with the back of his hand. My eyes blur, my ears ring, and the pain in my head grows.

"Bitch," the soldier says as he smacks me again, on my other cheek this time.

Another soldier comes in, kicking me in the chest. I sink into the cold hard ground, coughing as the weight of his feet connects with my chest. A foot kicks my pelvis, and I shrink further as the pain throbs throughout my body. Another hand or elbow? Maybe a foot hits me on the head. My vision blurs as I writhe on the ground. When another hand smacks my face, I see darkness and fully submit myself to it.

CHAPTER 41

Gabriel

Griffin and I race from the arena as soon as my father gets distracted. My heart pounds the moment we make it to the dungeons, and I see five other soldiers coming out of it, looking sickeningly pleased with themselves. Their knuckles are red and bleeding.

"We got that bitch good," the soldiers say, and I can't help myself. I swing at him, hitting him straight on his cheek, watching as blood drips from his mouth.

"Watch your mouth," I spit at him.

Griffin pulls my arm. "He's not worth it, Gabe."

I glare at the soldier, my eyes burning into him as he scrambles to his feet and flees, his boots kicking up dust. That's most likely going to get me another punishment from my father, but I didn't care. Griffin pulls open the heavy, iron-bound dungeon entrance, and I hurry inside, the musty smell of mildew and damp stone filling my nostrils as I quickly check each cell.

There she is again, at the end of the cold, damp dungeons, writhing on the rough stone floor, her body racked with pain. I race toward her, the metallic clang of the cell door echoing in the silence as I throw it open.

"Alex," I say, bending down and nudging her gently. Nothing, no reaction, not even a movement. I look up at Griffin, who has a panicked look on his face. "Grab a healer. I'll take her to my rooms," I add.

Griffin pauses, his eyebrows knitted in concern.

"My rooms," I repeat to him, my stomach knotting painfully at the sight of her injuries.

He nods and sprints out of the dungeons.

After bending to scoop her into my arms, I hurry from the dank, dimly lit dungeons, whispering her name as I walk back to the castle. Instead of turning right toward her bedroom, I led her down the long hallway to my wing, where Quentin, my ever-vigilant soldier, stands guard at my door. He frowns, his eyes narrowing as he sees the woman in my arms, a tense silence hanging in the air. Instead, he opens the door and helps me by carrying her head to the pillows.

"Your Majesty," he says as soon as Alex is on my bed.

"Don't tell the king," I say, waving for him to go.

Quentin nods, then exits the bedroom. I grab a small towel and wet it slightly before running it over head.

"Alex," I say softly, "Alex, please wake up, come on, Sparky." I pat the wet towel on her face, trying to wipe away the dried blood on her face and hair.

The door opens, and Katya comes in, clothes in her hand. "Quentin said my lady is here," she announces.

I nod, thanking her. "She'll be sleeping here from now on, okay, Katya?"

She gently lays her clothes on my nightstand. "I brought her some clothes. I'll go get her some of the salve she made and some food and water."

"Thanks," I say, settling myself beside her on the bed again.

Suddenly she rises, coughing, her eyes blinking. I grab the trash can beside my nightstand and put it in front of her. She coughs violently, her body bending over the bed. Thick, red liquid escapes her lips, the majority of it spurting into the trash can.

The door opens again, revealing Griffin and a healer in tow.

"What happened?" the healer asks.

"They beat her up," I rasp quickly, nudging at Griffin to get water.

The healer shakes her head, approaching the bed, putting her supplies at her foot.

"She just vomited blood," I offer, watching the healer carefully.

The healer frowns, then checks her vitals before cupping her head with her palm.

"She's not feverish yet, but I imagine she will be soon. She's been through a lot," the healer says. "Can you draw her a bath? There are no major wounds, but I imagine she might have some internal bleeding we need to figure out. Once she's clean, I can check her properly."

I go into the bathroom, turn on the faucet to a good temperature, and then I come back out, helping the healer remove her clothing. Afterward, I carefully laid her in the bathtub. She wakes slightly, murmuring things before her head lolls again, laying on the back of the porcelain bathtub.

The water covers her breasts, and I do my best to avert my eyes from her body, yet my heart breaks at seeing her like this. At the knowledge that it's my father doing this to her, my father who's the reason behind all her pain. The healer takes the sponge and bathes her, and I sigh with relief. Once she's clean, I lift her out of the bathtub, where the healer places a towel over her. I place her on the bed, then move aside to let the healer get her dried and inspect her.

Griffin and Katya return with food and drinks, placing them on the coffee table. Katya leaves to grab all her clothes, but Griffin remains. He stands next to me, putting an arm around me.

"She'll be okay, brother," he says. "She's strong." I nod, swallowing hard.

"I don't know if I can keep doing this, Griff," I murmur to him. "I can't protect her from my father."

Griffin shakes his head. "Just say the word, man." He takes one last look at her, then turns and leaves the room.

The healer continues to check her, patching any open wounds as she goes along.

"I think she's okay internally, but please let me know when she's up and awake so I can treat her for any ailments. She has a lot of bruises." The healer turns to me. "You need to be extra careful with her, and she can't run, nor do any physical activities, at least for the next few days while she's recuperating. Do you understand?"

I nod. "Thank you." The healer hands me a few medications.

"Make sure she takes the white one as soon as she wakes up. The blue one in five hours, and then the green right after that. I'm going to let her rest for now, but call me if there are any symptoms within the next ten hours," the healer orders.

"What about the blood she vomited?" I ask, crossing my arms.

"I think it was just blood she accumulated in her mouth, but definitely reach out if her stomach is feeling weird," the healer responds.

I nod. "Okay, I'll let you know."

The healer exits the room, and I sit next to her again on the bed. I realize she's still naked, so I grab her clothes and put a loose shirt and sweatpants on her before falling asleep beside her.

I must've fallen asleep for a few hours, because when I open my eyes, Alex's eyes are also open, watching me.

"Creepy, Sparky," I mumble, patting the tip of her nose. "How are you feeling?"

Tears pool in her eyes, her face scrunching as she shakes. "I-I-I'm a murderer," she says, tears streaming down her face.

"Hey, hey." I move closer to her, bringing her face to my chest. "You are not a murderer, okay? You didn't know, and this wasn't your fault, okay? It's not your fault."

"It wasn't the king, Prince, it was me," she mumbles between sobs.

"No, Sparky, you'd never have done this if you'd known there were people in there. This was not on you," I say firmly, caressing her cheeks.

"I helped, prince, I helped," she wails, and my tunic gets soaked in her tears.

With a grunt, I pull myself upward, forcing my head down until my eyes met hers, the scent of her hair filling my nostrils. I gently push the hair from her face, noticing the dark bruises blooming around her eyes, the jagged cut on her cheek, and the swollen, split lip. My fingertip traces her mouth, eliciting a small wince, yet her gaze holds mine, a silent connection forming between us.

I'll kill them. I'll kill every single one of them who'd hurt her.

"No, this is my father's fault. I'll forever hate him for this," I say, hopping off the bed, just remembering I was supposed to give her the white pill. I grab it from the nightstand along with some water.

"Here," I say, handing her the pill and the water. "How do you feel? Does your stomach hurt?"

"Where am I?" she asks, looking around her.

"You're in my room. I need to keep you safe, and the only way to do that is if you're here," I respond, expecting some kind of backlash, some sassy comment, some snarky response.

But no. Instead, she just frowns, then says. "I'm–I'm just tired," she says, bending her head and closing her eyes. I slip into the bed next to her, pulling her head to my chest. Her eyelids flutter closed as she snuggles into me, her body radiating warmth. In my arms, she's safe.

Now the question is--how do I keep her that way?

CHAPTER 42

Gabriel

"Gabe, Gabe, I really need to talk to you," Griffin says, catching up to me as I pick flowers from the gardens to take to Alex.

He motions to the blooms in my hand. "For Alex?"

"Yeah, she's awake," I say. "Quentin's guarding her."

"You trust Quentin?" Griffin's eyebrow rises.

"Yes, not as much as I trust you, but enough," I tell him.

"Maybe more discovering and less romancing?" he teases, a grin on his face.

I roll my eyes, but I can't help smiling.

"You're so fucked," Griffin comments, pointing to my silly little grin.

I don't think I've been this happy in a while. It's not like anything's happened between us; it's just--she's let me in. She talks to me; she doesn't hide from me, and most importantly, she sleeps in my bed. I've never been taught to court, so I'm just doing what I know from books I've read. I've never had to convince anyone to be with me. Every girl I've ever been with would gladly go to bed with me. But she's different. I treat her differently. I don't want her to feel like she's just one of the girls. I want her to feel that she's *the* girl. The only one.

"I need to talk to you about the final task," Griffin says.

I pause. "Do you have details on the final task?" I ask, frowning.

He gives a slight nod. "I dug around a little. The task is for Alex to put these collars on the dragons."

"Just collars?" I narrow my eyes. That doesn't seem like my father. This is the final task. It's meant to be the worst of them all--the way for Alex to prove herself.

"Gabe, these aren't your regular collars," he says, putting a hand on my arm. "And I found their maker." Griffin's eyes hold a mischievous glint.

"Wait--what?"

"I found who your father has been working with to create the collars," he repeats.

Impressed, my eyes narrow in concentration to take it all in. "How?"

Griffin smiles slyly. "I slept with someone who works in their lab."

My jaw drops. "Holy shit, Griff. How did you know who she was?"

He waves dismissively, as if it's no big deal. "I followed your father after the whole debacle with Alex at the tasks. He was saying something about getting it ready, and I got so curious I took note of the woman later and found her running around the castle the other day. Want to take a field trip?" he suggests, smiling and quirking his eyebrows.

"Okay. Give me a moment; let me just let Alex know. I'll meet you here in an hour?" I offer, making my way up the stairs to my room. She's sitting on her side of the bed, a book in her hand.

"Hey," she says as I enter the room, her eyes lighting up.

"Hello, Sparky, how are you doing?" I ask, grabbing an empty vase and adding flowers to it.

"Aw, Prince, are you giving me flowers?" she teases, putting the book down and crawling over the bed with her cheeks in her palms.

"If I were, would you accept it?" I challenge. She turns red immediately. I place the vase next to the bed. "I thought I'd do something nice for you."

"You don't have to get me flowers," she says, sitting up as I sit next to her on the bed.

"I know." I shrug. "How are your wounds doing?"

This time, she shrugs. "I mostly feel tired, I think. My ribs hurt a little, and so do my eyes, but the healer says they'll go away, eventually."

I reach out, my fingers brushing against her soft hair as I tuck a strand behind her ear.

"Listen, I have to do something with Griffin for a bit. Is there anything you need?" I ask, a finger tracing her jaw.

She shakes her head. "Where are you guys going?"

"I'll tell you when we get back," I say, smiling. I want to kiss her so badly, and I want to invade her space, inhale her breath, but she hasn't been obviously open to anything yet. I don't know how much experience she's had, and I don't know how she sees me, and besides that, she's recovering from injuries. So instead, I kiss her forehead and pat her hand.

"I'll be back in a bit, okay?" I tell her. She nods, crawling back to the other side of the bed where her book waits for her.

"Prince," she says right before I make it out the door.

I stop, turning to her. "What is it?" My heart hopes for her to say so many things. Her mouth opens, but then it closes again.

"Never mind," she says, settling back on her seat.

I leave the room, my thoughts churning before I meet Griffin down the hall.

"Just in time, brother," he says, a smile spreading across her face. I nod.

"Let's go," I say, heading out of the castle.

Griffin stops. "Where are you going?"

I narrow my eyes. "I thought we were going to find the lab?"

"Brother," he says, putting his hands on my shoulders. "The lab is here."

My eyes widen, and my jaw drops.

"Yes, Gabe. It was right here all along, right under our noses," Griffin says. He walks down a hallway that eventually leads to the kitchen. He turns a corner, near a half bathroom, where a wall just happens to be. Griffin touches the wall, then puts his ear against it. I watch, frowning, as he knocks on it. Then, slowly, he pushes it, and something clicks. The door opens. My jaw drops, but we don't have time to talk. Griffin enters, quickly pulling me inside before closing the door.

We're inside a small room, which looks like a library with all the books stacked in the bookshelves and two chairs. I'm actually kind of shocked I've never stumbled across this room. Griffin and I played throughout the castle when we were young. I know certain paths, I've gone through tunnels, I thought I knew where all the secret passages were.

"If these are just books, why have they been hidden?" I say aloud. Griffin shushes me. He walks towards the shelf, reading through the titles of the books. When he finds what he needs, he pulls the book out. Another clicking sound echoes, and the bookshelf opens halfway. My jaw drops again.

We enter the room through the bookshelf, only to find another bookshelf.

"How did you find out about this, Griff?" I whisper.

He smiles slyly. "I got her tired. I was able to explore while she slept." He grins. I roll my eyes, chuckling. Of course, he did. Griffin looks through the bookshelf once more. When he pulls the book, the door opens to reveal a staircase going down. It's dark and dingy, but we go down anyway. The staircase leads to what looks a bit like a control room.

There are many screens with videos of outside the building, and a pile of paintings are stacked on one side, like they're waiting to be put up. Or maybe they'd just been taken down.

We continue walking through the hall, noticing a kitchen sink, some cabinets, and a fridge smaller than the one we have in the kitchen. Does that mean someone lives here?

Griffin pulls at my arm, bringing me to attention. At the end of the hall sits a table, at which an older man is sitting, hunched over in a chair. His hair is a greyish white, but so is his beard. It looks like he hasn't shaved in weeks. Blood streaks his forehead and cheek, and he's busy poring over something in front of him. In one hand, he has a red pen, and a pair of black glasses is perched on his nose. He barely seems to notice we're here.

"Hello," Griffin greets. The small man jumps, practically stumbling over his chair.

"H-hello," he greets. "Who are you?"

"Are you the one making collars for the dragons?" Griffin gets straight to the point.

The small man looks surprised. "Uh–yes."

I step forward, my eyes narrowing at this man. I've never met him before. Never seen him in my entire life. "Who are you?" I ask.

"M-m-my name is Finn," he responds.

"Who are you, Finn? And how are you here?" I ask.

"I've been here for ten years," Finn says, and my eyes widen. "I make whatever the king requires, including the collars."

"Where are you from? Who do you work with?" I demand.

He doesn't seem fazed by my interrogation. "I only work with the king and Sir Andrew. I've never seen any other human in this place," Finn replies. I can't quite tell if he's lying.

"You're making the collars? What are they for?" Griffin asks.

"Yes, I make all the things the king needs. The collar is for the dragons," Finn responds.

Griffin gets frustrated, stepping closer. "I know that. But what does it do for the dragon?"

Finn looks surprised. "It doesn't do anything for the dragon. *But*, it lets us control them." Finn's eyes shine with pride. "It took us awhile to figure it out, as I had to map out the system again so I could understand what we're missing. We only realized it maybe a week or so ago, and I just got the final piece of the puzzle. I've been working on it for years, and it took us over ten years just to finish it. For a while, I didn't think we would. The king was getting mad."

"What kind of collar is this? This doesn't seem like anything I've ever seen," I say, picking up the collar nearby. It was thick and large, white with a black mirror on the sides.

Finn looks at us proudly. "Of course, sir, they're not from this realm."

My jaw drops just as Griffin's does. "Are you saying the king is using otherworldly tools?"

"Of course, sir, what else would he be using to conquer this realm?"

My heart sinks. "What do you mean by conquering this realm?"

He purses his lips, as if knowing what he's about to tell us will be hard to take in. "That's why I'm here, sir. I was kidnapped from the other realm to serve him, so he can conquer the other kingdoms here," Finn says.

"You were kidnapped from your realm to conquer the other kingdoms?" I repeat, unable to fully grasp the concept.

"Holy shit," Griffin says.

"Holy shit," I repeat.

"Fuck," Griffin swears.

Finn's face breaks into a smile. "Oh! That's what we say on Sandaigdigan too!"

"San-San-daig-digan?" I repeat.

"My realm is called Sandaigdigan. I don't exactly know what this realm is called, sadly," Finn explains.

"How-how have you survived here so long?" I ask. "Alone?"

"I don't understand the question, sir. I'm here to serve the king, sir, and make sure he gets what he wants," Finn repeats, giving me a confused look.

"Do you think your dad messed with his mind?" Griffin whispers to me while we look at Finn.

"Shit," I mutter under my breath.

"Yeah. Shit," Griffin agrees. "Tell us, what kind of control does the collar exert?"

Finn looks confused. "Everything, sir. It controls everything."

My eyes widen. "He's not going to need Alex after the tasks."

"No, he won't." Griffin agrees.

My heart sinks. We don't have a choice.

Finn turns to us once more. "Hello, who are you?" he asks, a smile spreading on his face.

I stare at Griffin, then back at Finn. "Finn, we just met. I'm the prince, and this is Griffin," I say again, gesturing at Griffin.

Finn hangs his head. "I'm sorry, sir. My memory isn't great. Not with the change in realms."

"We'll leave you to your work, Finn. But I'll be back. Can you not tell my father that we came?" I ask, frowning.

He looks at me sadly. "I don't know if I'll even remember myself, Your Majesty."

We bid him goodbye before walking back up.

"How do you get into another realm, Griff?" I whisper as we get out of the lab.

He shrugs. "I don't know."

CHAPTER 43

Alex

The door opens suddenly, a grave and serious prince entering his room. He and I have spent days in his room, and not even for one moment has he signified any interest in me, apart from leaving a single kiss on my forehead. As someone who's never actually been in a relationship, and never been kissed, I always forget why I don't want to be involved with men: I forget that they're so freaking confusing. I forget that I'm actually my own woman after telling myself many years ago that I don't need any man. I hate that every time I look at him; I wait for a kiss, but nothing happens. I hate that I want a kiss, but nothing happens. Is it because I'm not kissable? Or maybe it's because I'm not royalty? Neither case makes me feel good, and yet as he enters the room, I find my heart pounding.

He sits at the end of the bed, putting his hand on my feet under the blankets, with a frown plastered on his face.

"What is it?" I ask, my eyebrows knitting at how grave and serious he looks.

"We know what the third task is," he responds.

"Why do you look so worried?" I ask.

"The king will be asking you to put collars on the dragons," he begins.

"Collars? Like dog collars?" I repeat, crossing the distance between us until I sat right next to him, my leg bent in front of my body. The prince nods.

"Except these collars aren't exactly your regular collars. These collars will allow the king to control the dragons," the prince says, his hand moving from my feet to my knee.

Tingles shoot up my spine, and I force myself to hide the redness threatening to take over my cheeks.

My vision narrows. "What do you mean, control the dragons?"

"He'll be able to get them to do anything, Sparky. Like anything," the prince emphasizes.

My brain pauses for a moment, like it's trying to comprehend what the prince is saying. "So, if he needs to blow up another barn, he can…without me?" I frown.

He nods his head. But my mind is already spinning. "That means he can hurt anyone using the dragons. That means he can hurt the dragons. That means he can hurt me because he won't need me." I jump off the bed, pacing around the room like a maniac. "He's going to kill me after.

He's going to kill the dragons. He's going to kill anyone he wants. He could kill my family after."

The prince gets off the bed, putting his hands on my shoulders. "I won't let that happen."

I search his eyes for a real plan. "He's going to kill me, Prince. There's just no stopping this. I'm going to die. He's going to kill my dragons, and he's going to do things to them and make them do things they don't want to do. He could really hurt them."

"Not if we leave," the prince says suddenly.

I look up at him. "Leave? What do you mean, leave? He's going to kill my family if I don't do this. He'll kill me! Or the dragons!"

He shakes his head. "Not if we leave and take the dragons with us," the prince says.

I stare back at him. "Are you nuts? Are you thinking right? Your father will have us all killed!"

"What's he going to do without the six dragons? He just lost his real and true reason for being the strongest kingdom. We're not strong for anything. We're playing with fire by saying we have dragons, but in reality, they do nothing for us. Not without you," he says firmly.

"You're out of your mind. Holy shit, I'm going to die," I say, the only thing my brain can think of right now.

But he grabs my wrists firmly. "No, you're not. We're going to grab your family, and we'll run somewhere where he can't hurt us. Not with you as the Quskaha, and not with me as the prince of Quaila," he says.

"Prince, are you nuts? Where will we go?" I demand, shoving him off.

"Anywhere, anywhere, Sparky, anywhere as long as I'm with you," he says.

I laugh mockingly. "You and your pretty words," I sing at him.

His eyes widen. "They're not pretty words, Sparky. Everything I've told you is true. I'm trying to protect you. Without power in this kingdom, I can't protect you. That's why we need to leave. I'll go anywhere, *anywhere*, as long as I'm with you. Fuck, I'll follow you to the end of the world if that's where you want to go."

"You'll actually leave this kingdom?" I frown at him.

"Yes, if it means I get to be with you and protect you," he says, closing the distance between us.

"You don't want to be with me," I accuse. "I've been staying with you for the last week or so and not once have you made me think you actually like me." My eyes narrow as I step up to him. "Tell me, prince, is it because I'm not pretty enough? Is it because I'm 'brown'? Ooh no, can't have that as your future queen, imagine what your heirs would look like. Ew, right?" I say mockingly.

His hands reach up to cup my face. "Gods, not one part of me thinks about you like that. Don't you get it?" he says.

"Get what?" I challenge, shoving his hands away from my face.

"The moment I kiss you is the moment everything changes. The moment I kiss you means I'll never let you go," he declares. "All the gods know I've wanted you from the moment I met you. The gods know you are and have always been the only one."

My eyes widen, but he steps forward once more, cupping my face in his hands.

"Once I claim you, Sparky, you'll never be with anyone else. Ever again," he growls, his eyes moving from my face down, down. "And, gods, do I want to kiss you. Every time

I see you. Every time I see your face turn red. Or the way your dimples show up when you smile. Or maybe when you fight like hell. When you're angry. Every time you talk to me. Right this second."

"Pretty words," I hiss, but my entire body heats up, my knees buckling beneath me.

"Gods, you're so frustrating," he maintains.

My eyes light up in a fresh bout of fake mockery. Why do I always do this when I'm uncomfortable? "Ooh no, can't have that for royalty, can we? You know what, Prince? You can say your pretty words over and over again. The truth is there, and you know it. I'm just a girl that you can't have, and your little ego can't handle it."

But there was nothing frustrated in his eyes. His hungry gaze travels up my body, lingering on my breasts and legs, the intensity of his stare making my skin pop with goosebumps. Finally, his eyes meet mine, filled with a primal hunger. His chest beat fast. I can almost feel the heat radiating from his body.

A fiery sensation surges through my body, settling in a way that feels completely new and unfamiliar, and pooling between my legs.

I laugh mockingly again. "Is that what they tell princes? Is that how you grew up, thinking you can just tell that to any woman, and they'll fall at your feet? Delusional, huh?"

He doesn't look put off by my defensive behavior. Perhaps he can see that I'm just terrified of my own feelings. "Not just any woman, Sparky. Only you. There's only ever been you." His eyes darken with his warning.

"Pretty words, prince, pretty words," I insinuate.

The air crackles with tension as he steps forward, and I instinctively move back, his closeness a palpable thing. As the rough-hewn wall presses against my back, the prince lets out a small, smug smirk, and I swallow hard, a nervous lump forming in my throat. The heat radiating from our bodies intertwines, creating a spark so intense, a feeling I doubt I'll ever experience again. I can feel the hardness of his sculpted chest. I can feel the hardness in his pants. I feel his skin as his hands get closer and closer to mine. My heart beats as if it's ready to jump out of my chest.

"Are they just pretty words?" he murmurs as his face bends down to meet mine. His breath tickles my face. I smell cedarwood and vanilla as his skin meets mine.

"Aren't they?" I manage, keeping my head high. I refuse to back down, even though every part of me wants to melt in his touch. He looks down at the finger running gently down my arm.

"You know, I think you like this," he says as goosebumps visibly rise along my arm.

I frown. "Do I?" But my skin betrays my words, and he chuckles.

"I think you do. I think you're just as attracted to me as I am to you," he says softly.

I roll my eyes. "You're so full of yourself. Just because you're a prince doesn't make everyone fall for you."

His hand rises from my arm, gently stroking my jaw and my cheeks. My body betrays me once more when my cheeks turn red.

"I don't care about anyone else. I just care about you and how I can make you feel," he drawls sultrily, his fingers trailing a path of fire across my skin, sending shivers down my spine. "Such beautiful skin. Such beautiful eyes."

I don't see his movement because he's so close, so close. I can feel his breath on my lips; I can feel the touch of his skin. His hands cup my face, pulling me even closer. Our eyes meet.

"I don't care about anything else, Sparky. I don't care about my father, I don't care about my throne if it means losing you," he whispers.

I slip out from under him, the pressure of his body against mine too much for me to handle. I swallow, instantly wishing my face wasn't so red.

"Sure, speak pretty words, prince," I say, instead moving towards the closet that's way across from him. The furthest I can get from his touch, so I don't lose myself to him, and to his moment, that probably means nothing to him, but everything to me.

He chuckles, his darkened eyes staring back at me. "So, would you run with me?"

"I have to talk to the dragons first," I mumble beneath the embarrassment of our near-moment. Then I whirl back on him. "Where do we go?"

"We'll pick up your family first. Then, we'll figure something out." The prince shrugs.

I roll my eyes. Must be nice to not have a plan. I shoot him a glare before slamming the bedroom door behind me.

CHAPTER 44

Alex

"Where are you going?" the prince asks, pulling at my arm.

I shove him off, fighting so hard not to feel his touch against mine. If I let him get too close, things will happen. Things I'm not ready for or don't know how to control.

"Where else, Prince?" I snap.

"I don't know, Sparky, why else would I be asking?" he shoots back.

I frown at him, stomping down the stairs, my voice lowering into a whisper. "I'm going to talk to the dragons, of course."

"Oh, okay," he says, shrugging, but he continues to follow me.

I pause. "Where are you going?" I demand, my hands on my hips.

"If you think you're going alone, you're crazy," he says, not turning to me.

"I can handle them now, Prince," she protests.

He rolls his eyes. "And I can follow you wherever you want, Sparky."

I sigh, defeatedly. "Why do you have to be so difficult?"

He gives me a face. "Why do you have to be so difficult?" he sneers. I ignore him, racing him to the dragon's field, but his steps are longer and faster.

I give up at the top of the hill as my breathing hitches. He sticks his tongue out at me as he walks down to the field.

"Mature," I yell at him, but he ignores me. I follow him eventually, after catching my breath at the top of the hill. In the dragon field are Cirianiel and Tuliikaarme and the golden dragon. Dimonyaga is nowhere to be found. Once I reach the field, I haul myself up over the rusty fence, the cold metal biting into my hands, before turning and dropping lightly back down on their grass.

"What do you think you're doing?" the prince growls behind me.

"How did you think I was supposed to talk to them, Prince?" I shoot back, narrowing my eyes.

His nostrils flare slightly, lips curling in a half-scowl, before jumping over the fence easily.

"What are you doing?" I ask.

"Where do you think you can go that I wouldn't follow?" he asks, his tone light and teasing, and with a mischievous glint in his eye.

"You know I can ask them to burn you, right?" I warn.

His face turns into a playful grin. "Not before I kiss you."

My face burns crimson, and I stomp toward the dragons, the heat rising in my cheeks.

"Hello, Quskaha," Cirianiel says, his snout lifting from the ground.

"Oh dinner," the golden dragon says, standing up. At this age, he's maybe about a month old, and he's already much, much taller than I am.

"Not dinner, Kirkaas," Tuliikaarme responds before turning around.

"Is this your baby?" I ask Tuliikaarme. He nods his head.

"This is Kirkaasain. We call him Kirkaas," Tuliikaarme responds.

"Who's your friend, Quskaha?" Cirianiel asks, looking beyond me.

I move myself in front of the prince, but he looks at me weird and steps in front of me.

"They won't hurt me, dick, I'm trying to protect you!" I snarl at him. Turning back to the dragons, I say: "This is prince…uh…Gabriel." I realize I've never called him that.

"I like it when you say my name, Sparky," he whispers into my ear, and his mere breath against my skin makes me shiver.

"Ohhh, I smell it again," Cirianiel laughs. "You like him, don't you?"

"Cirianiel!" I call out, my cheeks turning red. "I didn't come here to talk about him."

"What about me?" the prince says.

"They say you're annoying," I whisper back. His face crunches into a frown. "I have to talk to you about something," I say to the dragons.

Tuliikaarme moves to face us. "What is it, Alex? It looks serious," Tuliikaarme says, bending to face me.

"It is," I say, turning to the prince for a moment before I turn back to Tuliikaarme. "I need you to run away with me." I close my eyes, not ready to see their reactions.

Tuliikaarme's mouth opens, a slight pungent breeze coming out of her mouth, but she turns to Cirianiel. "What did she say?"

"She's asking us to run away with her," Cirianiel repeats.

"Wait, what?" Tuliikaarme asks. "This is our home, Alex."

I take a deep breath. "I wouldn't ask if it's not important. The king…he's working on a collar to contain you, to control you. It's going to be my next task, Tuliikaarme. If I don't do it, he'll kill my family," I explain.

"Wait–how?" Tuliikaarme asks.

"The how isn't important, Tuliikaarme," I say.

"My father kidnapped a man from a realm called 'Sandaigdigan' to make the collars," the prince whispers to me.

I frown at him before turning back to Tuliikaarme.

"The king kidnapped someone from Sandaigdigan to make the collars. I won't collar you, Tuliikaarme, or any of you. You're not meant to be controlled," I say. "We need to make it out of here before the next task; otherwise, they're going to kill me."

"Why can't you go, and we stay?" Cirianiel asks, blowing smoke above him.

"Ciri, if they can make this kind of collar, it's only time till they can get it on you! I won't let that happen," I protest.

"But we can defend ourselves, Quskaha," Cirianiel responds.

"Not all of you," I reply, looking at the smaller golden dragon.

The skies turn dark quickly, and when I look up, Malakas is landing, with Dimonyaga in tow.

"They have names?" the prince asks when I greet them, and he cowers with me under him. I shove him away, quickly hissing that I'm not afraid of the dragons, but he ignores my warning anyway, his arm continuing to cover my head.

"That's Malakas." I point to the massive black dragon.

Malakas lands with a thud, vibrating through the ground. "Quskaha," he greets with a roar.

"Malakas, Quskaha is asking us to run with her, away from this kingdom," Tuliikaarme says to the massive black dragon.

"That's Tulii." I point to the bigger red dragon.

"Alex!" the younger red dragon says, aiming to run to me, but is distracted by a prairie dog rushing past him.

"The younger dragon is Dimonyaga, and the green one is Cirianiel," I point as I introduce.

His eyes widen. "Cool."

"I'm not doing it lightly, Malakas. The king has built some kind of collar to control you. It's my next task assigned from him. To collar and control you so they can do it without me. They'll kill me after." I gave him a shorter version.

The huge dragon lowers its head to me. The prince pulls me back, but I stand still.

"I'm not afraid of you, Malakas, I'm trying to protect you," I say as a strong breeze from his sniff tickles me.

"Oh yeah? Have you found Kidlat yet?" Malakas says.

My heart sinks. "I haven't."

Malakas roars, the ground vibrating with it. "You haven't completed your side of the bargain, Quskaha," he scolds.

"The king beat me after the tasks, Malakas. I went to face him, and he had his soldiers beat me," I recount.

He lowers his head again, snaking its way to me. This time, he smells the prince, and I shove him to stand before him, while the prince grumbles in protest. Malakas hums.

"This one likes you," he observes with a click of his tongue.

"So does she," Cirianiel snickers behind him.

I give them both a look. "This is serious!"

Malakas hums again.

"Perhaps we can go," Tuliikaarme suggests. "But we'll have to travel slowly for the little ones," she adds, pointing to Dimonyaga and Kirkaas.

Malakas hums, taking another sniff. The prince tries to shove me back again, but I don't let him. He's safer behind me. I know they won't hurt me.

"The prince. He protects you," Malakas observes.

"Yes, it's a little annoying," I respond, shooting a look at the tall, sculpted man beside me.

"But you. You want to protect us," Malakas says.

"Yes, yes. I would never let them hurt you, Malakas. I want you to be safe," I say.

"You realize you cannot exactly hide five dragons, right?" Malakas questions.

"I know. But they also can't fight against five of you, a prince, and me," I say firmly.

Malakas hums.

"We'll pick up my mother and brother and then we'll escape to the wilderness, somewhere they can't catch us," I say.

Malakas hums again.

"I say we go. I don't want to be where the Quskaha isn't," Tuliikaarme says.

Cirianiel steps up, nodding his massive snout. "I say we go too. I don't want to be collared."

Malakas clicks his tongue.

"Ooh! Do I get a vote?" Dimonyaga chirps.

"No," Tuliikaarme, Cirianiel, and Malakas respond at the same time.

Dimonyaga's face falls, and he turns and plops on the ground next to Kirkaas who pats his shoulder.

"We cannot go without you, Malakas," Tuliikaarme says after a moment of silence.

Malakas huffs, smoke erupting from his nostrils.

"We cannot separate," Malakas agrees. Then his head comes down to me again. "You'd better find Kidlat very soon, then."

My heart sinks. I was afraid he was going to say that.

CHAPTER 45

Gabriel

"There's a dragon hidden beneath the castle, and they can't get out of the dungeons. The other dragons will come with us only if we release her. Her name is Kidlat," Alex says.

My eyes fall to her chest; the frantic thump-thump-thump of her heart is almost visible beneath her shirt. She notices my gaze and raises an eyebrow, lips pressing into a thin line before folding her arms across her chest.

"Can you blame me?" I tease, and she instantly turns red. Gods, I love the impact I have on her, even though she denies it so often. Putting on a more serious face, I say: "I think it's time we tell Griffin. He knows many of the ins and outs of this castle. He'll know where it is."

"You haven't told Griffin?" she asks, her eyebrows drawing together.

I look at her. "You're the most important part of this. If I couldn't get you to go, I'd stay."

She studies me for a moment, her eyes narrowed, like she doesn't believe what I'm doing. "You'd stay?" she repeats.

"Of course. I go where you go," I respond easily, her eyebrows narrowing even more. I laugh at her reaction. "I don't even know why you're surprised."

She continues to stare at me, her eyes narrow, her heart beating just as fast. When the door opens and Griffin enters, his reaction goes from carefree to confusion at Alex's expression.

"I wouldn't know," I say immediately to him, then turn to grin at her. "I told her the truth, but she doesn't like it."

"I-I…" she protests, only to huff and glare at me. Griffin chuckles, taking a seat in one of my chairs.

"So," he says, directing it to me. "Where are we going?"

"I thought you said you hadn't told him!" Alex protests. I smile.

Griffin shrugs. "He hasn't. I have no idea what we're talking about."

"Liar," Alex accuses, glaring at me.

I shoot her a look. "I didn't!"

Griffin laughs. "Arguing like a couple already. Alex, Gabe and I have been friends since we were what? Five years old? I've been waiting for the moment he'd stand up to his father. After you came into his life, this desire has only been getting stronger. I was wondering when he'd have the balls to leave," he explains to Alex. She crosses her arms again, shooting me death glares.

"I don't know where we're going yet, but we have to do something for the dragons first," I begin, sitting on the chair in front of him.

Griffin's eyes narrow. "Okay? What kind of thing?"

"We need to release the dragon we're hiding below the castle," I say.

"Wait--we have a dragon beneath the castle?" His eyes widen.

"Yes," I confirm, wincing at his reaction.

"Oh, damn." His lips lift on one side.

"I need to find a way to get there to help. Do any of you know any secret passages? No secret entrances? Hidden staircases? Dungeons? Random doors that don't open?" Alex asks.

"Okay, Inspector, relax," Griffin gives her a look.

She rolls her eyes in response. "I'm just trying to jog your memory," she protests.

"Let the man think, woman, stand down," I hiss at her, but playfully.

She sticks her tongue out at me. I laugh, realizing I haven't laughed this much in a day. Not only does she make me giggle, she's also not afraid to make me angry. Every single woman I've ever come across or dated has always been so terrified of saying something wrong, looking dumb, or looking weak. But this girl is an entirely different breed. A woman--someone who's strong, kind, could hold her own, never needing anyone. The kind I could live a life with because I know she'll tell me what she thinks. I know she won't hold back if I'm being a dick. She'll tell me what I'm doing wrong, and she'll be proud of it.

When I turn to Griffin, his eyes are on me. "What?" I say, smirking.

His smile brightens even more. "I haven't seen you this happy, Gabe. It looks good on you." His gaze turns to Alex. "You make him happier than I've ever seen him. Twenty years of being friends, Alex." She turns red, sneaking me a look. "His mother would be ecstatic to see him right now. He hasn't had a smile like that in years."

I pat his shoulder. "So, are you going to help us or what?" I gaze at Alex, who's looking anywhere but at me.

Griffin smiles slyly. "So…I don't know of any secret entrances or secret passages…but…" he pauses dramatically.

"But?" Alex demands. Griffin ignores her, but turns to me.

"Do you remember when we'd go down to the lake?" he says, a wide smile on his face.

I smack my forehead. "Holy shit!" The memories flash back.

Griffin turns to Alex. "When we were young, we used to go down to the lake all the time. There's a direct path to the lake from the kitchen area, and we used to always take that path. Down those stairs is an entirely separate dungeon. It isn't used today."

"So?" Alex asks doubtfully. "How do you know it leads to a dragon? I mean, let's be honest, their size isn't exactly like normal humans, so I highly doubt a dungeon would fit them."

Griffin laughs. "Oh, you little troublemaker," he starts, garnering a scowl from Alex. "That's what you get for not exploring more."

"You mean not accidentally getting into a dungeon with a dragon who could blow fire on me? Yes, because we've proven I'm fire resistant," she responds sarcastically.

Griffin laughs even harder. "Those dungeons opened into a bigger one with an open wall out onto the lake. How do you think they got the dragon in? There needs to be an opening large enough to trick a dragon inside."

She frowns.

"Anyway," he continues, looking at me. "I remember exactly where it is. But most importantly, I remember how to get through the open wall."

Now it's my turn to frown. "How?"

"We're going to rappel."

CHAPTER 46

Gabriel

"Are you sure you're not taking me somewhere to kill me?" Alex whines as we hike down the cliff to the edge of the old dungeons. According to Griffin, the best time to go down is during sundown, so we can catch the sunset and have a little adventure. The cliffs on this side of the island are jagged and unstable, losing bits and pieces of land to the lake every year during the monsoon season. I huff, wondering if a little adventure is really what we should be chasing right now. Hadn't we had enough excitement? When was it all going to end?

I laugh. "If you want me to carry you, all you had to do is ask."

Her cheeks burn, and she narrows her eyes at me. "Get your head out of the gutter, Prince; not everything is about you," she snaps just as quickly.

"I'd do it, you know, I'd carry you down, Sparky, just say the word," I say to her.

She slips on the screen, juggling her balance, before careening directly into my chest. She plants her hands there, and I hold on to her shoulders, grinning at her.

"If you want to touch me, all you have to do is ask," I add with a smile.

Her glare grows, and she pushes me away. "I can do it," she says stubbornly, ignoring me and proceeding to go down a few more rocks.

"That's my girl," I say cheekily, knowing I'd get a rise out of her. Ever since I'd confessed everything to her, everything has felt a little more open between us, except she doesn't seem to believe that it's just her. She's a little shyer. At night, she sleeps in my arms, and I promised myself I wouldn't take advantage. Never with her. I'll wait until she's ready, but it has to be completely her decision.

Alex turns to me, pausing in her tracks and narrowing her eyes. "I'm not your girl," she hisses.

"Sure felt like it last night," I quip, and her face turns bright red.

"Mom, Dad, can you both stop fighting? I'd really like to get us to where we're going in one piece," Griffin teases, and then he pauses, his hands on his hips in front of us.

"Take it up with the prince; I don't think he got enough milk this morning," she snaps.

Griffin gives me a look, and I can't help but start laughing again. "Fine, fine, I'll behave," I say, catching the warning in his eyes. "You're no fun." I scowl.

Alex turns back to me, shaking her head. "You're such a child," she says bemused.

Griffin chuckles. "He's only that way with you, trouble."

She groans. "Not you, too. Is Alex not enough? You guys have to conjure up some other names to make me seem more interesting?"

"Of course not. It's just fun, Sparky," I add, finally catching up to her. She glares at me, her dark eyes filtering out the sunset. Sweat beads down her forehead, and her breaths are labored from the hike. She's wearing tight black pants that only reach below her knees, showing the scars of her recent burn. Her white tank top is thin, and I glance at it periodically to glimpse the black sports bra showing clearly from beneath the material. Her hair's in a messy bun above her head, but tendrils of hair fall across her face. I don't think she realizes how gorgeous she looks at the moment. The setting sun peeks over the horizon, its orange and pink hues exploding through the sky. I'd give anything to see her like this every day for my entire life. If she'd let me.

"Look," I say, pointing behind her to where the sun's getting ready to set. She turns quickly, and I step up beside her.

"Beautiful," she breathes.

"Not as beautiful as you," I can't help saying. Red rises in her cheeks.

"Why do you say things like that, Prince?" she asks, looking up at me.

I tilt my head, confused. "Why wouldn't I if it's true?" I respond.

A grimace takes over her face. "But I'm no one. I'm not royalty; I'm not anyone. I was a handmaid. Why start something you know you can't continue?" she asks.

I smirk a little. "One, you're not a handmaid. Not anymore. Two, who says we can't start something? We're about to escape from this kingdom, so anything can happen," I remind her.

She frowns as she turns to follow Griffin, who's quite a bit ahead of us.

"You're so confusing, you know. You don't even know me," she mutters.

"What's so confusing about me, Sparky?" I ask, eyes narrowing.

"Well, you're a prince. You're going to inherit a kingdom. You're sacrificing it for someone you barely know," she says.

"Then tell me more about you," I say.

She chuckles. "That's it?"

"I mean––we're just getting to know each other, Sparky." I shrug, following her as I look throughout the lake. They're gorgeous at this time of day.

She stops, then directs her full attention to me. "I spent twenty-four years as my mother's apprentice. I don't have experience with anything. I've never traveled, never gone anywhere, because I was always taking care of my mother and my brother. I don't have friends because I was always too busy doing chores, making my mother's concoctions, helping to take care of my brother. I don't know how to make friends."

"Well, that's simply not true. Katya is your friend, isn't she? Griffin certainly is—and so am I," I say, crossing my eyebrows. "That's three friends. Not including your dragons."

She frowns, huffing a breath. "I'm not well-traveled. I'm not royal material; I can't speak other languages. I talk to animals, for god's sake. I'm basically crazy to most people. I'm fucking brown." She points to her skin.

I laugh. "None of that deters me, you know. I wish you could see what I see."

"What do you see?" She frowns, looking really quickly as Griffin, who was scaling over the cliff, searching for something.

I reach out to her face, tracing her jaw with a soft touch. "I see a woman who was forced to be here so she can help her family. A woman who, despite the things my family forced her to do, had the grace to make sure I was safe and okay, even if it meant sacrificing her freedom. I see a woman who would do anything to protect her dragons, even if it meant sacrificing comfort and life. I see someone who's so passionate about what's right and wrong that she doesn't see the king with the crown willing to kill her for what he wants, a woman so kind that she'll share her food, share her salve with people who need it. Someone who doesn't judge me for the way I am--even if my father forces you to think otherwise." I pause, cupping her face in my hands. "I see a woman so beautiful and so strong, so unafraid to tell me what she thinks; it's damn sexy."

Her eyes glisten in the sunset light. "I see the king, you know. I figured I'm going to die anyway, so what does it matter if I stand up to him?"

"Everything, Sparky. Everything. You're brave and passionate, and that's what makes you different from everyone else. You don't allow anyone to step on what you believe is right—not me, not the king. And despite what you say, I think that's the only royal material that matters."

She studies me carefully, and steps up, drawing her hand closer to my face. The expression on her face softens, and her eyes drop to my lips. My heart skips a beat.

"Hey! Gabe, can you help?" Griffin calls from a few feet away.

I look up, momentarily pissed that Griffin was breaking our moment, only to realize he's sitting at the edge of the cliff. "Jeez, Griff, do you want to die or something?" I rush to help him.

"Well, you guys were so into your conversation I felt I needed to take the time to actually figure out where we're going to make our drop tomorrow night," he says, rolling his eyes. "It took a minute, but it's down there," he adds, pointing below him. "There's a ledge up there where I set up the ropes."

"Wait, you want me to go down that cliff from there?" Alex's mouth drops as she leans over to see the ledge. "Like go down there, then use a rope to go down?" Her frown is palpable.

"Yes," Griffin states plainly, a smirk drawing on his face.

"No," Alex says. "No, are you serious? You really are trying to kill me."

He gives her an indulgent smile. "I'll be right there, Sparky. We'll both be there," I tell her. "You've been on the back of a dragon spinning around in the air and you're afraid of this?" I remind her, laughing.

She glares at me. "I trust those dragons!"

"You don't trust us?" Griffin says, sounding hurt. "Ouch," he mocks a pained expression with his hands on his heart, his lips in a pout.

She turns her glare onto him. "I don't trust that ledge. I don't trust the rope."

"Well, trust me," Griffin says, looking her in the eyes. "Trust me. I'll get us down there tomorrow safe and sound. Besides, we used to do this as kids," he adds at the end.

Her eyes widen. "That's what I'm afraid of!" she says, half chuckling. "You did this as kids, and I'm fairly certain this was not a good idea."

Griffin laughs. "It was a great idea," he says, winking at me. "Be ready tomorrow night. Bring a backpack with food and water. We'll need it."

CHAPTER 47

Alex

"What kind of food do you think we need?" the prince asks as we raid their kitchen in the middle of the night.

What do I know? I've never lived on the run. "I don't know, honestly. Maybe things we can cook? Things we can eat, especially in the first couple of days." I shrug.

"Fine," he grumbles, picking up bread, pastries, and cookies on the table.

I frown. "Maybe things a bit more substantial?"

"We'll need to learn how to hunt," he says aloud, not necessarily to me. "I'll get Griffin to bring weapons, too. We'll also need to find food for the dragons."

I turn to the prince. "Do you have gold?"

"Lots of it, why?" he responds.

"We need to bring it. If we're taking sheep from farmers out there, we need to compensate them," I say.

His face changes for a moment, and he gives me one of those looks that make me feel like I'm the only girl in the world. Like everything about me is so beautiful he can barely stand it.

"You're so smart, it's sexy," he teases.

I turn crimson, turning away. The door to the kitchen opens, and we momentarily freeze, only for Griffin to come in holding a pack. "We'll need matches, lots of them, in case we get cold," he says.

He turns to the prince and me. "Bring a heavy coat in case we get cold. Don't bring too many clothes, as we'll need more food and we can only carry so much." He opens one of the cabinet doors. "And we'll need some medical supplies in case any of us get hurt," he adds.

The prince and I look at each other. "We could get some of the supplies from my mother," I offer. "We'd probably need to ask the healer for some."

Griffin packs canned food into his bag, throwing a few to the prince and me for our bags. "It's not going to be pretty or easy the next few weeks," he warns.

"Why do I feel like you've planned this?" I ask, my eyebrows meeting.

He laughs. "It's part of training. How do you survive if you're at war and you have to stay fed and healthy? I did this training when I was maybe ten years old, and then again just a few years ago. Everyone needs to have some kind of survival training—who knows when war comes?" He winks at me, and I roll my eyes.

"I'm not allowed to join training outside of the castle." The prince shrugs. "Griffin always has all the fun without me."

Griffin laughs again, his laughter echoing throughout the kitchen. "So much," he comments mockingly. "I've got a tent in case we need it, but we'll probably have to use our body heat and coats as beds for a while."

I give them a wry look. "Yay," I add sarcastically.

"Yay for me," the prince says.

"We'll need to make sure you pack some good clothes, trouble, like actually good clothes." Griffin directs the comment to me.

"Oh, you mean, from the clothes you didn't allow me to bring?" I add dryly.

"No, from the clothes the palace gave you, obviously," Griffin responds quickly, mimicking her panicked look. "I highly doubt you had clothes suitable for the castle."

"Fine," I mumble, scowling.

Griffin passes a few more water bottles to us. "This should be most of your weight. We'll hunt and get food. I'll grab us bows, arrows, and swords."

"Like the vacation I always dreamed of," I mutter under my breath.

The prince rolls his eyes, dropping a few more bottles in my bag. His gaze turns to Griffin, who's still ransacking the kitchen. "See you tomorrow?"

He hums, barely acknowledging us. The prince pulls me out of the kitchen, grabbing my bag so he can carry it upstairs. I protest, pulling back the bag.

"You'll have plenty of time to do that, Sparky," the prince says, yanking the bag from me.

I say nothing and just followed him to our room. He drops the bags by the door. "I'll have Griffin take this to the ledge tomorrow morning, so you don't have to carry it."

"I can carry it," I offer, frowning.

"No. My father will be keeping his eye on you. We'll have to pretend it's a regular day, and you can't be seen with a bag." He shakes his head. "We'll need to grab a few clothes for you."

"Prince…" I say, hesitating a little.

"Yeah?" he responds, moving to the closet to look at my clothes.

"What if this isn't the right way to go about it?" I ask in a low voice.

He turns to me, sighing.

"I don't know what the right path is, Sparky. I just know I won't be able to control my father. I can't stand you getting hurt, and we'd never allow the dragons to get hurt. If that means we're out in the wilderness a bit, I'm okay with that," he tells me, pushing a strand of my hair behind my ear. "As long as I'm with you, I'll be alright," he adds, before turning back to the closet. He grabs a few of my clothes, including a warm coat, and stacks them into his bag.

"What about clothes that you need?" I ask, watching him fill up his bag. He looks back at me. "All I need is you," he says, turning me around and pushing me into the bathroom to get dressed and ready for bed.

"Pretty words," I mumble before closing the bathroom. When I get out, I see he's also gotten dressed in grey sweatpants and a white t-shirt before getting ready for bed. He slips into bed from one side, pulling the blankets over him. I climb in next to him.

"What happens if this isn't the right path?" I whisper.

He slips his arm across the bed, pulling my body to his so that his arm sat across my stomach.

"Then we figure it out together," he murmurs into my ear.

"Aren't you worried about losing your kingdom?" I ask quietly, running a finger across his wrist that wrapped around my stomach.

"I am. But I think if this is the way my father is heading, I've already lost it. I don't have enough power. I need to get more power, more support if I want to throw him," he whispers, planting a soft kiss on the side of my ear.

Then, just before his breath stabilizes and quiets, he adds: "It's you I don't want to lose."

CHAPTER 48

Alex

I sneak out of the castle around sundown, carrying my bag and the prince's bag. I haven't seen him since he left the bedroom during a call with his father. I hike down the cliff, being extra careful with all the scree in the area. I've always hated scree; it's one of the most annoying things, especially when you're dragging water from one place to another. This time, going down a cliff where one step earns you a one-way ticket to the lake, or maybe even death, I'm not a fan. I look to where the sun's setting, where the prince and I had our conversation the other day. The sun is much lower than where it had been that day, but it was just as beautiful. A tall figure climbs up the ledge, and I sigh deeply when I see Griffin.

"Have you seen Gabriel?" he asks, his eyes narrowing.

My heart pounds. "I-I last saw him this morning, but not since. I have his bag," I say, lifting the other heavy bag. "He was supposed to have you bring them both down in the morning."

"Shit," Griffin swears, putting his hands on his hips. He turns to me, his brows creased.

"Griffin, what's going on?" I ask cautiously. "Is the prince okay?"

He shakes his head. "I sure fucking hope so. Okay, this was not how I imagined this, but I need you to bear with me, okay?" he says to me. I nod. "You need to go down there and convince the dragon to come with us. I'll go get Gabriel. Did you tell the dragons we're leaving tonight?"

I nod. "Where is he, Griffin?" I ask.

"I have an idea. Let me get you set up so I can bring the bags down and help you down," he grabs my shoulders, looking at me gravely. "If we're not down there within an hour, trouble, you need to go."

"What? No, I'm not leaving him-uh-you. I'm not leaving you both!" I say, my eyes widening. "No, I'm supposed to be on the run with you. I can't do this alone!"

Griffin's eyes softened. "You can do anything you want, trouble. Gabriel knows this, and so do you. So do I." Griffin bends down to meet my eyes. I feel his breath; I feel the heat of his skin. Goosebumps rise along my spine. His eyes wander my face, as if it's slowly studying me, memorizing my features. My heart pounds in my chest. I swallow hard, my brain freezing for a moment, unable to decide what to do.

Luckily, he decides for me. With a swallow, he turns, climbing onto the ledge, then ties the bag onto the rope, grabbing the other side to use it like a pulley. When it's my turn, he gently turns me around, his hands warm on my back, quickly tying a harness around my body and legs before attaching me to the rope. He says nothing nor did I know what to say.

"So how do I do this?" I ask nervously after a while.

"You've never rappelled?" he asks incredulously.

I sigh heavily, a retort already on my lips. "Yes, Griffin, because this is a normal activity," I retort, an unimpressed smile on my face. He laughs.

"What do you mean? Everything we do is normal," he adds, a smirk on his face.

"I'm not going to go without Gabriel, Griff," I say seriously.

He nods, a grave look replacing the smirk. "I know, trouble. I'll find him." Then, he attaches one side of the rope to my harness. "This is you," he says, pointing to that side of the rope. "The other side of the rope is a pulley. Give a little, and you drop a little. You can use the cave walls to anchor yourself."

"If we ever survive this whole ordeal, Griffin, I will murder you myself." She glares at me as she lowers herself.

"Nothing like a little rappelling, Quskaha," Griffin yells at me from above. "You know, in comparison with flying a dragon."

"I'm going to ask the dragons to turn you into ashes," I warn him, only partially kidding. A loud scream escapes my lips when I accidentally give a little too much, and I plummet unexpectedly, faster than I want, my heart leaping into my throat as I fall. I pull the other side of the rope as quickly as I can, trying to stop myself from falling too fast.

"That's karma," Griffin yells.

"Dick," I mutter under my breath.

"Trouble, remember, an hour, okay? Don't let yourself get caught," he says from above.

"Find him, Griff," I yell back, my own voice echoing at me. A skittering and then it falls quiet. I look around me. On one side, an open wall faces the lake, the water darkening with the approaching sunset, and the air growing cooler. The sound of slow rushing water fills the cave. The other side boasts a cave wall arching carefully to one side, small stalactites hanging from the ceiling, creating an opening to somewhere. It's mostly dark, lit only by a tiny fire from the side of the cave. I grab my pack, opening it to pull out a match. Griffin will kill me, but I'm not prepared to walk into a caged dragon, only to find myself on fire. I've learned from experience that burns aren't fun. I pull the match, light it, walking ever so slowly through the opening of the cave. I spot a dead torch on the ground and light it up with my match fire. Once the fire takes, I blow the flames from the match and throw it aside.

"Kidlat?" I say before entering the cave. Darkness would have fully surrounded me had it not been for the torch in my hand. "Kidlat?" I repeat.

A soft growl responds to my call, and I walk toward it slowly. "Kidlat? Malakas sent me."

The growl grows as I near it, and with the help of my torch, at the end of the cave, I gasp at the sight of a dragon tied up by its hands and legs by metal chains. The dragon is a beautiful orange color with gold horns. It had lots of wounds and looks weary.

"You're a Quskaha," the dragon says softly.

"I am. Alex," I introduce myself as I approach slowly.

"A little stupid of you to come here without food, Quskaha. Have you forgotten what dragons eat?" the dragon says.

I frown. "I'm not here to visit, Kidlat. I'm here to let you out," I say.

The dragon looks up carefully. "What did you say?"

"I'm here to let you out, Kidlat. Malakas, Tuliikaarme, and Cirianiel, the younger dragons and I are going to escape this kingdom," I tell him.

The dragon roars with laughter. "You think you can escape this kingdom?"

"We'll protect each other," I add, folding my arms.

"Malakas agreed to this?" he asks.

I nod.

The dragon settles weakly on the ground. "I must've been gone for years. He must be going crazy," the dragon whispers.

"Three-thousand and forty-one years," I respond, remembering the books, how one of them disappeared randomly.

"Yes," the dragon says miserably.

"Have you been here all this time?" I ask.

"No, I've been moved multiple times, but I don't get enough food to function properly," Kidlat responds.

"Kidlat, if we leave this place, we can figure out what to do. We can find a way to overthrow the king. I promise to always protect you and make sure our kind never controls you," I promise.

He swallows and nods hard. "Have you ever heard my story, Quskaha? How they trapped me?" Kidlat asks, a little life coming back to his face.

"No, but I want to hear it," I say, looking behind me to see if Griffin and Gabriel had arrived.

"Do you? Are you sure you know what your kind can do?" Kidlat asks, his eyes boring into mine.

"I'm sorry, Kidlat. I know you don't deserve it," I blurt out.

The dragon crosses its eyes, looking even more pissed. "Your kind took my baby. That's how they got me in here," it roars. "They kidnapped my baby, and tortured it until I agreed to be trapped, until I agreed to stop burning their kind. That's how your kind got control over me."

Kidlat steps forward, writhing through its chains. Tears pool in my eyes, threatening to fall.

"I'm so sorry, Kidlat, I'm so sorry. For the rest of my life, I promise I will work to make sure that never happens again. I'm so sorry. Nothing I can say will ever be enough to make that better. But I will spend the rest of my life fighting for you, I promise that," I say, facing the dragon as I sit on my knees.

The dragon hums.

"Lies. The many, many lies humans have told to get what they want," the dragon roars.

"I'm not lying, Kidlat. I've been doing tasks above to show my worth to the king. The last task requires me to put a collar on your friends, Malakas, Cirianiel, Tuliikaarme, even the younger ones. Once I put that collar on them, the king can control you, no matter what. They will kill me. I will give my head before any of that happens, I promise you," I explain, desperate for her understanding.

Suddenly, I hear a noise behind me, and I look back. Griffin walks to me, the prince slumped against him, one arm around his shoulder.

"Prince," I breathe, once again seeing the many bruises and cuts on his face and body.

"He's fine; he just needs to rest, but we need to go. Is the dragon ready?" Griffin asks, looking to the end of the cave where the dragon still sits with chains at its limbs.

"Ohh, what a gift, Quskaha. The heir to the family who did this to me," Kidlat says, life completely taking over its weary body. It pulls the chain with grace, taking it out of the wall. After pulling it again, he rips the chains off its legs completely. He growls, and my eyes widen as I step in front of the prince and Griffin.

"Please, not them. Not him," I plead. "He had no idea about you until recently. Please. The prince has nothing to do with the family that did this to you. He wants to make it better for you, eventually. He's on our side," I claim, stretching to put my body in front of them. "Please, Kidlat."

The dragon shoots me a look. "A Quskaha protecting a prince. Of course."

"Please, he protected me throughout the challenges. He's not the problem, but we'll happily make sure we get the real problem out of here," I plead.

"Why don't I just blow this entire place up, Quskaha?" Kidat threatens.

"Please don't. We can't just do that, there are hundreds in this castle who don't deserve this. Please. Please trust me," I continue pleading, ignoring the sound of the prince behind me.

Kidlat takes a hesitant step, his eyes narrowed, but I quickly put my hands up, shielding the unconscious prince with my body.

"Please, not them. They've been my rock, my protectors, my everything, Kidlat, please. Even Malakas, Tuliikaarme, and Cirianiel have met them. You can trust them. Please,

Kidlat, I swear I will give me life to protect you, I swear on everything I know and love," I plead.

"You say their names like you're worthy of saying them," Kidlat spits out.

"They told me their names, and they allowed me to call them by their nicknames. I swear, I didn't call Cirianiel until he told me while we were flying," I explain. "They're coming with us. They've agreed to go as long as I release you and take you with us. Please. You are our signal. You are the reason we have to go, because of what they did to you," I continue.

"They gave you their nickname?" Kidlat asks, stepping back, his body rocking with wear.

"Yes, I've met Dimonyaga and Kirkaas, the children," I say.

"There are children?" Kidlat repeats.

"Yes! They're both really good, really great dragons," I plead, my heart stopping as something or someone bangs on the door of the cave. "We have to go, Kidlat. Please."

Kidlat takes off through the opening, and for a moment I think it'll leave us. Instead, it stops, lowering its head and claws. "Climb now!"

I help Griffin take Gabriel up the dragon, placing myself in front of Gabriel so he has something to lean on if needed.

"Go!" I yell to Kidlat once we're all on the back of his neck. "Hold on tight!" I say to Griffin as Gabriel's arms close around my body.

Kidlat wiggles its back and legs, hitting every wall until it makes it out the opening. It jumps into the lake, barely making it out, its feet touching the water, its wings flapping unevenly around us to keep us afloat.

"Higher, Kidlat!" I yell.

"Just a moment," Kidlat yells as it swirls back to the entrance.

"No, no!" I yell, but I was too late.

Kidlat stops before the entrance, rearing its head back and with a single blow, a singular flow of flames enters the cave, burning it and everything around it.

"Now we can go," Kidlat roars, its wings flapping slowly to take us to a height.

The prince's arms wrap around me even tighter, and I touch his arms, a sigh of relief escaping my mouth.

"I knew you could't get enough of me," he whispers weakly, his chin settling on my shoulder.

A smile breaks out on my face. Then I point. "Look."

Across the horizon are my other friends: Malakas, Cirianiel, Tuliikaarme, Kirkaas, and Dimonyaga, flapping their wings, creating a good wind around us.

"Beautiful," the prince murmurs, his hold tightening around me.

"Hold on to me," I say.

"Always," he whispers.

CHAPTER 49

Alex

"Are you okay?" I ask the prince as we fly higher and higher.

"We'll need to drop soon," Kidlat says suddenly.

"Wait, why?" I ask, eyes widening.

"I need to eat, and you need to transfer to someone stronger than me. I'm actually feeling pretty weak now. It was only my anger that got me through those chains," Kidlat says.

"I'll take him to eat and join you at your mother's place," Cirianiel offers just to our left.

"I'll take you," Malakas says. "Over there!" He points with his claw to an empty field, far away from the castle.

When we make the switch, Tuliikaarme will take Griffin, and the prince and I will hop on Malakas.

"Are you okay?" I ask again once we make it up high again. His arms tighten around me, his legs gripping my butt along with Malakas' ridges. I feel the soft kiss of his lips on my temple.

"I am now," he whispers.

"What happened?" I ask.

"Oh, you know, just some minor father issues. He found out about what we did to Finn and wanted to make sure I knew who was boss," the prince says, his eyes looking out at the horizon.

"Are you worried about your future?" I ask, squeezing the hand across my stomach.

He smiles. "I'm not worried, Sparky. I'm with you."

A smile crosses my face. One of freedom, one of love, as we fly higher and higher into the dark sky. "This is fantastic," he whispers weakly into my ear.

"It's crazy, isn't it? Getting to fly this high?" I agree.

"You're amazing," he responds.

"Pretty words, prince," I say, but I relish the feeling of his arms around me, the way he smiled, everything he's said. When I pull at his arm and kiss the back of his hand, he kisses my neck.

"Am I yours yet, Sparky?" he whispers.

"Maybe when you call me Alex," I tease.

"Alex," he breathes. "Alex," he repeats. Then he spreads his arms out, yelling, "Alex!"

Malakas huffs. "Tell your partner to shut up, Quskaha," he says grumpily.

I laugh. I don't know if I'll ever have a moment like this. So, I hold on to it. I put it in my pocket for safekeeping. For protection in the future. For happiness. When I see Fortuna come into view, we lower our bodies until I see my little patch of space. The patch of life I'd grown up with. The patch of life I'll need to let go of. We land around the house with a massive thud. I slide off Malakas, nudging his snout affectionately.

My head spins, and my stomach churns from the mix of familiarity and the knowledge that everything has changed.

"There's sheep that way. Take some, not all, please," I remind him.

Malakas huffs. "Please. We're great hunters."

I scoff, helping the prince get down his claws.

"You okay?" I ask.

"Yo, that was pretty fucking amazing," Griffin exclaims as Tuliikaarme lands next to us. "What a thrill! Alex, can you tell this dragon she's amazing?"

Malakas huffs at me again, a mist of smoke exiting her nostrils. "Tell your dumb-witted friend that we can understand. It's just them that don't."

"She understands you, Griff," I call out, smiling. Griffin slides off Tuliikaarme, but he gives her a big smile, kissing her snout.

"I see the appeal, Quskaha," Tuliikaarme says approvingly. "This one has joy."

"That he does," I laugh, wrapping the prince's arms around me so I can help him walk. "Come on, I'll introduce you to my mother, then we can raid her concoctions for your wounds."

"I knew you liked me enough to pursue things. I guess we're meeting the mother, huh?" the prince jokes, winking.

"I'd jab you, but I think you'd fall," I hiss, rolling my eyes.

"I'd jab you," he responds with a chuckle. My face turns red at the thought.

Griffin laughs. "Gods, you guys, just have sex already!"

My jaw drops. "We are not! Say that again, and I'll drop you," I protest, my face heating so much I can practically feel it.

"Please don't," the prince groans, and Griffin takes his other arm.

"Did you tell your mother we're coming, trouble?" Griffin asks.

"Yes, because I can send mail," I roll my eyes. "This was supposed to be a secret, remember?"

"Well, I don't think it's much of one anymore," Griffin says gravely. "I saw the soldiers gearing up. They'll be here in hours, I suspect."

I focus on the little house that I used to live in instead. Closer. Closer. I'm going to see Angus soon! When we make it, I drop the prince with a groan, racing into the house.

"Mother!" I call. "Angus?"

My mother pokes her head out of the bedroom. "Alexandra?"

Griffin and Gabriel look at each other. "Alexandra?" Griffin mouths.

"Shut up," I snarl, before my face breaks into a massive smile and I run from the kitchen to her bedroom, tackling her to the bed.

"Mother!" I cry. My mother's arms wrap around me weakly.

"Oh, Alex, what are you doing here?" she asks, frowning.

"We've come to take you and Angus away from here, Mother. It's a long story, but we're escaping this kingdom," I say, pointing to the two men behind me.

"I don't understand," she says, coughing as she swings her feet slowly across the bed.

"Mother, I'm a Quskaha, someone who can talk to dragons. The king is threatening us, so we escaped the palace," I try, but how was I supposed to explain my last months in fifteen minutes?

"Oh, Alex, I'm so glad you're well. Would you like some dinner? I made some food this morning," she asks.

"Mother…" I open my mouth, but Griffin shoots me a look.

"Okay, Mother. Let me go heat it up, and we can have dinner, okay?" I say, patting her back. Then, I step back a little to show the two men. "That one is Prince Gabriel, and the other one is Griffin."

My mother smiles wide, slowly walking to the table before she sits in a chair. I move to the kitchen, finding the meal she'd made this morning and heat up the stove to warm it up.

"Are you hungry?" I ask Griffin and Gabriel.

"You know, at this point, we'll take all the food we can get," Griffin says.

I grab plates, start to pile the food on the table, then pull a chair out for the prince. "You can sit, you know; it's not poison."

"Alexandra!" my mother instantly scolds. "I'm sorry, Prince Gabriel, I taught her better than that."

I roll my eyes, turning to go back to the kitchen.

"Don't worry, that's what I like most about her," the prince says to my mother.

My mother's eyes widen. "You like her." Not a question, not a guess. A statement.

"Yes, yes, I do. I'll take care of her, I promise," the prince says.

"No returns?" my mother jokes.

"Mother," I hiss from the kitchen.

But the prince responds. "Never." I turn, facing the stove to hide the redness creeping up my cheeks. I hand out plates of food to each person before I join the table, sitting between my mother and the prince.

"He's pretty enamored of you, isn't he? What a beautiful man," my mother whispers to me, rendering my cheeks permanently red this time.

"You raised a wonderful woman," the prince says, sneaking a look at me.

My mother looks at him for a moment. "You're hurt, Prince Gabriel," she says.

"It's okay, we can treat it after dinner," the prince acknowledges.

My mother stares at him. "Who'd hurt you, son?" she asks, frowning.

"Mother, let him eat," I say, putting a hand on hers. "I've missed you."

"Oh, honey, I'm so happy you're living a life!" she says, then turns back to Griffin and the prince. "When she was here, all she did was take care of me. No friends, no life outside of that. I'm so grateful she has you," my mother says, reaching out a hand to the prince.

"Ouch, Mother," I mumble.

"But look at how beautiful you are right now! You're so beautiful, so strong. You are more than I could ever have given, Alexandra," my mother says, patting my cheeks. "You would never have made it out if you weren't forced to. And look at you!"

My cheeks burn bright red. "Thanks, Mother. Now, will you come with us?" I ask, changing the subject. How else could I ask without sounding lazy?

"Come with you where?" she asks.

"To run away, Mother. Run away with us. We have the dragons, so we'll be invincible," I respond.

"Oh, sweetheart." She takes me in her arms. Then, when she turns, the emotions drop from her face. "Eat, eat! I'm so glad you made it here to see me."

I frown, but I do what she says, and I finish my plate.

"Honey, can you take the dishes to the sink? I want to talk to the boys for a bit," she says.

My eyebrows knit, but I do it, bringing the plate to the kitchen and washing it out.

When I wipe my hands dry, I turn to see Griffin placing bottles of concoctions into his bag while my mother spreads a salve across the prince's body. She's saying something about how the salve was going to heal him faster.

"What is it, Mother?" I ask, sitting down beside her as she pats the salve along his back.

She finishes without saying anything, then the prince puts his shirt on.

"It was really nice meeting you, Anna. We'll take care of her," the prince promises as he and Griffin walk off with their bags. When I look up, the cabinet filled with concoctions and syrups and salves is empty.

"Mother! You didn't need to give us so much!" I point to the cabinet.

"It'll be useless here," she says gravely. "I need to tell you something, my love."

"What is it, Mother?" I ask, frowning.

"The palace took your brother," she says.

"Wait, *what*?" I croak.

"They took your brother a few weeks ago, and I don't know why," she repeats. "But honey, do not go after them right now. They have all the leverage and know you will come find him even though you are not ready."

"But they will kill him!" I protest.

"Maybe," My mother shrugs, "but they need him as leverage for you. They know you will come for him. What I'm saying is--wait until you're ready. Then you can take them, do you understand?"

I nod, tears filling my eyes.

"Do you understand, my love? You're not ready. Your brother is smart and cunning. He'll be alright. You need to do what you are meant to do," my mother says, squeezing my hands.

"Wait--what I'm meant to do?" I repeat. "Mother, what do you know?"

"Oh, honey, that's not what matters right now. What matters is that you're safe, do you understand?" she asks.

I nod, my chest squeezing. "Yes, Mother. But what about you?" I return the question. She pulls me into her chest, hugging me tightly.

"Oh, honey. You know I can't come with you. You know I'm sick, and I'll just slow you down. There's nothing for me to do there. All I have is you and your brother." She watches me carefully.

Desperation and urgency seep from my words. "Mother, they will kill you. Soldiers are on their way here right now," I decide to be blunt to at least make sure I've been clear and kept them safe.

"I know, my love. I know. That's why you have to kill me," she finishes.

The blood turns to ice in my veins, and everything sounds like it's underwater. My jaw drops. "Are you nuts? I won't kill you! What the hell are you talking about?" I rise from the seat, my eyebrows as knotted as the worry crawling all over my heart.

"Sweetheart, I'm only a liability. I've lived a wonderful life. I have two fabulous children. There's nothing for me anymore. You can ask your dragons," she adds slowly at the end.

Tears fill my eyes. "Mother, no, no, I can't do that to you!"

"Remember to let the animals out so they can run for safety, okay?" she continues.

"No, Mother, I'm-I'm-I'm not going to do that!" I protest fiercely, standing up. "I won't let them kill you, Mother. I'll kill them myself."

"Sweetheart, if they take me, they'll punish me to torture you. They'll take me, and they'll hurt me even more. Please do me the kindness of making it easier for me, honey. I've been in pain for so long. Only you can do this," she begs.

My eyes turn from hurt to angry. "You're giving up on us!" I declare.

"No, honey, I've met my purpose in this life. You," she says gently.

"No, Mother. No. I won't kill you," I vow, disbelief wrapping itself around me. How had it all come to this?

"Yes, yes, you can," my mother responds.

"I cannot do that, Mother. Please, please don't ask me to do that, not me, not anyone else," I beg, tears streaming down my face. My breaths come in shallow gasps.

"You can." She looks me in the eye, those beautiful dark eyes that I've grown up seeing. "My wonderful Quskaha.

You are more than what I asked for." She cups my face with her frail fingers, leaning her forehead to mine.

"Please, Mother, please, don't make me do this," I protest as two arms surround my waist. "Please," I plead, my vision blurry.

"I love you, my daughter. I love you so much. You're the gift I never asked for," my mother says, kissing my forehead before the arms behind me pull me away.

"Fly. Fly, my daughter."

CHAPTER 50

Gabriel

"No!" Alex yells, resisting my pull. "No! Mother, no! I won't leave you! I'll never leave you!"

But Anne Mauricio nods, and I pull Alex back further. She screams in my arms, writhing away as I lead her out of the house, grabbing her waist as I drag her back to the dragons. Tears stream down her face as she stumbles, turning back every few steps to run back toward her mother.

"We have to go," Griffin says behind me. "The soldiers are coming."

Suddenly, Alex stops writhing in my grip. "Wait," she says, her eyes widening. "I have to let the animals out." She races back toward the farm and enters the chicken coop. I watch as she picks up each chicken, kissing them on the head before she races them out of the chicken run.

"Go, Chris! Go, Virginia, go as far away as you can!" she yells as each chicken clucks away. Then she turns, moving toward the barn, and I help her push the door open.

"Sweetie, you gotta go, baby, you gotta go. Run for me, okay?" Alex says to the black and white cow, her tears now pouring down her cheeks. The cow does what she asks and runs out of the barn and into the woods. Alex then wakes the only horse in the stable and releases it.

"Run, Wayne. Run, Wayne!" she yells after the horse. The horse neighs, running into the woods after the cow. Finally, Alex moves towards a section in the back of the barn and bends to her knees. When I approach her, she turns, and a massive grey, white, and orange cat climbs onto the back of her neck.

"This is Mouse," she says, introducing me to the cat. "That's the prince."

She takes one last look at the barn, then with a final turn, Alex walks back to the dragons. I catch up to her, taking her hand in mine.

"Let's go," I say.

"Not dinner," Alex responds to something Malakas says. She climbs up Malakas' claw, and I follow, sitting between a spike on his neck. Griffin does the same.

"Ready?" I call.

"Let's go," Alex says darkly, and I know she's thinking about her mother.

Malakas kicks off his hind legs, reaching the air before any other dragon. Alex grabs her cat, settling him in her bag. "Stay," she orders.

Malakas circles the air, and I see the traces of yellow lightning further out.

"The soldiers," I whisper to Alex. Her shudder is visible from where I sit, so I wrap my arms around her, tightening around her shoulders.

"Do it," she says to Malakas. "Burn it," her voice cracks at the end. Malakas speeds up, reaching the top of the house. When he rears his head back, his wings tucking into his body, I feel the heat of his fire spread throughout his body and come out his mouth. A massive circle of fire, crackling and spitting embers, blows into the house, filling it with smoke and the smell of burning wood.

Alex takes one look, then breaks down into hysterical sobs, her head turning into my chest. I hold her like I'd like to hold her every night. Like I want to be the one to comfort her every hurt, her every pain.

We watch the fire spread across the land, taking in every beautiful memory, a wonderful past, and a loving mother. I watch Alex as her cries turn into sobs, wailing for her mother.

As we fly higher, I hold Alex tighter as the blazing inferno of their house below shrinks into a tiny speck of orange far, far away.

AN EXCERPT FROM *WHEN HER POWER AWAKENS*

Available on Amazon

"Kenna, Kenna, you have to wake up. Kenna, we have to go," a desperate voice says.

I blink. I'm so tired and dazed.

"Kenna, we have to go. Come on, they're going to take you. We need to leave now," the voice says again, and I feel a gentle pat on my cheeks.

I grimace. That stings.

"Kenna, Kenna," he repeats.

I cough, blinking rapidly. My eyes hurt as they open to the blinding light. I fixate on the brilliant and dazzling glow. And…it is radiating from…

From me.

Me.

I scream. The light continues to glow, and I wave my arms at it, trying to get rid of the light bursting out of my stomach.

I continue to thrash, eager to get the light away from me. What the *Faahi* is that?

"Kenna!" a voice yells, and I look up.

A pair of hands grabs my shoulders, shaking me.

His face comes into focus. I know him. His face brings a cool breeze breaking into the steady warmth of the light. I float toward the breeze.

Toward him.

Finally, I recognize him, and my eyes fill with tears.

Zander is here. I grip his arms tightly, my entire body instantly grateful for his presence. My cheeks are wet, but I hold tight, forcing myself to focus on his face.

The light vanishes back into my body.

www.ingramcontent.com/pod-product-compliance
Lightning Source LLC
Chambersburg PA
CBHW021137310726
48971CB00002B/369